LiFE

LIFE

Lu Yao

Translated by Chloe Estep

amazoncrossing

Text copyright © 1982 by Lu Yao
Translation copyright © 2019 by Chloe Estep
All rights reserved.

Previously published as 人生by China Youth Publishing House in 1982 and 人生(第二版) by Beijing October Literature Publishing House in 2012. This edition published by arrangement with Beijing October Literature Publishing House, all rights reserved.

Published by AmazonCrossing, Seattle

www.apub.com

ISBN-13: 9781542044622
ISBN-10: 1542044626

Cover design by Adil Dara

Printed in the United States of America

Although the road of life is long, its most important sections are often covered in only a few steps, especially while one is young.

—*Liu Qing*

FOREWORD

The world depicted in Lu Yao's *Life*—the world of rural China at the beginning of the 1980s—is a world that no longer exists. Nearly four decades on, the center of gravity of Chinese society has shifted from the countryside to the city, in the process gutting villages, dissolving clan cohesion, and collapsing social structures that had existed for millennia. The great dramatic balance of Lu Yao's tale—Gao Jialin's hesitation between the virtues of rural life and the thrilling unknowns of urban modernity—has since been decisively resolved. These days, the Gao Jialins of twenty-first-century China are abandoning the countryside in droves.

Yet such deep roots are not so easily severed. The shadow of that diminished rural world hangs everywhere over modern China: in its family histories, its personal mythologies, its contemporary culture. In two seminal works of fiction—*Life* (1982) and *An Ordinary World* (1986)—Lu Yao captured the experiences of a generation torn between these two poles, and opened a debate that has continued to this day. His works have steadily gained relevance in China, for the simple reason that the questions he raised have yet to be resolved. Traditional rural culture tells one, in no uncertain terms, the right way to live. How to exist in the cities, however, is an open question.

In the 1980s, thirty years after the formation of the New China, a younger generation was seeing the possibility of a new life of the spirit, outside of the political strictures of communism, and with that a chance to change their material fortunes. For a few years, perhaps for the better part of the decade, China hovered on this threshold: the old world holding steady even as a new world became visible over the horizon.

It is on that horizon that Lu Yao's protagonist Gao Jialin appears. A "young man of promise" from Gaojia Village, he is educated—a high school graduate—and ambitious. Though he's failed to get into a university, a career as an unlicensed community teacher promises a bright future and, most importantly, an escape from working the land.

The Western reader might need to go back to the Russian novels of the nineteenth century, to Gogol or Tolstoy, to find a literary equivalent. Stendhal's 1830 masterpiece *The Red and the Black* is in some ways a spiritual twin—in fact Lu Yao makes a sly reference to it—though Stendhal's Sorel, in his attempts to break into urban cultured society, is more devious and in many ways less sympathetic than Gao Jialin.

But in the end, perhaps Gao Jialin's feelings are not so unusual. His horror of becoming a peasant is merely the horror of any young person of promise who feels that life has been charted out in advance, who can look down the course of the coming years, all the way to the moment of death, and know that nothing unexpected lies in wait.

One of the great successes of the novel is the careful balance Lu Yao maintains in presenting Gao Jialin's choices. Though China as a society has opted decisively for growth, and the city, and future unknowns, the question of how a moral individual should respond to those unknowns is as thorny and unresolved as ever. *Life* remains on Chinese bestseller lists to this day. Chinese readers continue to argue about the book and remain evenly split between those who cannot forgive Gao Jialin for his betrayal of his roots and those who think he was right to reach for a new and better life.

—Eric Abrahamsen, *Paper Republic*

PART ONE

PART ONE

CHAPTER 1

On the tenth day of the sixth month of the lunar calendar, the evening sky was covered with a dense blanket of dark clouds, and the earth, usually lively and bustling at the height of summer, suddenly grew quiet. Even the noisiest insects made no sound, as if in a state of anxious anticipation. Not even a wisp of dust blew over the ground. The frogs jumped one after the other onto the bank, recklessly flinging themselves onto the farmland and roads that lined the river. The air felt as sultry as the inside of a steamer basket. Pitch-black clouds spread across the sky from Old Bull Mountain in the west. Scattered flashes of light illuminated the horizon, but there was no thunder. The only sound was a distant, muffled rumbling, sending the frightening message that a great thunderstorm was coming.

Right then, Gao Jialin, a community teacher from Gaojia Village and the only son of Gao Yude, was wading through the stream that ran past the village, naked from the waist up, trying to get home as fast as he could. He was returning from a meeting of the commune's teachers' association and was dripping with sweat, holding on to his undershirt and a beautiful deep-blue Dacron-polyester summer shirt. He ran into the village, up the hill, and finally threw himself headlong through the door of his home, built into the hillside. He had just made it inside the cave house when he heard the deep, low roar of thunder outside.

His father was squatting barefoot on the heated brick platform of the kang bed, taking long drags on his cigarette, leisurely stroking his white beard with one hand. His mother tottered on her bound feet, carrying a bowl of rice with both hands toward the kang.

When the old couple saw their son return, their faces, as dry and wrinkled as walnut shells, bloomed like two flowers; they were clearly happy their son had made it home before the rain started. In their eyes, it was as though their precious son was returning home after years at the ends of the earth, instead of after a week of working in Madian.

The old man rushed over to the kerosene lantern and cheerfully poked at it with the extra-long nail of his little finger. The interior of the cave house was suddenly illuminated. He grinned and looked lovingly at his son, his mouth wordlessly opening and closing. The old woman grabbed the cornmeal buns she had placed on the kang and put them on the stove to heat. She then began to fuss over some fried eggs and wheat cakes for her son. Her every move conveyed just how much she adored him as she grabbed her son's quilted jacket from the kang and placed it around his sweaty, naked shoulders. "So headstrong!" she chided him. "You'll catch your death of cold!"

Gao Jialin didn't respond. He shrugged the jacket off and lay down on the bedroll at the edge of the kang without even removing his shoes. Facing the impenetrable blackness outside the window, he said, "Ma, don't make me anything; I'm not hungry."

The old couple's faces shriveled back up into walnut shells, and they exchanged looks that said: What happened to our child today? What's bothering him? A flash of lightning lit up the window, and then came a frightening peal of thunder as loud as a landslide. The wind blew and dust pelted the window paper . . . *papapa*.

The couple stared blankly at their son for what seemed like a long time.

"Jialin, are you feeling all right?" his mother asked, her voice quavering as she held the gourd ladle.

"I'm fine . . . ," he answered.

"Did you get in a fight?" his father asked.

"No . . ."

"Well, what's the matter then?" Jialin's parents asked, practically in unison.

Jialin said nothing.

Jialin had never acted like this before. Usually, whenever he returned from town, he would share all the details of his day and bring them treats: he would ply them with breads and cakes, telling them how these were "nutritious" and soft and easy to digest for people with old teeth like theirs. But clearly something serious had happened to turn their child mute! Gao Yude couldn't stand the distraught expression on his wife's face. He took a final drag on his cigarette, knocked the ash off onto the edge of the kang, and used a handkerchief he always kept stuffed between his shirt buttons to wipe the snot from the end of his nose. He nudged his son: "Jialin, what happened? Tell us! Look at the state your mother's in!"

Gao Jialin lifted himself up onto one arm and then slowly managed to sit up, as though he had suffered a great injury. Without looking at the two of them, he leaned on the bedroll, staring blankly at the base of the wall. "I'm not a teacher anymore . . ."

"What?" his parents exclaimed simultaneously, mouths agape.

Jialin remained in the same position and said, "My position as community teacher has been terminated. I found out at the meeting today."

"What did you do? My God!" The old woman dropped her ladle onto the stove, and it broke in two.

"Are they cutting the number of teachers? Haven't they been hiring more teachers every year? How can they suddenly start getting rid of them?" his father nervously prattled on.

"They're not cutting the numbers . . ."

"Then, won't Madian's school need a teacher?" His mother rushed to his side.

"No . . ."

"Why not? If you don't teach, then won't they be short of teachers?" His father looked baffled.

Frustrated, Gao Jialin glared at his father and shouted, "You're both so stupid! They don't need me—they'll just get someone else!"

His parents suddenly understood. His father massaged his own feet with his withered hands, asking softly, "So who will they hire?"

"Who? Who! Somebody else! Sanxing!" Gao Jialin flopped down on the bedclothes again and pulled the blanket over his head.

His parents were dumbstruck. The atmosphere in the cave house became oppressive.

They could hear raindrops pelting the earth; the wind and rain gradually grew louder and more aggressive. Every so often, lightning flashed on the window paper and peals of violent thunder rang out. Outside, all of heaven and earth was submerged in chaos.

Gao Jialin was still hiding his head. Snot hung from his father's nose and trembled, seemingly about to fall, but the old man couldn't be bothered to wipe it. Instead he slowly stroked the wisps of beard on his chin with a rough hand and massaged his bare feet. His mother hunched over the edge of the kang, wiping her eyes with her apron. Inside the cave house all was quiet, the only sound the snoring of the old orange cat.

The storm was raging even more fiercely outside. A low rumble interrupted the wind and the rain—water flooding down the river from the mountains.

It took only fifteen minutes for all the anger to leak from the dimly lit cave house and for the home to fill up instead with grief and pain.

They saw this event as a serious attack on their family. Since Gao Jialin didn't get into college after graduating high school, he felt he had already suffered a great deal. Luckily these three years teaching meant that he'd avoided strenuous physical labor and had time to continue his studies, delving ever more deeply into the subjects that he loved. He had already published a few poems and essays in the local paper, the result of these past few years of hard study. Now he had no choice but to begin life as a peasant, like his father before him. Even though he had never worked the land himself, he was a peasant's son, and he knew what it meant to farm this infertile mountain region. Peasants! He knew all about their great hardships. Though he didn't look down on them, he felt he needed more mental preparation before becoming one. There was no need to hide the fact that for the past ten years he had devoted his life to reading, precisely to avoid following in the footsteps of his father, a "master of the land" (or, to put it another way, a slave to the land). He had seen a bright future for himself in teaching. In a few more years, he could take the test to become an official state-funded teacher. Until then, he had planned to continue to work hard while trying to find a better job. But now, his hopes were dashed, and as he lay facedown on the kang, his face twisted in distress on the quilt, one hand ruthlessly pulling at his hair.

This disastrous news was like a slap in the face to Gao Yude and his wife. They felt sick over the plight of their only child: they had spoiled him since he was little, and his thin skin hadn't ever felt suffering. How could he endure a future of hard labor? Plus, during the years Jialin was teaching, he had earned the maximum workpoints, allowing their household of three to live comfortably. If their son wasn't teaching and couldn't quickly adapt to hard labor, their lives would become more difficult. They were old now; it wasn't like before, when their four hands could work the land and support their child's pursuit of "scholarly honor." The more they thought about these terrifying consequences, the more upset and panicked they became. Jialin's mother sobbed silently, but his father seemed too upset to cry. The old man massaged the soles of his feet for a long time before thinking aloud:

"Oh, Minglou, you're so skilled, and capable, and strong—but you've gone too far this time! You think because you're the local brigade secretary, you can do whatever you like! My Jialin did his best as a teacher these three years, and your Sanxing just graduated high school! How dare you do this to my child? If you won't listen to reason, can't you at least feel some shame? Minglou! This violates the laws of heaven. God will open his eyes and see what you've done! My poor, unfortunate child!"

In the end, Gao Yude couldn't stop himself from crying, and streams of muddy tears coursed through the wrinkles, falling into his wispy white beard.

Gao Jialin heard his father's sobs and jolted upright, a terrifying glint in his eyes. "What do *you* have to cry about?" he shouted. "It's *my* life on the line! How can I measure up to Gao Minglou's son!" And he leaped off the kang.

At this outburst, Gao Yude panicked. Barefoot, he also jumped off the kang, and rushed to grab his son by his bare arms. At the same time, his mother tottered over on her bound feet, her back pressed against the doorframe. The two parents held their half-naked son firm.

Gao Jialin irritably turned on his parents, who were struggling to hold him still: "*Aiya!* I'm not going to kill him! I just want to write a complaint against him! Mother, go bring me the fountain pen from my desk."

This terrified Gao Yude more than if his son were to start throwing furniture around. He kept a firm hold on his son's bare arms, imploring him, "My son, under no circumstances must you stir up trouble. Their family has direct access to the authorities, and both the commune and the county will crush you and your complaint. If you accuse him, aside from the fact that your complaint won't get any traction, it could ruin our family. I'm old, and I can't handle this; you're weak and you can't stand up for yourself. Please, I beg you not to do this . . ."

His mother continued his father's argument, pleading, "My dear child, your father's right! Gao Minglou's not a good person, and if you accuse him, our family will be ruined . . ."

Gao Jialin's body went as rigid as a tree stump, and hot air seemed to steam from his nostrils. He didn't hear a word of what his parents said. He shouted, "I'd rather take on that jackass than suffer this mistreatment. Even rabbits attack when they're threatened—how can we stand for this? I don't care if my complaint is successful or not; I have to write it!" As he spoke, he tried his best to wrench his arms from the grasp of his parents' weak ones. But they held him even tighter. The two older people cried until they could barely breathe. His mother rocked and swayed so hard it seemed she might fall over, until she finally got the strength to beg him one last time: "My baby, don't be so stubborn, I'm begging you on my knees . . ."

Gao Jialin saw his parents' pitiful faces and runny noses. He saw his mother trying her best to stay upright but teetering, about to fall, and he grabbed her and shook his head in distress.

He said, "Mother, there's no need for this. I hear you both. I won't write the complaint . . ."

Only then did the old couple let go of their son, using their wrists and palms to wipe the tears from their faces. Gao Jialin leaned rigidly against the edge of the kang, his head hanging low and heavy. It was still pouring outside, although there was no more lightning or thunder. In the riverbed, the flash flood roared like a herd of terrifying mythical beasts.

After he had calmed down, his mother pulled a blue shirt out from the trunk and put it over her son's ice-cold shoulders. Then she sighed and turned back to the stove to make him something to eat. His father fumbled with the matches, trying to start the stove, but his hands were shaking so much that he struck ten or so before managing to light one—not noticing that the flame from the kerosene lamp had been dancing in front of his eyes the whole time. He took a drag on his cigarette, bent over, and said resolutely, "You cannot write that complaint. But you're right—doing nothing is unacceptable . . . Yes, doing nothing would be unacceptable!"

Gao Jialin looked up, eager to hear his father's brilliant idea to punish Gao Minglou.

Gao Yude took another drag on his cigarette and hung his head, his expression thoughtful. After a while, he lifted his wrinkled farmer's face, looking mischievous, and said to his son, "Listen! You can't ignore him; instead, when you come across Minglou, you should call him Uncle! Don't show that you're upset, just smile. At this point, he should already be aware of what's happened." He turned his hoary old head to his wife, who was preparing food: "Mother, listen! If you come across someone from Minglou's family, just smile! Minglou didn't plant any eggplant this year, so go pick some from our allotment tomorrow and send a basket over to them. But don't give them the impression that we're trying to butter them up. After all, Jialin's future depends on what Minglou thinks of him. We're humble people, so we must use this to our advantage . . . Mother, are you listening?"

A sound like a sob came drifting over from the stove.

The tears finally overtook Gao Jialin. He turned quickly and fell onto the edge of the kang, sobbing as if his heart was breaking.

No one knew when the rain might stop, but as long as it pounded the earth and rushed along the riverbed, it seemed that there would be no peace that night for anyone . . .

CHAPTER 2

When Gao Jialin woke up, he had no idea what time it was, though it was almost noon.

Every day of the past month had been the same: he'd go to bed early and get up late, but he didn't spend a lot of time actually sleeping. He'd spend the whole night, *the whole night*, with his eyes wide open. From the wildly twisted quilt, one could see he had been suffering, not sleeping. As dawn approached, his parents would begin to grope around, noises would float in from the village, and he would finally rouse himself into a state of half consciousness. He could sort of make out his mother bringing some firewood in from the courtyard and puttering around with the bellows. He also heard his father's limping walk—a light step, a heavy step—as he moved across the floor to gather his tools before heading out into the mountains. Jialin would hear his father talking to his mother about making something better for dinner tonight . . . then he'd close his eyes, holding in tears, and go back to sleep.

Even though he was seemingly awake, he felt fuzzy-headed. He couldn't seem to get back to sleep, but he also didn't want to get up. He fumbled around for the pack of cigarettes next to his pillow and pulled out one of the few left inside. He greedily sucked at it and blew smoke toward the ceiling of the earthen cave. He was craving cigarettes more and more these days, and two of his right fingertips were stained yellow and permanently smelled of tobacco. But he was almost out of cigarettes—or, more precisely, he was out of money to buy them. As a community teacher, he had received a few dollars extra on top of his salary that he would use to support his habit.

After chain-smoking two cigarettes, he was totally awake. He really wanted to smoke another, but there was only one more left in the pack, and he wanted to enjoy that after he had brushed his teeth.

He started to get dressed. After putting on an item of clothing, he'd stare blankly into empty space for a while before putting on the next.

It took him forever to finally get down from the kang. He ladled some cold water from the pot onto a dry towel and used the damp corner to wipe his swollen eyes.

He then ladled some water into a mug and took it to the courtyard to brush his teeth.

The light outside was blinding. He suddenly felt transported to a different world. The sky was so blue it seemed like it had been washed by the rain. Snow-white clouds drifted peacefully across it. Corn spread over the fields like green felt all the way to Old Bull Mountain in the west. The mountains on either side of the road blocked out the view beyond, and the distant horizon was suffused with light-blue mist. The sunnier hillsides were planted with wheat, some of which had already been ploughed, the soil a deep brown. Some hadn't yet been turned over and were bleached a shining white by the sun, like sheepskin. The millet and buckwheat were already coming up evenly in swaths of very pale green. The villages alongside the river were shaded by jujube trees, the roofs barely visible underneath. The only real signs of civilization were piles of barley straw heaped in the fields on the outskirts of the villages, which from afar looked like golden mushrooms.

Jialin's eyes focused on a copse of date trees, a faraway pool of green. He was scared to look, but couldn't help himself. In those green shadows, two lines of stone buildings were faintly visible, dug into the earth. It was the school where he had spent the past three years living and working.

The school was jointly administered by the surrounding villages and enrolled one hundred students with the oldest in the fifth grade. Each year they sent a few students to the commune middle school in a nearby town. Gao Jialin had been the head teacher of the fifth grade and had been in charge of all the math and language classes this past year. He also taught music and drawing to the whole school—he was very well respected. But forget all that now!

Depressed, he turned away. Squatting on the bank, he began to brush his teeth.

The village was extremely quiet. The men had all left for the mountains, and the children were running wild in the fields nearby. The village was already filled with the *badabada* sound of box bellows and wisps of blue smoke that rose from the roofs of the cave houses. A few efficient women had begun to prepare lunch for their husbands and children. A chorus of irritatingly monotonous cricket chirps rose from the clumps of willows that dotted the riverbank.

While Gao Jialin brushed his teeth, he watched his mother's stooped back as she pulled up eggplants from the family allotment, her white hair shining in the sunlight. He was gripped with feelings of distress and shame. He quickly pulled the toothbrush out of his mouth and said to himself, *I've behaved outrageously the past month! How can I mope around at home in a bad mood while my parents toil all day? If I don't go work in the mountains, all the villagers will laugh at me!* Yes, he had already felt the eyes of the villagers on him. They had quickly accepted that Gao Minglou had arbitrarily fired him, but if they thought you were some kind of loafer, they would never let you forget it. The farmers looked down on anyone who didn't go into the mountains to work. *No more of this!* Gao

Jialin thought painfully. Life is suffering, and he had to accept his station—he was a peasant through and through.

Gao Jialin stood up, still lost in thought, then heard someone behind him call out, "Teacher Gao, are you home?"

He turned to look and recognized Ma Shuan—the leader of the production team from Madian Village, on the other side of the river.

Although Ma Shuan couldn't read, he was Madian Village's representative on the school management committee. He often came to school for meetings, and Jialin knew him well. He was honest and good-natured—not rigid or stubborn—and a good farmer, professional in his business dealings.

Ma Shuan, usually plainly dressed, today appeared transformed. He was pushing a brand-new bicycle, its frame covered in multicolored tape and the spokes bedecked with colorful velvet balls. It was all completely tacky. His outfit was just as tasteless: he wore a gray Dacron shirt under a pair of blue polyester overalls in the heat of the day; on his head was a yellow military-style Dacron cap; and on his deeply suntanned arm was a glinting gold-plated watch. He seemed a bit embarrassed by his outfit and laughed awkwardly. Although Jialin was in a bad mood, he couldn't help smiling at Ma Shuan's attire and asked, "You look like a bridegroom—what brings you here?"

Ma Shuan's face turned bright red, and he laughed and said, "I've come to see my bride! I've been introduced to Liu Liben's second daughter."

Then Jialin realized why Ma Shuan looked so different. These days, peasants visiting their betrotheds always dressed this way. He asked, "Is it Qiaozhen?"

"Yes."

"You've plucked the field's first green shoot! Haven't you heard everyone say that Qiaozhen is the prettiest flower in these mountains?" Jialin poked fun at him.

"The fruit is good, but I'm not sure I'll get a taste!" Simple Ma Shuan laughed at his own crudeness.

"How's it going? Is everything settled?"

"I've made the hour-long trek to see them in the city a few times, but the elder members of her family don't seem very enthusiastic about our match, and they haven't shown their faces around here even once. They probably think we're uncultured, with our dark skin. I'm darker than her, but as far as education goes, she's like me—she can't read much, but she's got a good heart!"

"Take it slow, there's no rush."

"Right, right, right." Ma Shuan laughed gleefully.

"Why don't you come over and have something to eat?"

"I can't. I already ate my words at my father-in-law's!"

Now it was Gao Jialin's turn to laugh. He didn't know an illiterate peasant could be so funny.

Ma Shuan lifted his watch-clad arm in farewell. He then straddled his bicycle and sped off toward the cart road between the mountains.

Jialin leaned against a date tree on the riverbank and stared at the silhouette of Ma Shuan as it disappeared into the green ocean of corn. He couldn't resist turning to look at Liu Liben's house on the other side of the river.

Liu Liben's nickname was "Double Ace." He'd never been an official, but all the villagers respected him—Gao Minglou most of all. He was quick to adapt when times changed, and in the past few years he had made a lot of money through speculation and profiteering. Recently, he had earned more than he knew how to handle, and his family was now the richest one in the entire village. Even though Gao Minglou was the village's "Ace in the Hole," on the economic front, he couldn't measure up to Double Ace. Most farmers respect rich people, but the villagers also respected Liu Liben for another reason. Liben's oldest daughter, Qiaoying, had married Gao Minglou's oldest son the year before last, so his status in the village had increased even more. Ace in the Hole and Double Ace were now related, and the two families had become the undisputed masters of the village. These families comprised the walls of the village—one at one end, one at the other, one a crouching tiger and the other a hidden dragon. Such was the arrangement of the two great families in this mountain valley.

Frankly speaking, Gao Jialin did not share the other farmers' admiration and respect for these two families. Although Jialin had been born into a humble family, his father had labored to earn the money to support his son's education, and

Jialin had washed the stink of mud off himself, so to speak. He had what ordinary folks regarded as the unapproachable air of an intellectual. In his opinion, neither Gao Minglou nor Liu Liben were worthy of his respect, and they weren't inherently any better than the down-on-their-luck farmers. Gao Minglou was hardly upstanding—he used all the power at his disposal to bully those both above and below him, every bit the petty warlord; Liu Liben knew only how to hoard money—he thought reading was a waste of it, so he didn't let his two older daughters go to school. He finally let his third daughter, Qiaoling, enroll, and now she was about to graduate. Gao Jialin didn't care much for the sons of these families, either. Gao Minglou had seemingly used up all the personality and ability for the men in the family; his two sons were slow and stupid. If his second son, Sanxing, hadn't been able to rely on nepotism, he wouldn't have even gotten through high school. Liu Liben's three daughters were all beautiful flowers, and clever; it was a shame two of them were illiterate.

Jialin stood on the bank and thought resentfully that although he might look down on these families, what were his own prospects?

A fierce desire for retaliation grew in him, and he ground his teeth: If there was no Gao Minglou, and if Jialin's fate was to be a peasant, he would probably toil for the rest of his days, with no other thoughts beyond that. But as long as Gao Minglou lived in Gaojia Village, Jialin would be fixated on besting him. To be more successful than Gao Minglou and his ilk, Jialin would have to leave Gaojia Village, since it would be hard to surpass them here. He was determined to prove himself to society and come out on top.

He brought his mug and toothbrush back into the house, looked in his trunk for a shirt, and prepared to go down to the pond next to the nearby field to bathe.

He came across a khaki military shirt, and his eyes suddenly lit up. It was his uncle's—he had sent it from Xinjiang while he was in the military there. It was so valuable to Jialin that he hardly ever wore it. His father's only younger brother had always been a soldier, and in the decades since the revolution he hadn't once returned home. He'd send letters every few months and give them a bit of spending money at the end of the year, but that was the extent of his uncle's relationship with his family. Jialin had heard his uncle was a deputy political commissar in the army—it was a point of pride in their family—but since he lived so far away, he wasn't much use to them in their daily lives.

Gao Jialin was picking up his clothes when it occurred to him that he should write his uncle a letter advising him of their current situation and seeing if he could find Jialin a position in Xinjiang. Of course, he thought, he was his parents' only child, and even if his uncle found him a job out there, his parents wouldn't let him go. But he was still determined to write his uncle. Jialin longed to leave home for somewhere far away . . . He could convince his parents when the time came.

He leaned over the table and, putting his essay-writing skills to good use, wrote a very moving letter to his uncle and placed it inside the trunk. Tomorrow he would find someone going to the market in the county seat who could mail the letter for him.

This thought comforted him. Immediately he felt calmer, happier.

He put on the khaki shirt and gleefully left home. He walked along the cart path by the river toward the dappled vegetable fields.

In August, the fields looked beautiful against the yellow earth of the plateau. The distant mountains were dressed up in vivid green this time of year, and in the valley, the corn was already as tall as a person, one or two cute little green cobs growing on each stalk, pink tassels bursting from their ends. On the mountainsides, runner beans, adzuki beans, soybeans, and potatoes were all blooming red, white, yellow, and blue, adorning the endless green expanse. The fields had already been weeded twice, and it had poured not long ago, so there was no sign of drought. Everything was damp, green, and dripping with water, and looking at the landscape gave everyone a deep sense of relief.

Gao Jialin walked briskly, all his worries suddenly forgotten, youthful vigor coursing through his veins. He plucked a pink morning glory and twirled the stem in his fingers as he turned through a cabbage field shining pale in the sunlight, then jumped over a few dirt levees and came to the river's edge.

He stripped quickly and stood on the stony bank of the green pond with his chest puffed up, then crouched. He had already decided that this wouldn't be a quick wash—he wanted to go for a real swim.

His naked body was toned and beautiful. Although his tall, thin frame bore no trace of physical labor, it looked strong, as though it had seen regular physical exercise. His face was a little suntanned; he had a high-bridged nose, large eyes, and particularly impressive eyebrows, like two swords. His hair was disheveled, not because he hadn't paid it attention, but rather purposefully so. He was attractive, and exuded a particular sort of masculine good looks when he furrowed his brows, deep in thought.

Gao Jialin limbered up, then dived from the stony bank, his body carving an arc in the air as he elegantly descended into the jade pool. He tried out different swimming strokes, but they all looked roughly the same.

A while later, he climbed to the top of a waterfall and washed himself with soap in the shallow water there. He crawled into a cave to put on his pants, and lay down bare-chested under a peach tree on the riverbank. The peach tree belonged to Old Deshun, a lifelong bachelor. The good-hearted man picked it clean of its fruit, even before the peaches were ripe, to give to the children of the village. Now only a sprinkling of leaves remained on the tree, which didn't provide much shade.

Gao Jialin laid his jacket on the ground and rested the back of his head in his hands, his body sprawled on the earth. Through cracks between the leaves, he let his eyes wander over the sky above, which was as clear as water. He didn't feel hungry even though it was well past noon. The river wasn't far away, but it sounded much farther than it was. It burbled, as pleasant sounding as a violin.

All of a sudden, the sound of a woman singing a *xintianyou* folk song floated toward him from the cornfield off to his right.

Upstream a goose and downstream a gander

A lovely pair, she gazes bright-eyed at her brother

The voice was sweet and resonant, though it was clear the singer was an amateur. He listened closely, and thought it sounded like Liu Liben's daughter Qiaozhen. He suddenly remembered Ma Shuan's problems with his potential in-laws and couldn't help laughing. He said to himself, *Your "brother" came to see you, but you weren't there. So he left, and now you're looking for him . . .*

As he reflected on the humor in the situation, he heard a rustling sound coming from the cornfield nearby. *Damn!* It was probably Qiaozhen crossing the road on her way home.

Gao Jialin sat up in a hurry, stuffing his arms into his jacket. He was just about to do up his last button when Qiaozhen appeared in front of him with a basket full of sweet melons.

Liu Qiaozhen didn't look at all like someone from the countryside. It goes without saying that she was pretty, and there was nothing shabby or vulgar about the way she dressed. She wore grass-green polyester pants and a faded blue work jacket, its broad collar flipped up, framing her lively expression.

She blinked her clear eyes, staring awkwardly at Gao Jialin. From her basket, she pulled out a sweet melon, so ripe it was almost yellow, and pressed it into Jialin's hands and said, "It's from our family's allotment. I grew it. Eat! It's so sweet!" Then she pulled an immaculate floral handkerchief from her pocket and gave it to Jialin to clean off the sweet melon.

Gao Jialin reluctantly took the sweet melon, but he didn't take the handkerchief and instead said gently, "I don't want it now. Maybe in a little while . . ."

Qiaozhen looked like she wanted to say something, but hesitated. Instead, she hung her head and started walking back toward the path along the riverbank.

Gao Jialin put the sweet melon aside and instinctively turned his head toward the riverbank, where he noticed Qiaozhen looking back at him. He quickly turned around and nervously lay back down on the ground. At the moment, he hated this elegant but illiterate woman just because her sister was Gao Minglou's daughter-in-law.

He really didn't want to eat the sweet melon, much preferring the idea of a cigarette just then, but he was very aware that he had already smoked them all. He knew he didn't have any tobacco, either, but his hands still searched his clothes, and he was disappointed when they came up empty.

"Jialin! Jialin! Hurry up! Lunch is ready! What are you doing lying there?" He heard his father call him from the path.

He stood up, put Qiaozhen's sweet melon in his jacket pocket, and started to walk back.

The first thing he did when he got home was light one of his father's cigarettes and take a long, hard drag on it. He immediately bent over, coughing violently, his eyes tearing up.

His father sighed and said, "Don't smoke these—the tobacco's too strong!" He grabbed the cigarette from his son's hand. "Jialin, when I was up in the mountains, I was thinking that tomorrow is market day in the county seat. Your mother can make a batch of buns for you to sell there. We're just about out of lamp oil and salt, and we have no money coming in. Plus, if you make some cash, you can buy yourself a cigarette!"

Gao Jialin wiped away his tears and stood up straight. He could tell his father was waiting for a response. He hesitated, remembering the letter he had written to his uncle, thinking that he could go to the county seat tomorrow and send it himself. If he gave it to someone else to send for him, they might lose it. So he agreed to go to the market the next day.

CHAPTER 3

Not long after breakfast, bustling groups of farmers on their way to the market began to appear along the road that followed the path of the Great Horse River to the county seat. Because of changes in laws in the countryside over the past two years, private businesses had been booming, and buying and selling at the market had now become an important part of farming life.

Groups of young people rushed down the road, riding bicycles trimmed with multicolored tape. They wore brand-new clothes to be seen in—if not polyester, then Dacron—and they all looked very fashionable. Even the rougher-looking farmers wore nylon socks and plastic sandals over their normally bare feet. Faces washed clean and hair combed smooth, everyone happily went to the market: to shop, to watch a play, to buy trendy things, to make friends, to meet someone . . .

The majority of farmers shouldered poles bearing everything from firewood to vegetables, calling out to pigs and leading sheep, carrying eggs and chickens, pulling donkeys and pushing carts. There were steelworkers, cobblers, ironworkers, stonemasons, bamboo craftsmen, felt seamsters, basket weavers, and tile makers; there were traveling doctors, magicians, gamblers, thieves, musicians, livestock wholesalers . . . and they were all pouring into the city, stirring up spirals of yellow dust all along the road at the foot of North River Mountain.

Gao Jialin picked up his basket of steamed buns, stepped into the road, then immediately regretted joining the flow of people. He felt like a real hick. It seemed like everyone on the road was staring at him. Once a self-confident teacher, he was now like an old country granny, selling buns at the market! It was agonizing, like millions of insects were gnawing at him.

But there was no helping any of that. The difficult path of his life had led him straight to this road swirling with dust. He had no choice but to accept it and start over. Not only was there no money at home for oil and salt, but his parents were getting older and still had to work hard. As a member of the younger generation, how in good conscience could he continue to laze about, eating all day?

He held on to the basket of steamed buns and did his best to keep his head down and look at nothing but the road beneath his feet as he hurried toward town. While walking, he thought about how his father warned him he needed to hawk the buns loudly, and how hot and red Jialin's face had turned at the thought. Dear God, how could he do this?

But, he thought, *if I don't hawk them, what will people assume I'm doing with all these buns?*

As Gao Jialin walked down the road toward a small gully, he thought, *I might as well try shouting now, while I'm on a deserted switchback, so that once I get to town I'll at least have gotten used to it a bit!*

Red-faced, as though he were doing something shameful, he checked the road in both directions. Not seeing anyone, he hurriedly made his way down the switchback.

He walked into the gully a good distance and stopped when he couldn't see the main road anymore.

Standing still, he opened his mouth but didn't have the courage to shout. He tried once more, but again nothing came out. His forehead was bathed in sweat. Everything around him was peaceful and quiet: a few snow-white butterflies fluttered serenely by some light-blue wildflowers in front of him; an invigorating scent came from the wormwoods growing densely on the hillsides that lined the road. Gao Jialin felt as though the whole world were holding its breath, waiting for him to shout, "Steeeeeeeaaamed buuuuuuuuuns!"

Aiya, why was this so difficult? He felt like he was being forced to bark like a dog in the middle of a public square.

He wiped the sweat from his forehead with the back of his hands and concluded that he simply had to shout. He gulped resolutely, closed his eyes, opened his mouth, and yelled, "Steeeeeeeaaamed buuuuuuuuuns!"

He could hear his mournful, theatrical cry echo off the surrounding mountains. He bit his lip and with great difficulty held back his tears.

For a long while, he stood staring blankly at the deserted gully, but eventually he returned to the road and continued toward town. It was only ten *li* from their village to the county seat, but just then it felt much longer and more onerous. He knew that the larger obstacle was still ahead of him, in that mass of bobbing heads: the market.

By the time he got to where the Great Horse River met the County River, he could see the entire city spread out in front of him. A swath of one-story buildings randomly interspersed with multistory ones stretched from halfway up the mountain all the way to the riverbank. The city—so dear to him—seemed like something from days gone by, with a musty sort of appeal. This was the largest town he'd ever visited—in his eyes the county seat was a big city, and there was no other place like it in the world. He knew it intimately; he had lived here from middle school through high school. His knowledge of himself and of society, as well as his ambitious dreams for his future, had started here. Schools, roads, movie theaters, shops, bathhouses, sports fields . . . life here was so rich and diverse. But three years earlier, he'd had to say goodbye to all of this.

Now he had returned. These were no longer the lighthearted years of his youth, when his clothes were neat and well ironed, he smelled of scented soap, and on his chest he proudly wore the badge of the town's highest institution of education. Today he bore the basket of buns, on his way to market just like every other peasant.

Those memories saddened him. Feeling a bit dizzy, he leaned on the stone railing of the bridge over the Great Horse River. All around him people rushed in an endless stream down the road. In the distance, the sky over the town center was covered in a cloud of gray dust, and the commotion of the city sounded like the buzzing of a beehive.

He suddenly thought of something even more terrifying: What if he ran into one of his old classmates?

He instinctively looked up and quickly surveyed the scene around him. By now he was greatly regretting this trip into town. Most people didn't have much to do when they came to the market, but he had to sell these buns.

Should he turn back? How could he? He was already here. Besides, there wasn't a penny to spare at home. Though his parents wouldn't say anything if he went back empty-handed, *he* would certainly feel bad.

No, he thought, *I've made it this far, I just have to put my head down and keep going!* He prayed that he didn't run into any of his old classmates.

He picked up his basket and walked across the bridge to the road. He steeled himself to pass through the crossroads toward the south gate, where the swine, grain, and vegetable markets were located. There, with the exception of a few cadres who would come to buy vegetables, the crowds mostly comprised farmers like him. He wouldn't be noticed.

But when he passed the bus station waiting room, his face turned white—and then immediately red, as though all the blood in his body had rushed to his cheeks. He saw Huang Yaping and Zhang Ke'nan, high school classmates of his, standing at the door of the waiting room. There was no time to hide, and the two had obviously seen him since they were walking in his direction.

Gao Jialin wished with all his heart he could hide his basket of buns somewhere. But Zhang Ke'nan and Huang Yaping quickly approached him, and he had no choice but to stretch out his one empty hand to shake Ke'nan's.

They asked what he was doing carrying the basket. He improvised, saying that he was visiting relatives to the south.

"Jialin, you've really made great strides! I read the essays you wrote in the regional paper. They were remarkable! And your style is beautiful. I copied a few sections into my notebook!" Huang Yaping said warmly.

"Are you still teaching in Madian?" Ke'nan asked him.

He shook his head and gave a wan smile. "I've been replaced by the son of the local brigade secretary. I've gone back to the production brigade."

"You must not have as much time for studying and writing then!" Huang Yaping responded, clearly worried.

"Actually, I have more time now! Wasn't there a poet who said, 'We use pickaxes to write infinite lines of poetry in the earth'?" Gao Jialin said, self-deprecatingly.

With that, he managed to make his classmates laugh.

"Are you taking a business trip?" Jialin asked. He had a vague feeling that there was something going on between the two of them, though it hadn't seemed like they'd had any special relationship when they were younger.

"I'm not going anywhere. Ke'nan is headed to Beijing to buy a color television for his work unit. I'm just here for fun . . . ," Huang Yaping said. She seemed a bit embarrassed.

"Are you still an inspector at the Luxury Food Company?" Jialin asked Ke'nan.

"No, I recently moved into sales," Ke'nan said.

"He got a promotion! He's the director of sales! Even though there's an *assistant* before the word *director*!" Yaping teased as she looked at Ke'nan, who wore a disapproving expression.

"If you want tobacco or booze, come on by; I'll see what I can do for you. I don't have much pull in my current position, but I can get that stuff. I know it's hard for rural folks to get them these days!" Ke'nan said to Jialin.

Although he knew Ke'nan was sincere, Gao Jialin was especially sensitive in his current state. He felt like Zhang Ke'nan was flaunting his own superiority, thinking highly of himself and looking down on everyone else. "If I need something, I'll get it some other way. I don't want to bother my old class-mates!" he said ungraciously.

At this, Zhang Ke'nan's face turned bright red.

Huang Yaping was perceptive, and she noticed the dis-agreeable turn in the conversation. She said to Gao Jialin, "If you have any free time this afternoon, come by the radio sta-tion! You haven't come to chat since you graduated. You're so stubborn!"

"Well, you're bigwigs now. We common folks wouldn't dare to climb so high!" Jialin betrayed his own shortcomings again: as soon as he felt disrespected, he became bitter and made it difficult for others to get out of a situation gracefully.

It was clear that Zhang Ke'nan couldn't take much more, and luckily, the announcer's voice came over the bus station loudspeaker just then, telling travelers to line up to buy tickets, which gave the little gathering an excuse to break up.

Ke'nan quickly shook hands with Jialin and left. Yaping hesitated briefly and said, "I really would like to chat. I also enjoy literature, but these few years as a broadcaster, all I do is flap my lips! I haven't written anything. Please do come by!"

Her invitation was heartfelt, so Gao Jialin didn't know why he was a little uncomfortable. "If I have time. Go see Ke'nan off. I should leave."

Huang Yaping flushed. "I didn't come to see him off! I came to the station to meet some family arriving from my hometown!" It was obvious that she was making this up. Jialin thought, *You don't need to lie to me!*

But he didn't say anything. He simply nodded politely and turned to walk down the road. As he went, he thought about the lies that he and Yaping had told and thought they were funny. He couldn't help thinking, *Go and meet up with your "family" then. I'll go meet mine, too . . .*

The meeting with Ke'nan and Yaping brought back memories from his younger days.

At school, Yaping had been class president and Jialin had been class monitor, so they had spent a lot of time together. They were the best students in class and both loved literature. They had great respect for each other. Jialin and Ke'nan hadn't been especially close, but since they were both on the school basketball team, they did know each other fairly well.

Huang Yaping was from Jiangsu. Her father was a county-level military secretary and a member of the local standing committee. Yaping accompanied her father to the county seat during her first year in high school and joined Jialin's class. She was clearly a refined southern girl, and her intelligence, generosity, and sophistication quickly endeared her to the entire school. Although Gao Jialin was born in a rural household and hadn't ever been to the big city, he had pored over many different types of books. Living as he did surrounded by mountains made him long for the world outside, and so he seemed a bit more sophisticated than most of his classmates, and more open-minded. Huang Yaping quickly discovered this, and was able to get closer to him easily through their classes together. He also enjoyed being with her. He had never known this sort of girl before. Compared with her, the other girls in his school were vulgar, talking only about food or clothes, and they couldn't keep up with their male classmates. He didn't have much interaction with them. Whereas he and Yaping talked about books they had both read, or music, or painting, or international issues. Once, one of their classmates commented on their "relationship." At the time, though, Jialin didn't dare make more of it than it was. He had a bit of an inferiority complex when it came to Huang Yaping. Which wasn't to say that Jialin wasn't as good as her, but when it came to family backgrounds, economic circumstances, and social positions, Zhang Ke'nan had all of these things. Ke'nan's father was the bureau chief of the county commerce department, and his mother was deputy director of the local pharmaceutical company; they were both well-respected figures in the community. Back then, Ke'nan liked Yaping and was always thinking of ways to get closer to her, but he didn't hold out much hope.

Before long, they all graduated. No one from their class tested into college. Everyone with a government-issued rural *hukou* was required to stay in the countryside, and everyone with a city *hukou* worked their connections to find a job. Yaping, with her excellent Mandarin language skills, became a broadcaster at the county radio station. Ke'nan got work as a safety inspector at the Luxury Food Company. Life's vicissitudes drew them all further and further apart, and although they were separated by a distance of only a few miles, they lived in two separate worlds.

After Gao Jialin returned home to the village, whenever he heard the crisp sound of Huang Yaping's Mandarin coming over the radio, he felt a bit melancholy, as though he had lost something precious, with no hope of getting it back. Eventually, this feeling softened a little. At some point, he vaguely remembered hearing an old classmate from another village say that Huang Yaping was dating Zhang Ke'nan, and Jialin grew sad again for some reason. He'd eventually tamped down all these feelings, and hadn't thought of them in a long time . . .

Now, after their brief reunion, he felt wretched. He walked toward the bustling market with his basket of buns in tow, his eyes darting left and right in an attempt to ward off any more old classmates who worked in town.

But when he reached an eddy in the stream of pedestrians at an intersection, he managed to run into yet another person he knew!

This time he didn't panic. When City Education Officer Ma Zhansheng came over and somewhat awkwardly shook Jialin's hand, he didn't feel like his basket of steamed buns was shameful at all—humph! Let him see them! After all, it was he who had forced Jialin into his current predicament.

When Ma asked him what he was up to, Jialin answered honestly: he was selling steamed buns. He even plucked one out of the basket and pressed it into the officer's hands; it felt as though the bun was shooting out steam—a hand grenade of revenge!

Ma Zhansheng took the bun hastily, then attempted to put it back into the basket. He stroked his stubble and said rather uncomfortably, "Jialin, you must really hate me! I might get an ulcer from all this bitterness! I have some things I really want to say to you, but I haven't dared. Please listen to me now."

Ma Zhansheng pulled Gao Jialin toward a corner of the intersection near a bicycle repair shop. He rubbed his face again, and said in a low voice, "Jialin, you don't understand the situation! The commune secretary, Mr. Zhao, and Gao Minglou, from our village, have been good friends for more than ten years. Regardless of whose status was higher, the two of them have always been attached at the hip. For the past few years, Minglou's family didn't have anyone they needed to arrange a job for, so they let you teach at the school. This year, though, Minglou's second son graduated from high school, and after having him just hang around the commune for a while, old Zhao had to consider the boy's options. You know, our national economy has changed over the last couple of years, and they aren't hiring any new laborers or officials out in the countryside, so local teachers have become very important. Of course Minglou gave his son the job. And what other teacher could have stepped aside for him? So his only choice was to fire you and hire Sanxing. And even though I announced it at the meeting, I didn't make the decision! Me, Ma Zhansheng, how could I make such a decision? Jialin, please, please don't hate me."

Gao Jialin raked his fingers through his hair and said to the officer, "Old Ma, you worry too much. I knew all that already. We've worked together before; you should understand me."

"Of course I understand you! Of all the teachers in the commune, you're the brightest. You're a good kid—pragmatic, but persistent. Don't worry . . . Oh! And I forgot to tell you, I've been moved to the county's labor bureau. It's a bit of a promotion—I'm now the assistant bureau chief. The past few days I've been talking to Secretary Zhao, trying to get him to hire you back as a teacher if he gets the chance. Secretary Zhao agreed without hesitation . . . so don't worry. Just wait a little . . . Well, you'd better get back to your buns. I have to run to a meeting. A new boss must crack the whip! If I can't light a fire underneath 'em, I should at the very least say a few nice things."

When Ma Zhansheng was finished talking, he wiped his face, shook hands with Gao Jialin, and burrowed his way through the crowd as though trying to escape from something.

Gao Jialin didn't harbor any good feelings toward the commune's more slippery figures, so he didn't pay much attention to what Ma Zhansheng had said. He only knew that Ma had left the city commune and risen into the county government. But what did that have to do with him? What was important now was to sell all of the steamed buns in the basket he carried in his arms.

Gao Jialin quickly squeezed through the crowd on the street and walked toward the South Gate Market.

CHAPTER 4

The South Gate Market was so busy it made Jialin's head spin. Usually the space was completely empty; now, it was filled with every possible type of buyer and seller. The largest sections were those for vegetables, swine, livestock, and food stalls, roughly forming the four centers of the market. The next most popular part of the market was an animal-taming group from Henan. They had a shabby old blue cloth with which they'd outlined a performance space, and all the farmers shoved their way to the front so they could buy a twenty-cent ticket to see a black bear play basketball and a Pekinese jump over a large woven sieve. The market was as noisy as a rushing torrent, suffused with dust and the smell of smoke and farmers' sweat.

His basket in one hand and his face dripping, Gao Jialin threw himself into the sea of people.

He gripped the basket and forced his way in blindly, no idea where to go. He was the type of person who held hygiene in high esteem, so he'd kept the basket of buns tightly covered with a snow-white towel the entire trip to keep out dust. But the cover meant that nobody could tell what he was selling, and although he had opened his mouth several times to shout, he couldn't bring himself to make any noise. He heard the cries of the other sellers in the market, especially those of a few canny old traders whose calls were practically performance art. Before today, he'd thought calls like these were funny. Now he envied how carefree, happy, and comfortable these traders sounded. At that moment, Jialin was convinced he was the least capable person in the world.

Just as he was blindly shoving his way through the crowd, he heard a woman talking to someone behind him: "The stubborn old man wants to booze it up again today and have another bunch of guests over . . . It's so hot I don't want to make anything, but the buns in the state-run canteen are disgusting and burnt . . . I've been running around for so long, but I still can't find anyone in this market selling good white buns . . ."

When Gao Jialin heard this, he quickly turned around and started to take the towel off the basket of buns. But no sooner had he turned before he pivoted back around and hid behind an old wooden shovel seller—the woman who was looking to buy steamed buns was none other than Zhang Ke'nan's mother!

When he was in school, he had been to Ke'nan's house once or twice, so Ke'nan's mother knew him.

The pathetic young man hid behind the shovel seller like a petty thief and waited until Ke'nan's mother left before he dared to move. Maybe Ke'nan's mother wouldn't recognize him anymore, but his ego wouldn't let him do business with anyone from his past.

Suddenly, the high-pitched sound of horns blared across the city, heralding Huang Yaping's weather broadcast. Yaping's voice rang out over the loudspeakers—it was even more dignified and gentler these days; her Mandarin could compete with that of the female anchors on China National Radio.

Tired, Gao Jialin leaned against a cement electrical pole, his well-defined eyebrows twitching. His eyes closed slightly; he bit his lip. He thought about Ke'nan, who at this moment was probably sitting on the long-distance bus, leisurely enjoying the view of the plains. Huang Yaping was sitting in a beautiful broadcast studio, elegant as usual, reading a script. But he, on the other hand, was bouncing around a dusty market, enduring humiliation after humiliation for a few measly coins. He suddenly felt very bitter.

He had lost all heart for his work at this point. He decided to temporarily leave this place where he felt so impotent and find somewhere more peaceful. As for the buns, he didn't want to think about them anymore.

Where should he go? He suddenly thought of the reading room in the county's cultural center; he hadn't been there in a very long time.

He quickly forced his way from the main street north across the intersection, toward the cultural center. Since he had loved going there to read as a student, he still knew some of the people there. He had initially wanted to get some water first, but he quickly dismissed the idea—he didn't want to see anyone else he knew today!

Instead he headed straight into the reading room, where he placed his basket on the corner of a bench. From the newspaper rack, he picked up the *People's Daily*, the *Guangming Daily*, the *China Youth Daily*, *Reference News*, and the local provincial paper, and sat in a chair to read them. There wasn't anyone else in the room. In such a booming ocean of a city, a corner of peace like this was hard to find.

Due to the recent upheaval in his life, he hadn't read any newspapers or magazines for a long time. Since middle school, he had developed the habit of reading the newspaper every day, and whenever he couldn't read it, he felt he had missed something. Re-entering the world of the news again, he suddenly and completely forgot everything else.

First he read the international edition of the *People's Daily*. He was very concerned about global affairs, and had once dreamed of studying at the International Relations Institute. In high school, he had kept a large notebook in which he grandly wrote out "The Middle East Problem," "The Future and Development of the Relationship between the Five ASEAN Nations and the Three Nations of Indochina," "The American Element in the China-America-USSR Relationship," and other such pretend research topics. Now he thought that these were a bit ridiculous, but at the time his grand style intimidated his fellow students. He didn't really have the skills to "research" anything, though; he'd only cut out and pasted in newspaper clippings.

He started by flipping through each of the papers once. He picked out a longish piece called "Satisfaction," curled up on the bench, and began to read Han Nianlong's speech to the UN on the issue of Cambodia.

After he had read most of the important pieces from a few days' worth of papers, he felt pleasantly fatigued.

He was surprised when the attendant came to close the reading room: it was already time for the city dwellers to have their afternoon meal.

He quickly picked up the basket of buns and left.

The sun had already begun to lean toward the west, and the sounds of the city had mostly faded. Only a few small scatterings of people were still on the streets.

Aiya, he had spent far too much time in the reading room! The farmers had already retreated from the city like the tide, and if he took one of the main routes through town, he would most likely run into one of his old classmates.

Running over the options in his mind, he realized he didn't have much choice. He started to make his way home.

He left the city with his head hanging and walked toward the Great Horse River. Everything was as it had been on his way into town; not even a single bun was missing from his basket. All that time at the market, and he hadn't made a single penny.

When he reached the bridge over the river, he saw Qiaozhen standing at the end of it, fanning her face with a red handkerchief and holding a new Flying Pigeon bicycle her family had bought.

Qiaozhen saw him and marched over to stand before him, practically blocking his way.

"Jialin, weren't you selling buns?" Her face was flushed, but he didn't know why. She seemed nervous—she was shaking ever so slightly, and her legs looked unsteady.

"Uh-huh." Gao Jialin agreed with a grunt and stared at her, baffled, while he searched for something to say. "Did you go to market as well?"

Qiaozhen used the handkerchief to wipe beads of sweat from her face, her eyes shifting toward her bicycle, though her attention was still focused on him. "I went to the market, but didn't do much of anything . . . Jialin." She suddenly turned to look at him. "I know you didn't sell a single bun, I know it!

You're afraid of losing face! You might as well give the buns to me. Watch my bicycle, and I'll go sell your buns."

She stretched out her hands to take his basket as she spoke.

Gao Jialin didn't respond. His mind was hazy, and he didn't quite understand what was happening. Qiaozhen snatched the basket from his arms. She didn't say anything, and instead simply turned and marched toward the road.

CHAPTER 5

Gao Jialin watched as Qiaozhen's slender silhouette disappeared, not knowing what to do. He massaged the bridge railing with his hands, mulling over how on earth he had found himself in this situation.

Qiaozhen's actions, however, had long been thought out. Not just for the past few days—for years she had kept her feelings to herself. She couldn't hide them any longer. She couldn't go on living without expressing them, or else she might explode.

Liu Liben's second daughter was as beautiful as a flower. Although she hadn't gone to school, she wasn't a simple country girl. She was quite mature in her ability to perceive and understand the world, and for that reason she had rather unusual pursuits and desires. Given her passionate nature, her rich inner world should not have surprised anyone. The farmers in the village and fields noticed only her outer beauty, and couldn't understand the magnificent brilliance of her spirit. Unfortunately, because she wasn't educated, she had no way to approach those people she found more interesting. When she was around cultured people, she felt a deep sense of inferiority, and she secretly blamed her father for not providing her with any schooling. But it was too late to see any of that now. She couldn't even count the times she had secretly cried over her misfortune.

But she was determined to find a cultured, spiritually rich man to be her partner. Due to her beauty, it would have been easy for her to marry an average commune cadre or full-time worker at a state-owned company, as long as he also came from the countryside. Matchmakers had been beating down her door trying to introduce her to these kinds of men, but she rejected every one. To her, these men were no better than peasants. Generally speaking, if she married this kind of man, he would be away most of the time and would come home only a few times a year, leaving her to deal with the house and the children. She saw proof of this everywhere in the countryside. But the most fundamental reason she refused these sorts of men was that she didn't respect them. And she knew that if she found her true match, she would do anything for him, and happily sacrifice everything. That was just the kind of person she was.

Although her father had given her life and raised her, he didn't really understand her. He watched her refuse cadres and workers, and he worried about finding her someone from the countryside. He had a soft spot for Ma Shuan from Madian. She had been in touch with Ma Shuan often over the past few years as part of the commune's campaign to improve farmland infrastructure. He was honest, reasonable, successful in business, and known throughout the village and countryside as a good worker. His family was wealthy and thriving. From the perspective of country folk, he was top-notch, but she couldn't force herself to love him. He frequently visited her home, but whenever he came, she would hide to avoid him, so much so that her father often scolded her for it.

That isn't to say there wasn't a man she held dear. All these years she had indeed been crazy about someone—and that someone was Gao Jialin.

The moment Qiaozhen understood that this world had something called love, she immediately fell for Jialin. She loved his graceful demeanor, his fine figure, and the masculinity that exuded from his every pore. She thought that men should be men, and she couldn't stand men with an air of femininity about them. If she could be with someone like Jialin, she would do anything for him—even jump off a cliff! At the same time, she appreciated him for his wealth of skills: he could play a variety of musical instruments, he could fix a lamp and drive a tractor, he could even write articles for the paper. What's more, he was fastidious about personal hygiene—whether his clothes were new or old, they were always spotless, and his body always smelled of soap.

She imagined endless scenarios in which the two of them were together, where she would put her hand in his, letting him lead her through the fields in springtime, the flowers in summer, the fruit trees in autumn, and the snowbanks in winter. They would walk, they would run, and just like in the movies she would make him take her in his arms and kiss her . . .

But in the real world, her sense of inferiority prevented her from approaching him. She was always thinking of him, while constantly avoiding him. She was afraid that he would overhear her saying something inappropriate on the street, and then her true love would laugh at her. Still, her thoughts and eyes never left him.

When Jialin had gone off to school in the county seat, she'd remained devoted to him, even though she knew he would soon fly far away and she would never have him. When Jialin returned home on Sundays, she always looked for some excuse to stay home, where she'd sit in her courtyard peering stealthily at Jialin's across the way. If Jialin went to the pond near the village to swim, she would grab a basket and head down to the water to pick grass for their pigs. On Sunday afternoons, she would follow him with her eyes as he headed back to the county seat. She couldn't keep her tears from brimming, wondering if he would ever return to Gaojia Village.

After Jialin graduated from high school, he didn't test into any universities and returned to Gaojia Village, crestfallen. Qiaozhen was elated. She finally saw a shining ray of hope—perhaps her dreams might come true. She plotted: Jialin was a peasant now, so wouldn't he eventually be looking for a peasant wife? Even with a country *hukou* and no education, she was sure she could make him love her. She knew she had the advantages of wit and beauty over other local girls.

But this ray of hope quickly dimmed. Jialin became a community teacher, and teachers now were the only ones with the hope of being able to buy—not grow—their own grain. Considering Jialin's abilities, she was sure he'd become a state-employed teacher in the future.

She fell into a deep depression. She would often hide behind an old locust tree near the path to her home and stare blankly off toward the school. She watched him walk along the road to the school, which had been trampled bare by the feet of so many young students, and then watched him on his way back to the village . . .

She managed to keep her ambition from everyone. No one in the village knew the dreams and troubles of this smart, beautiful girl. Only her sister Qiaoling, who was currently attending high school in the county seat, knew anything about the situation. Qiaoling would sometimes smile to herself and other times sigh at her sister's far-off stares or seemingly bottomless despair. When Jialin became a peasant again, Qiaozhen's long-suppressed emotions had returned to the surface. It was as though a volcano had erupted, and she couldn't control the powerful flow of her emotions. She was happy that he was a peasant again, but she felt terrible for his misfortune—so much so that she swore at Gao Minglou in front of her older sister.

She didn't know how to make him love her. The previous afternoon, when she'd seen him head out to go swimming, she'd grabbed her pig-grass basket and cut through the corn-field near the pond, where she'd casually picked a sweet melon from someone's private allotment to offer Jialin. Today when she'd seen him heading to the market, she'd followed him to the county seat on her bicycle. She didn't have any real busi-ness at the market—the only reason she'd come was to figure out how to tell him what was in her heart. She'd followed him that whole day—not too far and not too close—as he squeezed his way through the crowds. She saw her beloved carrying his basket of buns as he navigated the throng, not selling a single one. Later, when she spotted him leaning sadly on a cement electrical pole with his eyes closed, tears dripped down her face before she could get out her handkerchief to wipe them.

When she saw him go into the cultural center, she knew that he wouldn't be able to sell any buns there. She'd really wanted to follow him in, but she couldn't read, so what would she do there? Plus, there were bound to be lots of people inside; it wasn't a good place to have her conversation with Jialin. So instead she rode her bike to the riverbank and waited for him to pass by. She waited from noon until late in the afternoon . . .

Now, Liu Qiaozhen was holding Jialin's basket of steamed buns and walking happily toward the town's main street. She felt as though heaven and earth had suddenly brightened, as though everyone on the street were beaming, or at least grinning at her. When she came across a group of little kids just leaving the elementary school, she grabbed one and hugged and kissed him.

When she got to the intersection, she crossed the main road and walked to the market at the south gate. She stopped there, stifling a laugh at her surroundings. She didn't intend to sell the basket of buns but was instead going to give them to her aunt's family. They lived on the hillside above the town's main intersection. She couldn't ask her aunt for money for the buns, but she'd already pulled together enough to give to Jialin. She had even bought him some high-quality cigarettes and tucked them into the flower-print bag on her bicycle.

She proceeded to her aunt's house, where she left the buns and quickly made to leave. Her aunt and uncle insisted that she stay and eat with them, but she was afraid that Jialin wouldn't have the patience to wait for her. She left her aunt's house with the empty basket and practically ran toward the Great Horse River Bridge.

~

After Qiaozhen rushed back toward town with his basket, Gao Jialin stood on the bridge, still confused about what had just happened to him.

Later he decided the situation was self-explanatory: Qiaozhen was a simple girl from his village; she'd realized he hadn't sold any of his buns and had offered to help him. The village girls often went to the market to buy and sell. They didn't feel hard-pressed or embarrassed by it as he did.

No matter the reason, he was very thankful Qiaozhen was doing this favor for him. Although he didn't spend a lot of time with Liu Liben's family, he felt that Liu Liben's three daughters were quite different from Liu Liben himself. His daughters had all inherited Liu Liben's shrewdness, but they were of higher moral quality and didn't treat the village's poorer residents with the haughtiness or disdain that their father did. They respected their elders and cherished children. All the villagers seemed to love them. The three daughters were outstanding, so it was unfortunate that Qiaozhen and her sister Qiaoying hadn't gone to school; he'd heard that Qiaoling was the flower of her school. It would certainly be a challenge for any peasant to marry one of Liu Liben's daughters. Gao Minglou had wasted no time in marrying off his eldest son to Qiaoying. Now, the match-maker was banging down the family's door for Qiaozhen, and this time it was Ma Shuan of Madian who, wearing Dacron practically from head to toe, was running back and forth to Liu

Liben's house. Remembering Ma Shuan's outfit the other day, Gao Jialin couldn't help but laugh.

The sun was beginning to sink into the endless mountain range to the west of the Great Horse River. From the bridge, Jialin could see the road that led to their village was already in shade, and the green of the crops along the route seemed to be deepening. No one was coming or going from town at this hour. To the southeast, the county seat was covered in a swath of blue smoke. The County River, not yet as wide as it would be in late autumn, curved peacefully around the city on its way south, its surface reflecting the light of the setting sun. On the shore, a bare-bottomed child was playing on the muddy beach; the women from the city had finished washing their clothes and were gathering up the colorful garments and bedding that had been drying on the grassy banks.

Every so often, Gao Jialin gazed down the road toward town. He didn't have much hope that Qiaozhen would be successful in selling the buns, since the market had closed for the day hours ago.

When he saw Qiaozhen carrying the basket and trotting back toward him, he figured she couldn't have sold them all— she hadn't been gone long enough!

Qiaozhen walked up to him and quickly took out a roll of cash and stuffed it in his hand. "You can check, I charged 1.5 per piece."

Gao Jialin was astonished to see the empty basket in her arms. With the roll of money stuffed in his pocket, he felt hugely grateful to Qiaozhen. He didn't know what to say. He hesitated for a while, then finally said, "Qiaozhen, you're really something!"

Liu Qiaozhen's face brightened at Jialin's praise, and her eyes filled with tears.

Jialin stretched out his hand. "Give me the basket and hurry home on your bike. The sun is about to set."

Qiaozhen didn't hand over the basket; instead, she hung it on the front of her bike and said, "Let's go together! Hop on."

All of a sudden, Jialin felt awkward. Sharing a bike with a girl from his village in full view of everyone didn't seem right. But he also couldn't think of a good way to refuse her.

He hesitated and then lied, "I'm afraid to take you on the back—I'm afraid you'll fall."

"I'll take you then!" Qiaozhen held the handlebars in both hands and gave him a friendly smile, then looked down shyly.

"Aiya, how would that work?" Jialin scratched his head, unsure of what to do.

"Well then, we won't ride. We'll walk back together." Qiaozhen's beautiful eyes looked at him stubbornly. Her chest rose and fell.

She seemed to really want him to go back with her. He felt he had no choice and said, "OK, let's go then. I'll push the bike."

He reached out to take the bicycle, but Qiaozhen nudged him away gently with her shoulder. "You've walked all day. You must be tired. I'm not tired at all. Let me push it."

Just like that, he followed her. When they reached the end of the bridge, they turned and followed the open road along the river and toward home.

The sun had just set behind the mountains, and a red cloud was blooming across the western sky. Pale saffron rays of light shone on the mountains while the great peaks on either side of the river cast their dense shadows on the valley. The air was cool and heavy. The long-stalked crops were exploding with tassels. The corn, sorghum, and millet grew in neat rows, already taller than a person. The beans were all in bloom, and the evening was filled with a light botanical perfume. On the distant mountainsides, flocks of sheep were descending into the valley, white specks among clusters of green grass. A beautiful summer night, the earth at its most tranquil and magnificent.

Gao Jialin and Liu Qiaozhen walked along the verdant road, the crops on either side of them separating them from the rest of the world, creating their own mysterious realm. Their hearts were thumping in their chests as they made their way together in this secret place.

They didn't say anything at first. Qiaozhen pushed the bike and walked very slowly. Jialin tried to slow down to put a bit of distance between them, so he wasn't walking right next to her. He felt more nervous than he ever had before, since he had never walked alone with a girl on a quiet evening. It felt as though they were out for a stroll together.

Gao Jialin couldn't help but glance at Qiaozhen's profile. He was amazed to discover that Qiaozhen was even more beautiful than he had thought. She was as tall and slender as a white poplar, and she curved perfectly from her head to her toes. Her clothing was well-worn: what had once been dark-blue pants were now faded, along with a short-sleeved light-yellow Dacron shirt, light-brown sandals, and socks that were an even lighter brown. As she pushed the bicycle, her eyes seemed to watch the ground ahead of her, but she wasn't really focused on anything. Every so often she would look up, smile slightly, and turn toward him, as though she wanted to say something, but then she would turn back and continue on as before. Gao Jialin suddenly felt that he had once met a girl just like Qiaozhen, but on second thought, it must have been in a painting. Perhaps an oil painting by a Russian artist with a swath of green farmland and a tall, slender girl walking along a little path, gazing into the distance as she went, a red scarf tied around her hair.

While Gao Jialin was daydreaming, Qiaozhen's emotions were in turmoil. Walking alone with her love for the first time, the illiterate country girl was intoxicated with happiness. She had envisioned this day for many years. Her heart was beating wildly; her hands shook on the handlebars; the tide of her feelings rose in her heart; innumerable words caught in her throat, but she didn't know how to begin. She was determined to lay her heart bare for him today, but she was so shy she could barely open her mouth. She forced herself to walk slowly, waiting for the sky to darken further. She thought, *Walking and not talking like this won't do! I have to say something.* So she turned her head, still not looking at him, and said, "Gao Minglou isn't to be trusted—he'll do anything to get his way . . ."

Jialin stared at her, surprised. "You're talking shit about your own family?"

"I'm not. He's my sister's father-in-law. He's got nothing to do with me!" Qiaozhen looked at him daringly.

"Would you insult your sister's father-in-law in front of your sister?"

"I would, and I have! And I'd do it to his face!" Qiaozhen deliberately slowed down so she was walking next to Jialin.

At first, Gao Jialin couldn't make out why Qiaozhen would insult Gao Minglou in front of him, so he asked, "Why shouldn't I trust Secretary Gao? I don't understand."

Qiaozhen suddenly stopped and said angrily, "Jialin! He maneuvered and manipulated to fire you and hire his own son in your place! Look at how worried he's got you now . . ."

Gao Jialin had no choice but to stop alongside her. He looked at her lovely face full of earnest empathy.

He didn't say anything, just sighed and continued walking.

Qiaozhen went back to pushing her bike. This time she walked a bit closer to him, drawing parallel with him, and said, intimately, "God knows he did something wrong, and eventually he'll get what's coming to him! Don't torture yourself, Brother Jialin. You've gotten so skinny recently. If you're a farmer, then you're a farmer, just one of the many under the sun. No worse off than the party cadres. We have mountains and rivers here, good air, and as long as your family sticks together, you'll have a wonderful life . . ."

Gao Jialin listened to Qiaozhen's speech and felt closer to her. He needed someone to comfort him. He wanted to chat about everyday things with her. He half-smiled and said, "I studied awhile, but not enough, and the military's no good, either. I can be a farmer, but I can't do physical labor, and I'm afraid I'll starve my future wife and children to death!" When he finished, he laughed.

Qiaozhen suddenly stopped and gazed up at him.

"Brother Jialin! If you don't hate me, why don't we get together? You could stay at home while I labor in the mountains for the both us! I won't let you suffer . . ." She looked down and pushed the bike with one hand, nervously pulling at her clothes with the other.

Blood rushed to Jialin's head. Shocked, he stared at Qiaozhen but didn't know what to say, his chest burning as though on fire. His muscles tensed, and his limbs went rigid as a corpse.

Love? So suddenly? He simply wasn't prepared for it. He had never dated, and certainly hadn't considered loving

Qiaozhen. He felt panicked, but also curious, and regarded Qiaozhen with these complex emotions swirling through him. She was still looking down shyly, like a sweet lamb clinging to his side. The soft fragrance of her body reached his nostrils, and the sight of her beautiful face and body affected him. He tried to control himself and said to her, "It's probably best that we don't stand out here in the street like this. It's getting dark. Let's go . . ."

Qiaozhen nodded, and the two began to walk again. Jialin didn't say anything, but took the handles of the bike from her hands; she didn't say anything, either, but let him take the bike. Neither of them knew what to say.

After a while, Gao Jialin asked her, "Why did you suddenly tell me all that just now?"

"What do you mean, *suddenly*?" Qiaozhen looked up, tears silently trickling down her face. As she wiped them away, she confessed everything she had been feeling these past few years, sparing no details.

His eyes became damp as he listened. Although he usually had a rather tough exterior, he was deeply stirred by Qiaozhen's words. With this surge of emotion came a strange new kind of excitement: before his eyes, a scene of infinite colors flew by; infinite melodies from his favorite songs rang in his ears; the mountains, rivers, and earth around him appeared hazy . . .

After Qiaozhen was done talking, Jialin lowered the kick-stand with a pop and propped the bike up on the road. Then, he tugged at his clothing nervously.

Seeing him like this, Qiaozhen smiled. As she smiled, she wiped the tears from her eyes and took her flower-print bag off the bike rack to produce a pack of Yunxiang-brand cigarettes that she presented to him.

Gao Jialin opened his mouth in surprise and said, "How did you know I was looking for a cigarette?"

She gave him a charming grin. "I just knew. Go ahead and smoke! I bought you a whole carton!"

Gao Jialin moved to stand close to her. He didn't take the cigarettes at first; he just stared at her, dazed, with love in his eyes. She gazed up at him and rested her hands on his chest. Jialin hesitated for a moment, then put his arms lightly around her shoulders and pressed his feverish forehead to her similarly feverish one. He closed his eyes and lost himself in the moment.

～

By the time they were again walking side by side down the road, the moon had risen. The moonlight turned everything around them misty; the sound of flowing water from the Great Horse River was loud and clear in the quiet night. The village was just ahead—they would say goodbye on the road just below the bend in the river.

At the crossroads, Qiaozhen fished another pack of cigarettes out of her bag, put it in Jialin's basket, looked down, and said softly, "Jialin, kiss me again . . ."

Gao Jialin embraced her and kissed her. "Qiaozhen, don't mention this to your family. You must remember—don't let anyone know! And brush your teeth later . . ."

Qiaozhen nodded toward him in the dark. "Whatever you say . . ."

"Hurry home. When your family asks why you're back so late, what will you tell them?"

"I'll just say I went to town to see my aunt."

Jialin nodded, picked up his basket, and turned to go. Qiaozhen pushed her bicycle toward her home.

A feeling of regret suddenly welled up in Gao Jialin's heart as he entered the village. He worried that he had been too impulsive, that he had made a mistake. He felt that if he kept going like this, he would almost certainly become a peasant. Also, by kissing her without considering the consequences, he had been irresponsible both to himself and Qiaozhen. What made him feel even worse was that he'd said goodbye to twenty-four years of innocence, and from this point forward he would always have a blot on his record. He wanted to burst into tears; whether out of happiness or sadness, he didn't know. By the

71

time he walked through his front door, his mother and father were waiting for him on the kang. The table had long been set, but it was clear they hadn't moved a chopstick. When his father saw him, he asked, "Why are you so late? It's been dark for ages, and we've been worried sick!"

His mother stared at his father. "Our son tied himself in knots today to earn a living, and you are hassling him about coming back late!" She looked at her son. "Did you sell the buns?"

"Yes," said Jialin. He pulled out the money Qiaozhen had given him and put it in his father's hand.

Old Gao Yude sucked on his pipe as he walked over to the lamp, his thin hands counting the money as he said, "You sure did! Your mom had better steam another batch tomorrow morning so you can go sell some more. This will be much easier work than laboring in the mountains!"

Dismayed, Jialin shook his head. "I won't earn a living doing that. I'll go to work in the mountains."

His mother took a letter out from her sewing basket, which was stowed behind the kang, and said, "Your uncle sent a letter—hurry up and read it for us."

Jialin suddenly remembered he had forgotten to send the letter to his uncle—all because of that damned basket of buns. It was still in his pocket. He took his uncle's letter and read it for the two old people by the light of the lamp.

Older Brother, Sister-in-Law,

How are you? I'm writing you today to let you know that my superiors recently decided to transfer me. I've spent decades with the army and have a deep affection for it, but I must toe the party line and do as I'm told. At this point I still don't know where I'm headed. When I find out, I'll write to you again.

How are the crops this year? Has anything bad happened? If you need anything, please let me know.

Has Jialin's school started yet? I wish him the best of luck as he endeavors to serve the party's educational goals.

I hope everyone is well!
Your younger brother,
Yuzhi

When Gao Jialin finished reading, he handed the letter back to his mother and thought that at this point it no longer mattered that he hadn't sent the letter to his uncle.

CHAPTER 6

Liu Qiaozhen had brushed her teeth. This might seem like a mundane event, but as soon as she was seen doing it, news spread through the village like wildfire. To the villagers, teeth-brushing was something only cadres and scholars did—why would ordinary folk and country bumpkins bother with it? Gao Jialin brushed his teeth; Gao Sanxing brushed his teeth; Liu Qiaozhen's little sister, Qiaoling, brushed her teeth and no one seemed to notice, but when illiterate female commune member Liu Qiaozhen brushed her teeth, everyone commented on how strange it was.

"Huh . . . Liu Liben's second daughter has set her sights quite high! What a girl . . . Where did she learn to do that?"

"She's barely spent a day away from home, and she can't read a single character. How did she get so civilized all of a sudden?"

"Hygiene this, hygiene that—even filthy sows have dozens of kids and they don't care about hygiene!"

"*Haiya*, you all didn't see, but one morning she was crouched down on the riverbank with a bloody paste dripping out of her mouth and down her face! See for yourself!"

~

A handful of villagers still held on to old-fashioned beliefs and were not used to modern, civilized people. Wherever they were—up in the mountains, on the road, at home—they were always gossiping about the latest "peep show" in their village.

Liu Qiaozhen didn't pay any attention to these comments. Her beloved Jialin had asked her to brush her teeth, so brush her teeth she would. An infatuated girl can drum up the courage to do just about anything for the man she loves. She didn't mind the snickering of commoners; she could bear anything for the love of Jialin.

So that morning she carried her washbasin to the riverbank by her home, knelt, and began to brush. She hadn't been at it for very long when the stiff bristles of her toothbrush tore into her gums just as the villager had said—"a bloody paste dripping out of her mouth and down her face." But she didn't fret over it and simply continued with the task at hand. Qiaoling told her a little blood was normal the first time, that after a while she'd be fine.

A few women were coming back from the mountains and stopped by the gate by her house to laugh at the spectacle she was making of herself. Then, some brainless kids from the village saw them and ran over to see what was going on. Not long after that, a couple of old men who had gotten up early to collect night soil came over to check out the situation.

The sound of the crowd grew to a low rumble as more people came to gawk at the tooth-brusher. The two old night-soil collectors suddenly knelt down in front of her as though they were examining a sick cow; pointing to her mouth, each gave his own diagnosis of her condition. Another old man saw her open mouth, frothy with blood, and thought she had some kind of horrible disease. He asked the other old men, "Shouldn't we run to get a doctor?" The whole crowd laughed.

Qiaozhen had wanted to explain herself to everyone, to confidently joke her way out of the situation, but she couldn't manage to say a word. She tried not to pay any attention to them and instead took her time as she brushed. She had thought she would be done by now, but she kept going, thinking, *I'll keep brushing for a while—then they'll get used to the idea!*

She clumsily poked around in her mouth with the tooth-brush for a few minutes. Eventually, she pulled out the brush and rinsed her mouth with some water from the basin. She then spit the toothpaste on the ground and took another drink from the basin. The crowd followed her movements with their eyes: basin to mouth, mouth to ground.

Right around then, Qiaozhen's father was leading two cows up from the river gully back toward his home. The farmer-cum-businessman had bought the cows a few days before but hadn't yet resold them. He had taken them down to the water to drink.

Liben was in his fiftieth year, though he looked younger, with his rosy cheeks and fair, unwrinkled skin. He was dressed entirely in clean blue khaki, like farmers wore, with his white cotton skullcap, yet he didn't look quite like a farmer, more like someone who worked in the kitchens in town.

When Liben drove the cows up the bank with loud shouts and saw a crowd surrounding Qiaozhen as she brushed her teeth, he practically foamed at the mouth himself. Over the past few days, he'd noticed Qiaozhen changing her clothes three times a day and constantly brushing her hair. Now she dared to brush her teeth! He had nearly flown off the handle several times lately, but he thought his daughter was too old to be scolded, so he had managed to swallow his anger.

But at the sight of Qiaozhen losing face in front of this crowd, he couldn't hold his fury in check anymore.

He instantly forgot about the two cows, and his whole face turned red. "You foolish girl," he scolded her. "Get out of here! Get back to the house! You've shamed the whole family!"

The crowd dispersed as Liu Liben shouted. The women and children left first, then the old men followed, rushing to gather up their night-soil-collecting baskets and awkwardly extricate themselves from the scene.

Two tears welled up in her eyes as Qiaozhen held on to the washbasin. "Father, what are you scolding me for? Brushing my teeth is hygienic—what's so bad about that?"

"Fuck hygienic! You're an ordinary country girl. Now you're foaming at the mouth, and the whole village will laugh at you for wasting money! You shame our ancestors!"

"I don't care. Brushing your teeth isn't some great sin!" Qiaozhen set her jaw. "Look at your teeth. You're fifty years old, and a ton have fallen out, probably because you haven't—"

"Nonsense! Good or bad teeth, it's all up to fate. What damn difference does brushing them make? Your grandfather never once brushed his teeth, and he lived to be eighty with all of them still in his mouth. And he was eating walnuts till the end! So throw all this stuff away!"

"Why don't you care if Qiaoling brushes her teeth?"

"Qiaoling is Qiaoling; you're you! She's a student; you're ordinary folk!"

"Ordinary folk can't practice hygiene?" Qiaozhen suddenly felt very hurt and began to cry. "Why didn't you pay for me to go to school? You could have gotten the money! And you know what else? You ruined my entire life. I might have eyes, but still I'm blind! And now you're bullying me for brushing my teeth. I . . ." She turned her back on him and covered her face with her hands as she wailed.

Liu Liben panicked. He realized he had gone too far—he hadn't treated his children like this for many years. He quickly tried to mollify her: "Dad was wrong, don't cry. If you want to brush your teeth, do it at home by the stove. Just don't run to the riverbank! Everyone in the village will laugh."

"Let them laugh! I'm not afraid of anything! I want to brush them outside!" Qiaozhen replied firmly.

Liu Liben sighed and turned to look at the back of the yard. Startled, he suddenly dashed toward the garden—in that short time, the two cows had already devoured the entire plot of cabbage he had worked so hard to grow.

Qiaozhen wiped away her tears and returned home feeling sorry for herself. First she washed her face and then brushed her hair out conscientiously at the mirror, undoing her two short, coarse black braids. She then tied back her hair with a patterned handkerchief, giving it some volume, just as all the fashionable city girls were doing. What should she wear? She was annoyed.

From that evening on, every moment of every day, Qiaozhen wanted to see Jialin; she wanted to chat with him, to be affectionate with him. But for some reason, Jialin seemed to be hiding from her. She thought about how lovingly he had kissed her that evening and how cold he was being toward her now, and she couldn't help but cry piteously, tears oozing out from beneath her eyelids.

Whenever she saw him these days, he was headed back from the mountains. He was dressed in rags with a grass rope for a belt, looking like a beggar. Every morning he would take his old hoe into the hills to help the farming brigade dig up a wheat field. He didn't return for lunch, preferring to eat the food provided for the group. He had new clothes, so why did he dress so shabbily? Yesterday she had seen him by the well collecting water with a huge tear at his shoulder, revealing a tanned patch of skin and muscle. As she stood on the riverbank watching, her heart hurt so much that she cried. She wanted so badly to run to him, but he didn't seem interested in her, and just hauled the water away—even though he had clearly seen her!

That night she slept terribly. She mulled it over again and again, but she couldn't figure out why he hadn't paid any attention to her.

Later the thought occurred to her that it might be because Jialin resented her for her new clothing. She had worn her best clothes these past few days.

That could be the reason! Look at how frayed his clothes were! He probably thought her too frivolous. After all, he was an intellectual, and he wouldn't court her like the peasants who always wore new clothes. How common she was! Jialin looked so shabby, but she still thought he was more handsome than if he'd been wearing something brand-new. He was so graceful! But she was exactly the opposite, changing into her newest clothes! Once he saw her this way, of course Jialin would be disgusted. Sadly she thought, *But Brother Jialin, I did this for you!*

She took off her short-sleeved beige Dacron jacket and deep-blue Dacron pants and put on the clothes she usually wore to work—old grass-green pants, a faded blue work jacket, and a pink shirt, with the collar turned down over the jacket.

After she finished getting dressed, she picked up her hoe and walked toward the village. Her brigade was hoeing the cornfields that day, and Jialin was on the mountainside opposite hoeing a wheat field, so he would definitely see her.

~

The day after Gao Jialin had gone to the market, he had started to work up in the mountains. He looked like a loser: he wore his worst clothes and tied a grass rope around his waist, as if disguising himself as a peasant. The only problem was that no peasants in the village actually dressed that badly. The sight of him provoked a good deal of gossip. There were those who said he didn't have it in him to endure hard labor; after two days, they said he might simply lie down and quit. They all pitied him; there were very few educated people in the village, and it didn't feel right that he was now just like the rest of them. The village girls all clucked their tongues at the state of their teacher, the man who used to wear the most fashionable clothes, now dressed like a beggar.

Life

Gaojia Village wasn't very big; about forty families were scattered on a mountainside at the mouth of a small gully along the south side of the Great Horse River. Half the families lived in the valley near the gully, and the other half were down in the gully itself. In the gully was a creek that flowed for most of the year, trickling past one end of the village before it emptied into the Great Horse River. The flat lands on either side of the river were the villagers' main source of farmland. The farmland in the mountains on either side of the valley was actually larger than on the river flats, but even though they planted more wheat there, they somehow reaped less.

Because the village was so small, the families there had been grouped together in one production brigade by the local commune. Now, with the reforms over the past two years, they had been divided into two "production responsibility groups." Some commune members wanted them to divide into even smaller groups, and some even insisted on each household having its own production quota. But up until this point at least, Secretary Gao Minglou had resisted that pressure, and they had not been divided further. The secretary was not so satisfied with the changes that had occurred over the past few years. He didn't like the current laws—in his words, they "stomped all over the socialist system"; on the other hand, he also felt that there was no way to resist the tides of change. Still, circumstances required action. He would often sing out, "We must never forget how kind collectivization has been to us, but we

83

cannot resist the trend toward household quotas," even though, in reality, he was doing his best to drag his feet. In fact, he simply called the two village production brigades by the new name, "responsibility groups," so that he could report back to the commune that Gaojia Village was following the new laws.

Gao Jialin's family was part of the first brigade. But now they were hoeing the cornfields, and Jialin wasn't very good at it, so he went to dig in the mountains with the brigade digging up the wheat fields.

He worked so hard that the other farmers were astonished. On his first day in the fields, he stripped bare to the waist and said nothing to anyone, just threw himself into digging up the ground. He worked without eating, and even when his hands swelled up, he didn't seem to notice. He simply kept digging. Even when the blisters on his hands burst, and his palms began to bleed, and the handle of the pickax turned red, he still dug like a madman. One after another they begged him to slow down or rest, but he shook his head and wouldn't listen; he just kept recklessly swinging his pickax.

Today was the same; his pickax was quickly stained red.

Old Deshun, who had been digging in the earth nearby, noticed what was happening. He called his oxen to a halt, ran over, and seized the pickax from Jialin. He threw it to one side, so angry that the two long white strands of his moustache trembled. He scooped up two handfuls of dried yellow earth and rubbed them into the bloody mess that covered Jialin's hands and then forced him over to a shady spot, preventing him from showing off anymore. Old Deshun had been a bachelor his whole life, and he was a good and honest spirit. He loved all the children in the village: whenever he came across something nice, rather than keep it for himself, he'd give it to them. He felt especially sentimental toward Jialin. When Jialin was little and attending school, his parents were in dire straits—sometimes they didn't even have enough money for a pencil. Deshun would often give the boy a few coins. When Jialin started middle school, Deshun would go to town to sell melons and other fruits and sometimes had half a basket or so left over. He would often give this to Jialin to take to school. The sight of Jialin working as though his life depended on it, his tender hands rubbed raw, was almost unbearable to Deshun.

The old man pulled Jialin behind an outcropping, made him sit down, grabbed his earth-covered hands, and said, "Yellow earth will stop the blood . . . Jialin! You can't lose your temper like that again. You've just started this work; you must get into a rhythm. The days ahead will be long. Oh, you stubborn ass!"

Jialin's hands hurt like they had been slashed by knives. He pushed his palms together and bent his head awkwardly, trying to wipe his sweat onto his bare shoulders. "Grandpa Deshun," he said, "I wanted to do the most difficult part first, get it over with, so no matter what bitter work I faced, I wouldn't be afraid. Don't worry about me; let me get on with my work. Besides, I'm so out of sorts, a bit of hard work and pain will help me forget everything . . . so let my hands be destroyed!"

He lifted his disheveled head and chewed on his lip, a fierce expression on his face.

Old Deshun lit a cigarette and sat beside him, his hand running over his yellow-dust-covered face. It was all he could do to shake his gray-haired head and say, "Don't dig again tomorrow—come with me and learn to plow. Look at your hands; you can't even hold an ax like that. At least wait until they're better . . ."

Jialin shook his head resolutely. "No, I don't want them to get better!" He stood up and walked toward the bank, spit on his ruined hands, and recklessly swung the ax. The sun flamed down on his naked, sunburned back, and sweat quickly soaked the waistband of his pants.

Old Deshun watched this display of tenacity, sighed, and picked up a jar of water from the ground. He placed it next to Jialin and said, "It's all yours. You're not used to the heat yet. Drink it all . . ." He sighed and went back to plowing.

Jialin dug a full row before he returned to the jar of water and drank half of it in one gulp. He wanted to drink all of it, but he looked over at Old Deshun and took the jar back to the oxen.

He felt as though all the bones had fallen out of his body, as though his hands were clutching two spikes, as though thousands of arrows were piercing his heart—so he sat down.

Still, he felt a kind of inexpressible joy. He had shown everyone that he possessed the most valuable quality for a good farmer—the ability to bear hardship. And that he had a strong character, although that might cause him to make mistakes in certain situations.

He pulled out a cigarette, lit it, and took a fierce drag. It was the most delicious one he'd ever had.

At that moment, Qiaozhen appeared in the cornfield on the other side of the river, looking up at him. Although he couldn't make out her expression clearly, she seemed to rise up into the air and take flight straight toward him.

It was as though his heart was being stabbed by needles.

CHAPTER 7

Gao Jialin lay down on the brick kang, too tired even to eat dinner. His mother's brow was furrowed as she set the table, urging him to eat like she would coax a small child, saying, "People are iron, but food is steel, and hunger will always win out." His father told him under no circumstances was he to return to the mountain the next day: "Stay home and rest; you'll have to get used to it slowly."

Jialin didn't hear a word they said. At that moment his thoughts were entirely focused on Qiaozhen.

Ever since that day at the market, he had regretted his impulsive behavior with Qiaozhen. He felt that his current situation was not conducive to dating and that he had kind of fallen from grace because of what he'd done with an uncultured girl from the village—almost like he had resigned himself to the life of a peasant. Quite the opposite was true, however; the fire of his dreams for his future was not yet extinguished, and although he was a dust-covered peasant right now, he might not always be. He was still young, only twenty-four. He had time to wait for his luck to change. If he bound up his fate with Qiaozhen's, he would be bound to the earth as well.

But what was most annoying was that Qiaozhen refused to be wiped from his thoughts. Despite hiding from her for the past few days, he missed her terribly. His frustration at this was more painful than his ruined hands.

Qiaozhen was so beautiful, her lively face so full of passion and her body lithe like a white poplar, continuously swaying in his mind's eye.

Especially at night after he returned home from work, when his exhausted body lay rigidly on the kang, his desire for her became all the stronger. He thought that if she were by his side, then his mind and body would be able to relax; she would be able to transform his restless heart into a placid lake, undisturbed by wind or waves.

She loved him. She loved him ardently. He noticed how she had constantly changed her clothes over the past few days, and knew it was for him. Today, after he got off work and the other farmers had all left, he'd seen her standing on the other side of the river, waiting for him. But still he hid from her. He knew she cried for him; he imagined her returning home on the path through the cornfield, heartbroken. He knew he was being unreasonable—she wanted so much to be with him, why did he hide from her? Didn't he also long to be with her?

As he lay on the kang, a powerful current of passion suddenly broke through the dam of logic he had constructed. He threw reason to the winds, and wanted only to see her as soon as possible, to be at her side.

He got out of bed, told his father he had some business in another part of the village, and ran out the door.

The night was quiet. Stars had begun to appear in the sky, and moonlight shone through the mist. The earth was covered in a swath of shadows and an air of mystery.

Gao Jialin walked south and stood on the hillside by Liu Liben's house. He didn't know how to get Qiaozhen to come out.

As he was hesitating beside the high walls of Liu Liben's courtyard, he suddenly saw someone emerge from behind an old locust tree outside the main gate and rush toward him. Aha, it was his love! She had been waiting all this time, hoping against hope that he would appear!

Gao Jialin's heart beat wildly, but he didn't say a word, just turned and walked along the road that followed the stream into the gully toward the edge of the village. From time to time, he'd turn his head to look back at Qiaozhen, who followed close behind him.

When he reached the gully at the edge of the village, he lay down comfortably under a pear tree and listened excitedly to the sound of those sweet footsteps rustling toward him.

When she arrived, he quickly sat up. She hesitated slightly, then timidly yet determinedly sat down, leaning against him. She didn't speak, but kissed the place where his clothing had been torn open at the seam and the darkly tanned skin of his arm was exposed. Then she hugged him around his shoulders, pressing her face to the spot she had just kissed, and began to sob piteously.

Gao Jialin leaned into her, returning her hug, and pressed his face against her head, unable to suppress the tears filling his eyes and falling onto her lacquer-black hair. There was no one in the world he felt closer to at that moment.

Qiaozhen dropped her head on his chest, still crying, and said, "Brother Jialin, why have you been ignoring me?"

"You must have been so sad . . ." Gao Jialin stroked her hair with his ruined hands.

"You can see into my heart, and you're right." Qiaozhen's eyes, still shining with tears, gazed sadly at him.

"I'll never do that again, Qiaozhen." Jialin kissed her forehead.

Qiaozhen's trembling arms encircled his neck. She smiled with pleasure and said, "Brother Jialin, swear it on the Jade Emperor in heaven!"

Jialin was amused. "You're so superstitious! You must believe me, Qiaozhen . . . and why aren't you wearing that beige short-sleeved shirt? It looks lovely on you . . ."

"I was afraid you wouldn't like it, so I changed into this." Qiaozhen pouted mischievously.

"Wear it again tomorrow, then."

"OK. If you want, I'll wear it every day!" Qiaozhen reached for her flower-print bag and pulled out six boiled eggs and a cake, which she set in front of him.

Gao Jialin was taken aback. He had been focused on Qiaozhen and hadn't noticed that she had brought anything to eat.

While she peeled an egg for him, she said, "I know you didn't eat anything this evening. Those of us who do hard labor all year long are too tired to eat when we get home—I can't even imagine how you're feeling!" She gave him the egg and a piece of cake. "My mother's been terribly sick for the past few days. My sister brought her the cake, but she didn't want to eat it. I stole it from the cupboard this evening!" Qiaozhen laughed good-naturedly. "If you hadn't come to find me, I was going to bring these things to you at your house!"

Jialin swallowed a bite of cake. "You mustn't! If your father knew, he'd break your legs!" he joked.

Qiaozhen pressed another peeled egg into Jialin's hands and watched him happily while he wolfed it down. She put her hands and head on his shoulders and said tenderly, "Brother Jialin, you're sweeter to me than my father is to my mother."

"What nonsense! You really are a stupid girl!" Gao Jialin shoved the other half of the egg into his mouth. He patted her head softly, then shouted as one of the blisters on his hand broke against her hairpin.

Qiaozhen looked up in shock, unaware of what had happened, but quickly understood. Flustered, she searched in her bag. "Look, I forgot . . ."

She pulled out a bottle of red salve and a pack of sterilized cotton. She grabbed Jialin's hand and pulled it toward her, applying balm to his wound.

Jialin's jaw fell open. "How did you know my hands were hurt?"

Qiaozhen looked down as she applied the salve to his hands and said, "The Jade Emperor in heaven told me." She tittered. "Who in the village doesn't know about your hands?! You gentlemen, your hands are so delicate!" She gazed at him and smiled, parting her lips slightly to reveal two rows of pearly teeth as beautiful as white corn kernels.

An enormous wave of emotion rose in Jialin's chest.

Oh love, sweet love! Like the silent spring rain sprinkling the fretful field of my heart. He had only ever experienced the emotion before while reading in fiction, but now he truly felt it. Most precious of all was that this happiness had come to him in the midst of great adversity.

After Qiaozhen had thoroughly applied the salve to his hands, he lay on the ground, utterly content. Qiaozhen leaned gently against him, her face pressed against his chest as though intent on studying every beat of his heart.

They cuddled together in silence, her body like a white-edged morning glory curling around a sunflower. The stars were scattered across the dark blue of the night sky like bright pearls. The contours of the Old Ox Mountains to the west looked soft and beautiful, as though drawn with a pencil. The wind had died down, and everything around them was still. Amid the gently rustling green leaves above their heads, unripe pears floated in the misty moonlight.

They lay sweetly in the quiet beneath the sky and in the embrace of the earth.

~

When love first awakens a young person, it bestows a great power. This is especially true in the case of those who have entirely lost faith in themselves—in them, passionate love can cause the spirit to come alive again.

Qiaozhen's love was intoxicating: Gao Jialin felt uplifted, like he had a new passion for life. A warm current of love flowed over the cold tundra of his spirit, and he felt a new force blossom.

Love also gave him a deeper appreciation of the land. He had always been a child of the earth: he was born here and had lived a dreamlike childhood among the mountains and rivers of this place. When he'd gone to the city to attend school, the smell of the soil on him faded. He'd had less and less contact with the land. Now, with the help of Qiaozhen's pure and beautiful love, he was coming to a deeper understanding: he shouldn't fear living off the earth; this cherished land could still bear sweet fruit!

Gao Jialin slowly began to work in a more measured way: he stopped driving himself as he had those first days, until the physical pain forced the anguish from his heart.

After a while, his hands grew tougher. He rose early in the morning, and his back and legs were no longer so sore. He even learned how to plow and to do the very difficult job of separating the seedlings. He lost his taste for cigarettes, so he took a pipe up to the mountains. As a teacher, he had chosen his words carefully, but once he started working in the fields, he abandoned his precise way of speaking for the authentic language of the peasants; he learned to speak crudely and to joke with the women. His clothes naturally grew more and more tattered, and he washed or replaced them as necessary.

He would come home at noon every day and, without asking, help his father tend the allotment and help his mother pump the bellows. He also raised a few rabbits on the side. He spent his days like any other peasant, constantly busy.

The day was for working, but he had very pleasant evenings. Everything he suffered was endurable precisely because he had something so happy to look forward to.

At night, after it got dark, he and Qiaozhen would meet in the fields outside the village. Beneath the dense veil of night, they'd hold hands like children and stroll silently and aim-lessly along the field paths, occasionally stopping to kiss or to gaze at each other sweetly and smile. When they tired of walk-ing, they'd find a secluded spot where Jialin would lie down and release his exhaustion from the day with a contented sigh. Qiaozhen would then nestle into his side and comb through his dusty, disheveled hair with her fingers. Or she would press her delicate mouth to his ear and softly, softly sing one of the ancient folk songs passed down by their ancestors. Sometimes during this lullaby, Jialin would fall asleep and join his resonant snoring to her song. His beloved would then quickly rouse him and plead, "Look at how tired you are. You should take it easy tomorrow!" She would take his hand, cover her face with it, and say, "Wait until we're married when you'll get to rest at the beginning of the week. I'll give you a real Sunday, just like you had at school."

Every day Jialin was intoxicated by her sweet ministrations, and every day all other thoughts were pushed further from his mind. Only when he happened to see one of the county or commune cadres rushing along the road across the river, the wind blowing pleasantly over their snow-white Dacron shirts, would he suddenly feel melancholy. A slight bitterness would rise in his throat as though he had tried to swallow a pill that wouldn't go down. He'd do his best to suppress this feeling, but he'd only really settle down when he saw Qiaozhen again, when he could then finally swallow the pill and chase it with a spoonful of honey.

He wanted to be with Qiaozhen all the time. He regretted that they weren't on the same production brigade since that made it hard to see each other during the day. They missed each other like crazy. Sometimes their two groups would work near each other, and when it was time for a break, he would pretend to be looking for something and run to the other group. He never said anything to Qiaozhen, just looked at her. No one around them had any idea; only the two of them knew what was in their hearts—and that made it all the sweeter.

Sometimes he didn't have a good excuse to go find her. Then she would belt out those two poignant lines:

Upstream a goose and downstream a gander

A lovely pair, she gazes bright-eyed at her brother

Whenever he heard the song from afar, he couldn't help but smile.

Once when Qiaozhen had just finished singing, the women teased her, "Qiaozhen, Ma Shuan is on his way—quick—look at him with your bright eyes!"

She scolded them angrily and threw dirt at them, but was secretly proud and thought, *Jialin is ten times stronger than Ma Shuan, you'll see, and your eyes will be red with envy!*

All the while that Gao Jialin and Qiaozhen were falling in love, matchmakers streamed into Liu Liben's house. Liu Liben told them all that times were changing, and the decision should lie with his daughter. But secretly, he had a different plan. He had selected Ma Shuan—he was not badly off, he was honest, and he still understood enterprise, which was good since Liu Liben really wanted to go into business with his son-in-law at some point. But Qiaozhen didn't think much of this darkly tanned young man, and Ma Shuan had his work cut out to persuade her otherwise. He even thought about asking his relative Gao Minglou to try to convince Qiaozhen.

Matchmakers would also frequently come by Gao Jialin's. Jialin's parents were thrilled with the idea that someone might find them a daughter-in-law, especially after seeing their meager home. There was one girl from a village on the other side of the mountain who didn't want a bride-price—just Jialin himself—and Gao Yude was especially interested in her. But what was cause for celebration for his parents was met with laughter by Gao Jialin.

Jialin and Qiaozhen were happy with things the way they were since they could keep their love a secret. For the moment, they didn't want to share the news of their romance, as this would undoubtedly make them the butt of intolerable taunts and coarse comments from the villagers. The two young lovers wouldn't let anyone destroy their quiet, mysterious happiness.

Once, when Jialin and Old Deshun were working together, the old man asked, "Jialin, do you want a wife or not?"

Jialin laughed and said, "Sure, but there's nobody suitable."

"What about Qiaozhen?"

Jialin's face turned red, and he didn't know what to say.

Deshun grinned and said, "I think you two would be a good match! Qiaozhen is smart with excellent character; you two were made for each other! Jialin, you have good taste!"

A bit panicky, Jialin said, "Grandfather, I've never considered it."

"Boy, there's no need to be like that. We old men see everything!"

Jialin frowned and said, "OK, Grandfather, but you mustn't say anything!"

Deshun took Jialin's hands in his wrinkled ones and said, "My lips are sealed so tightly that not even iron bars can pry them apart! I'm so happy for you children. It's just like the old song; you two 'truly were paired up by heaven.'"

At midday, after he and Deshun had finished their work and were returning home, they happened across Ma Shuan at the entrance to the village. He looked as he had the last time Jialin had seen him: dressed in head-to-toe Dacron and pushing his gaily decorated bicycle. Jialin thought, a little unhappily, *You're on your way to Qiaozhen's house.*

Ma Shuan warmly greeted the pair. At first, he didn't say anything to Jialin, waiting for Deshun to walk a little ahead.

Then he said, "Professor Gao! I've just come from Liu Liben's house. I'm going to ruin my legs running back and forth to that place. Once again, Qiaozhen didn't pay any attention to me, even though I've burned incense at the temple about it. You're from this village, and you're a teacher, so you must know Liben's daughters. Can't you help me out?"

Gao Jialin was not thrilled at this request, but he did his best not to show it. He managed a smile and said to Ma Shuan, "You're wasting your time. Qiaozhen has her eye on someone else."

"Who?" Ma Shuan asked, surprised.

"You'll find out soon enough . . ."

At this, he walked around the disheartened Ma Shuan and returned home.

CHAPTER 8

Rumors that Gao Jialin and Liu Qiaozhen were together quickly spread throughout the village.

They were first exposed by some elementary school kids who had been stealing watermelons from the fields after dark. They said that one night they saw their old teacher, Gao, hugging and kissing Qiaozhen in the fields on the far side of the village behind a hay bale. Still others confirmed that they had seen the two lying together in the sorghum one night on the near side of the river . . .

As the rumor passed from person to person, it grew increasingly outrageous. There were those who said Qiaozhen's stomach was growing bigger; others said that she had already borne a child; and there were even those who could describe the time and place of the birth in painstaking detail.

Liu Liben eventually heard these rumors. The day they reached him, Double Ace donned his skullcap, so angry it seemed that steam came out his ears. At lunch, allowing her no opportunity to explain or make excuses, he beat his good-for-nothing daughter outside by their mud-brick stove. Then he furiously marched to the north side of the village to talk to Gao Yude.

Double Ace had suddenly realized that Qiaozhen's behavior—brushing her teeth, changing clothes three times a day, running around after dark—was all because of Gao Yude's black sheep of a son!

He ran up to the decrepit walls of Gao Yude's house and called out for him.

Jialin's mother shouted from inside that the old man wasn't at home.

"On such a bright, hot morning he should be inside eating! Where's he gotten to?" Liben bellowed from the yard.

"He's probably gone to work in the allotment." Jialin's mother hurried out and invited the respected village elder into her home.

But Liben said he was busy, turned, and walked away.

He went out the main gate, toward the stream, and around a small hill—straight to Gao Yude's allotment. On his way he laughed to himself. *Hmph, of course he's working in the dirt. So poor there's not two cents in their whole cave, and they want to marry their son off to my daughter. They don't even have a pot to piss in!*

From far away Liben could just make out the stooped figure of Gao Yude working his plot of millet, and he picked up the pace.

Although he was full of rage as he came up the path, Liben was mindful of the old customs as he greeted his elder: "Elder Brother Gao, could you please take a break? There's something I need to speak with you about."

Gao Yude saw that one of the most revered members of his village had sought him out on this blazing-hot morning and panicked. He couldn't utter a word, simply dropped his hoe and beckoned Liben over.

The two of them sat in the shadow of the mountains. Old Yude offered up his pipe, but Liben waved it away saying, "Go ahead, I'm afraid I'd choke on it!" As he spoke, Liben pulled a pack of Gong-brand cigarettes out of his pocket, lit one, and took a long drag. He turned to look at Yude with a gloomy expression. "Elder Brother Gao, your Jialin is messing around in the village. Why haven't you done anything? He's violating all our customs!"

"What's going on?" Old Gao Yude pulled the pipe from his bearded mouth in surprise and turned to face Liben.

"What's going on?" Liu Liben leaped to his feet, practically foaming at the mouth. "That prodigal son of yours is luring my Qiaozhen away in the middle of the night, doing god-knows-what with her without our approval and causing us to lose face in front of the whole village. I'm so embarrassed I wish I could

105

hide my head between my legs, while you go around with a clear conscience, pretending you don't know anything about it!" The tip of his cigarette trembled as he spoke.

"Aiya, my good Liben! I truly had no idea about any of this!" Old Gao Yude said, defensively.

"Well, now I've told you! If you don't do anything about it and I see your son carrying on with my daughter, I'll have no choice but to break his legs!"

Although Gao Yude had been a cowardly man all his life, upon hearing this powerful man threaten his only child, he stood up with a grunt and pointed the end of his brass pipe at Liben's white skullcap. "Young man," he shouted, "if you dare lift a finger in my son's direction, I'll split your head in two!" The old man looked as fearsome as an angry bull.

Meek people rarely get angry, but once they're angry, they lose control. Liu Liben saw this useless old man with one foot in the grave turn suddenly ferocious and panicked. He stepped back a few paces and stood still for a while. He didn't know how to respond.

In the end he turned and walked away, arms behind his back, clasped proudly at the elbows. As he departed, he shouted to Yude, "We're not finished here! You wait and see! I'll find a way to deal with you and your son. It's disgraceful!"

Liu Liben passed Gao Yude's potato plants, which were just beginning to sprout little white flowers, and returned the way he'd come.

Double Ace was restless and furious, but standing at a bend in the river, he didn't know where to go. He was a staunch traditionalist. He was a trader and always open in his dealings, but if he ever perceived a slight to his reputation, he couldn't let it go. As he saw it, a person lived for two things: money and respect. And wasn't the point of making money to gain respect? But that useless daughter of his would rather mess around with a good-for-nothing peasant than worry about losing face in front of the whole village! As he stood by the river, he raged silently at Qiaozhen. *Wretched girl! How can I show my face in the village after you've disgraced us?*

Suddenly he thought of his in-laws. *Minglou would take care of Jialin,* he thought. *If Jialin's not afraid of me, then he'll certainly be afraid of Minglou!* After all, he was the secretary! Jialin wouldn't be able to cope with hard labor, and if he wanted to get his teaching job back, he'd have to go through Minglou.

He walked from the bend in the river over a small hill toward Minglou's house, which was also on the north side of this village.

Gao Minglou's house was like his: a long cave house with five openings, bigger by far than the rest of the village houses. Not long ago Gao Minglou had built a wall around his home, as well as an arched entranceway. Still, Liben didn't feel like his in-laws' house was any better than his own. Minglou had built his entranceway out of mud bricks, and the enclosing wall out of stone, while the actual front gate was tall and pretentious, with a couplet engraved in stones on either side. The house had stone slabs for eaves, and although stone was certainly a better material than most of the other village peasants could manage, Liben's home used slate-colored tiles, which made it look just like city government buildings! Most importantly, his in-laws' facing stones were roughly shaped and, as a result, looked rather crude, while all the stones of *his* home were finely chiseled, the gaps filled with lime mortar, so that you couldn't tell where one stone ended and the next began.

But he hadn't come to his in-laws' today to compare the advantages of their respective homes. Today he had come to ask a favor of Minglou. Because, unlike his skills in making money or building houses, Liben's ability to grant favors paled in comparison to Minglou's.

His eldest daughter, Qiaoying, and her mother-in-law welcomed him warmly into their home. The central room was Minglou's parlor. There was no kang; instead there was a bed made up with clean bedclothes, like one of the commune's guest rooms. Usually no one slept there, but when cadres from the commune or the county seat got sent down to Gaojia Village, no one else ever volunteered to host, so Minglou brought them here to stay. There were two new, cheap-looking sofas against the windows, still waiting to be upholstered and wrapped in burlap.

Liben sat down, and his daughter's mother-in-law swiftly brought out a pot of tea and set it in front of him. Liben left his drink untouched, but took out a cigarette, lit it, and asked, "Where has Minglou gone?"

"You don't know? He went to the commune for a meeting. He's been gone for days. He said he'd come home today, but we haven't seen him yet. He'll probably be back this afternoon."

"I've been in Inner Mongolia buying a horse and I haven't gotten out much since I came back, so I didn't know he had gone to a meeting . . . ," Liu Liben said casually.

"Is something wrong?" his daughter's mother-in-law asked him.

"No, nothing. Just a little thing . . . If he's not at home, then there's no need to discuss it now. I'll take my leave." Liu Liben stood up and prepared to go.

Qiaoying wiped her floury hands off and stood in the doorway. "Father, I've already made some noodles. Please eat with us!"

Her mother-in-law also did her best to force him to stay.

Liben mulled it over: his home was in quite a state, with Qiaozhen and his wife weeping and wailing, so going home would certainly be upsetting. Plus he was hungry, and nobody would be making food at home. So he sat down on Minglou's family's tacky sofa and drank some tea. He thought, *After lunch, I'll go to the edge of the village to meet Minglou when he returns.*

~

Old Gao Yude was still standing in his allotment as Liu Liben sat on Minglou's couch. He perched his chin on his hoe and stared off blankly into the distance.

Liu Liben had just angrily confronted Gao Yude, seemingly without rhyme or reason, and said that his only son had seduced his daughter. The old man could make neither heads nor tails of the accusation.

Gao Yude hadn't been feeling too bad lately. His son had gotten over his frustrations and had devoted himself to his work, finally getting his life together again. Gao Yude was long in the tooth, but at least his son was in the prime of his life. Later he'd have a wife and children, and when it finally came time for Gao to close his eyes below the yellow earth, he would be at peace. His son was tougher than he was anyway, and Jialin would get along just fine without him.

But his grief was profound at the news Liben shared. He never thought his son would run around with someone behind his back like this. Everyone in the village placed a great deal of importance on having a proper wedding. This was so disappointing! And with someone from the same village, no less . . . This kind of thing could really damage the family's reputation.

At the same time, he thought, Qiaozhen was a good child, one of the best in the whole village, really. And if Jialin was able to find a wife like her, well, that was a happy stroke of luck, wasn't it? But if he wanted to marry her, he should have followed local customs. One must stay on the straight and narrow. How could he go with her to the fields in the middle of the night? And if Gao Yude took Liben's word for it, then it seemed the whole village thought Jialin was in the wrong. How shameful! As soon as someone lost his reputation, he forfeited any chance to marry—even an idiot or a cripple—since no one would think he had any integrity. They would look down on him and refuse to work with him in the future. *You idiot!* Gao Yude thought. *How could you be such an imbecile?*

The old man lost his desire to keep hoeing. He limped down the road, dragging his arthritic leg behind him, toward the bend in the river.

Even though he hadn't eaten lunch, he was not at all hungry. He sat under a willow tree at the riverside, his gaunt hands rubbing the bare soles of his feet, turning the issue over in his mind, trying to think of a way to solve it.

Although he was old, his mind was still alert. He decided to think about it from Qiaozhen's point of view: *Maybe the girl really does like my Jialin! Should I invite a matchmaker over to officially make the match?*

But as soon as he thought of Liu Liben, he became disheartened. How could someone like Gao Yude, from a poor home, dare to aspire to Liu Liben's level? Even a family with decent standing in the village wouldn't dare attempt that.

The sun was slanting over his head, and the shadows of the western mountains had plunged the gully into gloom; it was already late afternoon. Yude remained in the shade of the tree rubbing his bare feet, still at a loss for what to do.

"Oh! What are you stewing over out here by yourself?" a voice behind him asked.

Yude turned around and saw Old Deshun. He felt a desperate need to discuss the situation with him. Although the two were a few years apart in age, they had been friends all their lives; back in the old days, when they'd been hired laborers for a landowner, they had always stirred up trouble together. He raised his hand and called out, "Deshun, come have a seat. I've got a real problem!"

Deshun took the hoe off his shoulder and came over to sit beside Yude. "I've still got some work to do," he said. "I've got to till my allotment again this afternoon—the whole thing is full of weeds!" He took the pipe Gao Yude handed him and asked, "What's there to feel bad about? You have such a good, reliable son—things are bound to get better in a year or two. Jialin really is a good boy! Don't worry about Minglou or Liben causing a stink; soon no one will be able to stop Jialin from making good!"

"Aaaah." Yude gave a long sigh. "You praise him too much! He's in a lot of trouble."

"Trouble?" The wrinkles on Deshun's face deepened around his eyes.

Gao Yude hesitated, then said, "The youngster and Liu Liben's second daughter have been fooling around together, and the news has spread through the village like wildfire—you must have heard about it!"

"Oh, I figured it out a long time ago. Who said they're fooling around together? They're young people who get along—what's the big deal?"

"Aiya, you figured it out? Why didn't you tell me?" Gao Yude stared angrily at his friend.

"I thought you already knew! The children make such a good pair! They should embrace their youth!" Deshun said, smiling at the angry Yude.

"But this kind of behavior has never been honorable. It must be done the right way! How can they run around in the dead of night?"

"Aiya, you're so old-fashioned! We were young, too, once! I've never been married, but I had my fair share of shameless days in my youth, to say nothing of what young people must get up to now."

"Don't you go talking nonsense to me. Liu Liben was just here shouting at me something terrible, saying he wanted to break Jialin's legs! I'm sure something horrible will happen! What do you think I should do?" Gao Yude's face was a mask of worry, one hand continuously rubbing at his bare foot.

"Oh, let him roar like a tiger; he'll just scare away the foxes: no matter how much he tries to intimidate you, he'll never be able to intimidate his daughter, and as long as Qiaozhen loves Jialin, no one can keep them apart! You might not believe me, but just you wait and see. There's really no need to worry, though you seem to love to suffer. I must get back to my work now. Hurry home for some dinner."

Old Deshun gave the pipe back to Gao Yude, stood up, shouldered his hoe, and left. He walked away, breathily humming a *xintianyou*.

Gao Yude watched as he vanished from view and felt that although Deshun was older than him, his body seemed much more robust. "Huh," he said to himself, "I guess bachelors don't have any worries! You don't have to feed a family—you just have to feed yourself! You sure can talk the talk, but come back when you've got a son yourself. Then we'll see if *you* don't worry yourself to death! My son made me anxious when he was small, and he still worries me now that he's grown, not to mention the agony he's brought his mother . . ."

Gao Yude's legs had gone from painful to numb. He limped all the way home.

When he went inside, he saw Jialin bare legged and lying down on the kang, his nose in a book. His mother wasn't there; she was probably sleeping in the neighboring room.

The old man hung his hoe on the hook by the door and addressed his son. "Still reading! These books are ruining you! My son, at your age, how do you still not understand the way the world works? You're such a worry to us!"

Gao Jialin sat up. He had no idea what his father was talking about. He stared at him and said, "What have I done?"

"What have you done? A lot! Today Liu Liben came looking for me at our allotment and told me everything you and Qiaozhen have been up to. He said the whole village has been discussing your disgusting behavior!" And with this, Gao Yude squatted on the floor and massaged the bottoms of his feet.

Gao Jialin's mind raced. He put his book down on the kang and after a long while said, "Don't worry about it. The villagers will say whatever they want."

Gao Yude looked up, his head a mass of white hair. "My son, you must be careful! Liu Liben said he was going to break your legs!"

Gao Jialin chewed on his lip and chuckled grimly. "If he does that, I'll mess up his face."

Hurt and angry, Gao Yude stood and walked toward him. "You better not make any more trouble for me! You should have given up ideas like that a long time ago! How dare we climb up to their level? You know how important they are! They've got connections across the whole Great Horse River Valley!"

Gao Jialin crossed his arms over his strong chest and said to his pitiable father, "Who's climbing where? Dad, don't worry—this is my business, let me take care of it!"

Gao Yude knew how stubborn his son was. "My silly boy, the day will come when you fall . . . ," he lamented.

CHAPTER 9

Gao Minglou left his meeting at the commune and strolled along the highway—his second son, Sanxing, had taken their family's bicycle to school. He had volunteered to let his son take the bike; his son was a teacher, after all, and needed to look a bit more dignified. It wouldn't do for him not to have a bike.

The leader of Gaojia Village was in his fifties, but he could still get around quite well. He was outfitted from head to toe in blue khaki, but the color had faded with age. Beneath the brim of his cap was an imposingly ruddy face and two glinting, fiery eyes.

Walking along the road, Minglou was not in the finest mood. This most recent meeting at the commune was about how to best implement the new wage-for-labor system. It seemed like things were getting serious. Some neighboring towns had already begun to pay salaries according to workers' productivity. Commune Secretary Zhao was telling production brigade heads to adopt these new ideas, pressing them to move away from collectivized labor and toward the household responsibility system.

Isn't this just individualism by another name? Gao Minglou thought, resentfully.

He knew very well that these new laws would mean bigger harvests and bigger payouts. And that the majority of peasants would support them, especially in the mountain regions.

His dissatisfaction with the new laws came from his own way of thinking. In the old days, the villagers would work together in the mountains while he would squat at home the whole day "working," with all the work points accrued from the day's labor going to him, even though he did none of the real work. He had complete control over every aspect of the villagers' lives, from the land and grain taxes they paid to personal events, big and small. All these many years, no one in the entire village, young or old, dared disrespect him. But if they changed to a household-based labor system, they would all rise above their current circumstances, and no one would pay any mind to Gao Minglou! The thought of losing his power tormented him, since he had always advised everyone else. Not to mention that now he was supposed to farm his own land! He would have to work the soil from dawn till dusk just like everyone else. He hadn't done hard labor in many years—how could he face such hardship, and so suddenly?

In the face of this formidable tide of social change, he felt very small. He couldn't stop it, but he thought he would drag his feet when he could, and if that didn't work, well, he'd cross that bridge when he came to it. At least he could keep it from happening this year.

He pondered this the whole way home until he found himself unexpectedly at the village entrance.

"Minglou, are you back?"

Gao Minglou heard someone calling out from the side of the road.

He looked up and saw Old Deshun. Deshun was six or seven years younger than Minglou's late father, but the two had gotten along well when they were younger, and Minglou always considered him a sort of father figure. Even though Minglou was the head of the village, he was a smooth operator, and so would always make sure to put on a respectful face for Deshun.

"Uncle, your allotment is looking quite nice! You'll certainly get some wheat out of there!" He faced Deshun, who stood above him on the hillside.

"Give me some more land, and I'll get even more wheat out of it! Minglou, other villages have already started working toward greater division of labor—how come that's not happening here? For so many years, everyone has been all mixed up together, either loafing about or causing trouble. Now even though they say we've been divided into two teams, everything seems just the same as it did when we were all together!"

"Uncle, don't worry! We have worked together this way for so many years, we'll need time to divide everyone up!" Minglou changed the subject. "Have the teams finished tilling the fields they've been working on the past few days?"

Old Deshun put down his hoe and took out his pipe; the old bachelor apparently wanted to offer suggestions to the secretary. Deshun always did this—involve himself in other people's business—especially when it came to issues of production. And Minglou would usually listen to him; the old man had worked the land his whole life, and what he said was usually right.

Minglou was now watching the old man as he came toward him down the hill, and knew that he was about to receive some advice—and that all he could do was wait patiently as the old man prattled on.

He pulled out a cigarette, and the two of them squatted on the road along the riverbank.

Deshun took a drag from his cigarette, lighting it with Minglou's lighter. "Minglou, the wheat's all been brought in. It will soon be autumn; couldn't we get a little fertilizer for the plantings? In the past, we always went to the city to get night soil right around now—how come no one's taken charge this year?"

Minglou shook his head. "In past years we've been one team, and whenever we decided to do something, we planned it together. This year we're in two groups, and we have different needs. How do we handle that? Plus both groups still have land to weed, and I'm afraid we won't have hands to spare."

"Well, that's easy—just send two people to town for the first few days! Then representatives from both brigades can go collect the night soil and bring it back for everyone to use."

Minglou thought about this a moment. "Yes, that would work. It would be just like before. You can collect the materials needed. Get hold of two wooden carts, and take two people with you from the village. Qiaozhen can take you to her aunt's house to stay, and they can give you dinner as well. After a few days when the work here eases off, we can sort out a few more carts, and more people from both groups can be sent. Would that work?"

"Yes, I'll go! I'll take Jialin as well. His brigade's work has been difficult recently, and the boy's not used to it. This way he can rest for a bit; collecting night soil shouldn't be as hard."

As soon as he brought up Jialin, Minglou blushed, but grunted in agreement.

When the old man saw that his "advice" had been taken, he stood and went back to his hoeing.

Minglou threw away the stub of his cigarette and continued his thoughtful walk home.

Jialin had grown up under Gao Minglou's watchful eye. He had been a stubborn boy but also very bright, and he seemed stronger than all the other children his age in the village. Gao Minglou had taken an interest in him, and even when Jialin attended school in the city, he still came home every Saturday, and Minglou enjoyed popping by the family's house to see him. Although Minglou was just an ordinary farmer, he still enjoyed hearing news of the world, and Jialin was a rich source of information. He would often tell Minglou about this country or that, talking the man's ear off until past midnight. Minglou would sigh to himself: *Gao Yude has all the luck!* The man himself was a complete dunce, but somehow he'd managed to raise such a clever son! Minglou's own sons were entirely mediocre. His eldest had gone to school for two years, but was so thick he'd failed and had to repeat the first grade. In the end, there was nothing for him to do but go back to farming. If it weren't for Minglou's prestigious role in the village, he wouldn't have been able to marry his son off to Liu Liben's Qiaoying. And Sanxing had had to bribe the county cadres with the brigades' earnings, or else he wouldn't have even gotten into middle school. His grades certainly weren't good enough, but he got through thanks to recommendations. Now, finally, he had managed to complete high school.

As soon as his second son graduated from high school, Minglou began to worry again. No position seemed suitable, especially given the difficulty of getting a job in the public sector these days. So Minglou became determined to make his son a community teacher. There was no way he would allow both of his sons to become peasants, and being a teacher would bestow some dignity on Sanxing. What's more, he'd never had to suffer, and he wouldn't be able to deal with hard labor. If Minglou didn't help him, Sanxing would end up a lazy bum.

Minglou originally thought he could have his cake and eat it, too—he wanted to negotiate with the commune's education officer, Ma Zhansheng, to fire one of the teachers from a neighboring village instead; it would be best not to have Sanxing replace Jialin. Minglou was compassionate in his way. He wasn't afraid of anyone in the village, but he knew that even though Jialin wasn't considered an important personage, he had a stubborn spirit and strong character. Minglou might make an enemy out of Jialin if he didn't tread carefully. If that happened, he wouldn't rest easy for the remainder of his days. He was getting older, and Jialin was young. Even if Jialin didn't have the means to retaliate right away, he might become more powerful as he got older, and his descendants might enact revenge! Minglou's two sons were no match for Jialin. He wanted to avoid firing Jialin at all costs.

But Ma Zhansheng had laughed at him. There was no chance of Minglou's idea happening! Every village wanted to put one of their own in the teaching position. To get Sanxing the job, Minglou would have to force Jialin out. There was no other way.

Afterward, this became a source of anxiety for Minglou. Even though Gao Yude and his wife were all the more obsequious toward him, it was clear that Jialin hated him. Minglou heard that when Jialin began to work in the fields, he drove himself so hard that even when his hands began to bleed, no one could stop him; he only continued to work as though his life depended on it. He said he wanted to really mess up his hands! A cold chill ran through Minglou when he heard this. He thought, *Aiya, what a savage young man!* That anecdote showed him Jialin wasn't a weakling, and his anxiety became even more overwhelming.

The reason Gao Minglou had been in control of Gaojia Village for so long was because he was nobody's fool. He was astute and circumspect, and, compared to the average peasant, he was a much more creative thinker.

Gao Minglou walked with his head down, mulling over the situation, not seeing any good solution to give him peace of mind.

He walked to the bend in the Great Horse River, where there was a fork in the road, and stared up at the village. Suddenly, he spied his cousin Liu Liben under an old date tree smoking a cigarette.

~

Liu Liben had finished eating at his daughter's in-laws' and was squatting as he waited for Minglou.

His daughter's shameful behavior made him feel as though he had shrunk several inches. He wanted Minglou to punish Jialin, and then to suppress the story of their fling so it wouldn't spread any further. Then he would quickly find someone to palm Qiaozhen off on. If he could marry her off this year, then he would, but in any case, he wouldn't delay more than a year. When daughters got older, they couldn't find partners, and who knew what would happen then. He wanted Minglou to stand up for him, to persuade Qiaozhen and Ma Shuan to get married. And since he was the secretary, he should have a lot of pull!

Gao Minglou walked over to the date tree and hunkered down casually in front of Liu Liben. The two cousins each smoked a cigarette. Minglou disliked when cigarettes were rolled too tightly, and rolled cigarettes were too weak for Liben, so each smoked his own.

"How are you? Did you buy some more cheap livestock? How much can you make on those animals?" Minglou asked his business-minded cousin.

"What good is money?" Liben coarsely shouted back, his emotions just about at the breaking point.

"I remember hearing that you didn't much care about money." Minglou flashed a sarcastic smile, but at the same time he knew his cousin was unhappy about something. He noticed him almost panting with rage, and asked, "What's wrong? You've made so much money this year your pockets are about to burst, but you're still not satisfied? And these new laws are good laws for you!" He couldn't help giving another sarcastic grin.

"Stop teasing me—I'm in utter anguish!" Liu Liben stretched his arms out toward his cousin as tears welled up and ran down his face.

As soon as Gao Minglou saw this, he turned serious and stood up. "You can cry forever, and I still wouldn't know what you were crying about. Tell me what's going on!"

Liu Liben threw his half-smoked cigarette on the grass beside him and said sadly, "Qiaozhen has made me lose face!"

"But she's such a good girl . . . What could she have done?"

"Ahh, I can't bring myself to discuss it. Gao Yude's dishonorable son seduced my Qiaozhen, and now the whole village is gossiping about them. Look at what I've become!" Liu Liben swallowed hard and smacked himself in the head.

Gao Minglou laughed at him. "Ha ha, I thought it was something serious! Aren't they just courting?"

"Courting? Bullshit. There's been no matchmaker, and they've been fooling around outside in the middle of the night, shaming our ancestors!" Liu Liben looked up and shouted angrily.

Gao Minglou wiped away flecks of Liu Liben's spit that had landed on his face and said, "Liben, all day every day, you trek to the four corners of our country on business. How are you still so old-fashioned? Have you been living under a rock? Do young people these days still act like we did? For the past few years, I've been travelling to Dazhai, and I pass through Xi'an and Taiyuan and see the young city boys and girls, whole crowds of them, walking with their arms around each other right in front of me! When you first see them, you think they're uncivilized, but then you get used to it and think that that's the only truly civilized way to be . . ."

Liu Liben felt both angry and hopeless. He had wanted Minglou to punish Gao Jialin, but hadn't imagined Minglou would chastise him instead. His lips trembled as he said, "What about Jialin? He's useless, good for nothing, and he's defiled my Qiaozhen!"

Gao Minglou stared at him. "You're afraid people will think Jialin's not good enough for Qiaozhen? You only care if others think he's not good enough—what about you? If everyone else approved of him and he'd still defiled her, what then?"

"What skills does Jialin have? He can't do hard labor; he can't do business; he has no future!"

"He was a high school student. Can your daughter even read?"

"What does being a high school student have to do with anything? He's still going to have to spend his life with a finger up a cow's ass!" Liu Liben's mouth twitched slightly, then he added, "And he can't even do that!"

Gao Minglou moved close to Liu Liben and tried to mollify his cousin.

"My good Liben, you're too narrow-minded. You shouldn't underestimate Jialin. And don't just think it's me saying this—there aren't many his age in the whole valley who can compare to him. He can write, draw, sing, play music; he's not too stubborn; and he's clever and has the spirit of a great man! Never mind the names they call us—Ace in the Hole and Double Ace. One day, he'll have the real power in the village! What hasn't he studied and mastered? When he sets off to do something, you won't catch him, even with a horse! Now I've fired him and hired Sanxing in his place. It's clear that I've been a bit harsh, and later, if there's a vacancy, I want to find a way for him to earn a living. If he and Qiaozhen get married, he'll be my relative as well, won't he?"

But Liu Liben wouldn't hear a word of it. "What kind of home does Gao Yude have? Just collapsing walls with nothing worth a penny inside. Gao Yude will die with no prospects, and what will Jialin do?" He snorted.

"Aiya! Where do you think valuable things come from? Aren't they earned by people? As long as a man is determined, he can have anything! As for Gao Yude and whether or not he has any skills, that doesn't mean anything. Qiaozhen is looking for a husband, not a father-in-law! Don't worry about how poor his family is; Jialin can set up his own house! What were we doing at his age? In the old days, weren't both our fathers laboring for the landowner Liu Guozhang?"

Liu Liben still wasn't convinced by his cousin's eloquence; he jumped to his feet angrily and said, "Don't feed me that garbage. I have eyes, you know! Do you mean to say that I can't foresee the future of Gao Yude's family? That worthless son of his disgusts me. Please spare me your fine-sounding speeches. Qiaozhen is my daughter; I can't bear to condemn her to a life of despair!"

"He disgusts you, but he doesn't disgust Qiaozhen! What choice do you have?" Gao Minglou felt that his cousin was being a little ridiculous.

"*I* don't have a choice? I'll break his legs, that son of a bitch!"

"Aiya, what do you think that will achieve? My good cousin, I can see you're in quite a state, that there's nothing I can say to change your mind. But you can't go throwing your weight around. These days young people love freely, and the law protects their marriage. All they need to do is agree; it doesn't matter what the mother or father want—even the Heavenly Emperor couldn't stop them! If you try and stop them, you'd better make sure the public security bureau doesn't catch you!" Gao Minglou was secretary of the whole village, so he understood laws and regulations. His threatening words were a warning to his cousin.

Liu Liben was certainly frightened by them. He went blank for a moment, then gave himself a hard whack to the skull, turned, and strode away from Gao Minglou. This was the first time the two cousins had parted without resolving their differences.

Gao Minglou followed behind, slowly making his way home. Liu Liben was a fine businessman, he thought, but hopeless at everything else.

Minglou thought it would be best if Qiaozhen married Jialin. On the one hand, he thought Jialin would make an excellent husband for Qiaozhen; on the other hand, he wanted Jialin and his own eldest son to share their burdens. In the future their families and Liben's would all be part of one larger family, working as a team, and they would wield a lot of power in the village. Jialin and Minglou would be family then, too, and he would feel even worse about having gotten him fired. When Minglou first spoke to Liben, he had been optimistic—he had been figuring out how he could extinguish the flames of Jialin's hatred for him. Now, faced with his own family's rejection of Jialin, he couldn't tell how the whole thing would shake out in the end.

CHAPTER 10

In the early morning, when the sun's rays were peeking above the horizon, Jialin went to bring water back from the well under the stone cliffs of the gully. He had hardly gotten any sleep, tossing and turning the whole night.

Stones circled the well, which was as dirty as a puddle. The bottom of the well was covered in mud and fleawort. Bits of broken twigs and blades of grass floated on the surface. The well, which everyone in the village drank from, was also full of mosquitoes and their larvae.

He hesitated a long time with the wooden ladle in his hand, in the end deciding not to collect any water. Sunk in gloom, he knelt with his buckets at the side of the well.

He was jittery and depressed. The whole village was gossiping over his and Qiaozhen's "immoral behavior," and he had heard that Liu Liben had beaten Qiaozhen. The whole situation was growing out of control. Now, he was sitting in front of a well that was disgusting and untended even though the villagers drank and cooked with this water all year long. He was distressed.

Everything felt burdensome and painful. When would the winds of modern civilization blow through this backward, unenlightened place?

His heart thudded in his chest. It seemed too difficult to imagine staying in the countryside much longer, but what other choice did he have?

He looked up out of the gully where the great mountain all but blocked his view. The world was so narrow!

As he closed his eyes, his mind wandered across an endless, borderless plain, with a bustling city, grand, majestic trains, and planes that shot through the sky like arrows. He often lifted his spirits with daydreams like this.

But then he opened his eyes, and he was back in reality. He kept looking at the well and noticed that the dirt on top had not yet settled to the bottom. He sighed and thought, *If I threw some bleach powder on top, maybe that would help a little. But where would I get it? You can only get ahold of bleach powder in the city.*

He had been kneeling for so long that his legs were beginning to go numb, so he stood up.

He couldn't help but glance toward the hill where Qiaozhen lived. He didn't see anyone. Qiaozhen was probably up in the mountains, or else she had been beaten so hard by her father

that she now lay unmoving on the kang. Or else she was afraid
and didn't dare stand on the bank of the river by their house
under that old locust tree to watch him—whenever he'd come
to collect water before, he would always see her there watching
him. They would smile at each other without saying a word, or
else make funny faces.

Suddenly, Jialin's eyes lit up: Qiaozhen appeared from
behind the old locust tree! She stood there quietly, her arms
at her sides, and stared bashfully yet happily at him, almost
smiling!

She nodded in the direction of the hill by her house,
implying that Jialin should meet her there.

He looked toward the mountainside and saw Liu Liben
with his bottom sticking up in the air as he tilled his allotment.

Gao Jialin felt a sudden burst of anger. Liu Liben had
beaten Qiaozhen and upbraided Jialin's father, but he apparently didn't give even a thought to Jialin in all of this! Double
Ace relied on them to make money, but never actually had time
for the Gao family.

Jialin decided he would get his revenge today. He wanted
to have a conversation with Qiaozhen out in the open and
make her father watch! The sight would make the older man
apoplectic with rage!

Jialin purposefully raised his voice and shouted, "Qiaozhen,
come down here! I have something I want to say to you!"

Qiaozhen was surprised and didn't know what to do. She instinctively turned to look up the hill toward her house. She couldn't tell if her father had heard; he was still bent over the ground, weeding.

In the end, Qiaozhen decided to come down from the bank. She didn't even use the road, but instead half-ran, half-hopped her way through a grassy hollow nearby, heading directly for the well.

She appeared in front of Jialin, her shoes, socks, and pants damp with dew. She wrung her hands uneasily. "Jialin . . . what's going on? People up in the village can see us. My father—"

"Don't be afraid!" Jialin brushed back a lock of hair that lay across her forehead. "I'll call them over myself! We're not doing anything wrong . . . Did your father hit you?"

He looked sadly at her delicate face and slender frame.

Under Qiaozhen's long eyelashes, tears glinted, but she smiled as she bit her lip and stammered, "No, he didn't . . . but he yelled a lot."

"If he ever uses force with you, I won't go easy on him!" Jialin said angrily.

"You mustn't be mad. My father has a sharp tongue but a soft heart, and he wouldn't dare hurt me. Please don't be upset—he's my family, and I'll deal with him," Qiaozhen said soothingly, blinking at her beloved. She looked at the empty bucket beside him and asked, "Where's your water?"

Jialin jerked his chin in the direction of the well. "It's so disgusting, it could be a latrine!"

Qiaozhen sighed. "There's nothing to be done; it's always been like this. And everyone still drinks it." She turned away but couldn't restrain her laughter. "We have a saying around here: 'If you say it's dirty, then you won't get sick.'"

Jialin didn't laugh. He took the bucket off the side of the well and placed it on a rock. He said to Qiaozhen, "We have to go to the city to get some bleach. After we put it in the well, we'll call some other young people to help us clean."

"You want us to both go to the city? Together?" Qiaozhen was surprised.

"Yes, together! Get your family's bicycle, and I'll bike us over—together! There's absolutely nothing to worry about! What will the villagers laugh at?" Jialin looked Qiaozhen in the eye. "Do you dare to come with me?"

"Of course I do! Take the bucket back—I'll go home to get the bicycle and change clothes. You should change, too. You can't talk about cleaning up the well in those filthy clothes! Take them off, and I'll wash them tomorrow."

"What a good little wife you are!" joked Jialin.

Qiaozhen pursed her lips, drew near to Jialin's face, and blew a raspberry at him. "Don't be so crude!"

They were both tremendously excited as they walked home.

For Qiaozhen, it was quite bold to ride into town behind Jialin on a bike in front of her family and the entire village. And considering her current situation, she would need a lot of courage to do it. The only reason she didn't fear being beaten by her father or ridiculed by the villagers was because of her obsession with Jialin. If Jialin asked her to jump off a cliff, she would do it with both eyes open!

But Gao Jialin had made the decision for different reasons: to challenge the outdated morals and vulgar opinions of the villagers he hated, as well as to take revenge on that arrogant Double Ace.

Jialin carried the empty water bucket home, opened his suitcase, and took out his rarely worn best set of clothes. He washed his face and hair with scented soap and felt like a new man, his whole body light as a feather. He combed his hair in front of the mirror and felt like a valiant hero.

His father had gone up to the mountains and his mother to the allotment, so no one else was home. He took a few bills out of a small wooden box and put them in his pocket. Then he went out and stood on the hillside to wait for Qiaozhen, since the path in front of her family's house was the only way out of town.

Qiaozhen came out wearing his favorite of her outfits: a beige short-sleeved shirt and deep-blue Dacron pants. Her shiny, jet-black hair was bound up on her head with the patterned handkerchief, and her delicate, pale face reminded him of the first pear blossom of spring.

They walked side by side along the path from the center of the village toward the river. This felt new to them, and they were excited, but neither said a word. They were too embarrassed to even look at each other. It was the most profound moment of their lives. When the two of them were alone together at night out in the fields, their love was private. Now, they were displaying their happiness to the entire world. Mostly they felt a sort of dignified pride.

Qiaozhen was proud: Let them all look! She, an illiterate country girl, was going to the county seat with a clever, strong, handsome gentleman!

Jialin was also proud: Let all the farmers and peasants look! The most beautiful girl from the Great Horse River, the daughter of the "God of Wealth" Liu Liben, was walking at his side, docile as a lamb.

The village was soon buzzing with the news. The women who hadn't gone into the mountains, the old people, and all the children came to watch them. The farmers on the mountainside opposite and in the river valley dropped their trowels and came to the edge of the ridge to see the two "foreigners" in the village. Some smacked their lips with envy, others grumbled, and still others mocked them. The more conservative among them peered at Jialin and Qiaozhen disapprovingly, while the cruder villagers leered. Most felt the situation was quite novel and interesting—especially the young people, who both admired and envied them: a young woman and man from the river valley farming team secretly going around together. Look, look, now they're holding hands behind their backs!

Gao Jialin and Liu Qiaozhen knew all of this was happening, but they didn't care—they only had eyes for each other. A naughty little boy threw a clump of dirt as they walked past, and another child chanted, "Gao Jialin, Liu Qiaozhen; girlfriend, boyfriend having fun!"

Gao Yude watched them from the mountainside with everyone else. At first, he didn't know what everyone was suddenly running to the ridge to look at, and he put down his hoe to go see for himself. When he saw the spectacle, he quickly stumbled back to the cornfield amid everyone's jokes and giggles. His aged face turned red with embarrassment, and he sat down on the handle of his hoe, his hands trembling as he nervously rubbed the soles of his feet. He said to himself, "Troublemaker! You troublemaker!" Where was Liu Liben? If Double Ace saw this scene, it would be a wonder if he didn't beat these two crazy young people into the ground!

Meanwhile, Liu Liben was still on his family's allotment on the small hill by their home, oblivious to what was happening, so Gao Yude was worrying over nothing. Double Ace was just as his daughter had said—sharp-tongued but with a soft heart. Even if he was angry and worried, he wouldn't raise a hand against them in front of everyone. Gao Yude put his head in his hands and took a series of long, deep breaths.

~

Early the next morning, chaos erupted at the well in Gaojia Village. Farmers who had gone down to collect water that morning had discovered something in it. More and more people gathered around the well, but no one knew what the substance in it was, and they didn't dare touch the water. Someone said that Jialin, Qiaozhen, and some other young people had put the "white things" in the well. Someone else explained that this was because Jialin was obsessed with hygiene and had suspected the water was polluted, so he'd put some laundry detergent in the well. Other people said it wasn't laundry detergent; it was a kind of pesticide.

Good lord! Who cared if it was laundry detergent or pesticide? How could he casually toss something into the well like that? Everyone swore and cursed: Gao Yude's idiot son is going to kill us all!

Some of the villagers ran to the edge of the village to tell Gao Minglou, to ask the brigade secretary to come take a look! But most of the villagers around the well just grumbled among themselves. The young people who had apparently helped Gao Jialin treat the well explained that the substance was bleach, and it was important for hygienic reasons. The villagers immediately unleashed a torrent of abuse:

"You kids are so dumb, blindly doing whatever Jialin tells you!"

"Your mother didn't care about hygiene—are you missing an arm or a leg?"

"You've offended the Dragon King, and now your water's ruined. Go drink your own piss!"

But the hygiene revolutionaries who supported Jialin ignored the curses flung at them, and simply collected their water and carried it home. Their fathers, however, immediately emptied it out into the yard.

While more and more people gathered at the well, Liu Liben's family was at home fighting: Liu Liben tried to beat Qiaozhen while her mother protected her daughter and fought off her husband. Luckily, Qiaoying and her husband were also at the house and were able, with great difficulty, to break up the fight. Liu Liben was so upset he didn't eat breakfast before going to work. He left by the small road behind the family's house so that no one around the well would see him go.

Gao Jialin heard what was happening at the well and wanted to go explain things to his fellow villagers. Before that could happen, though, his mother and father grabbed him by the arms and said he would leave over their dead bodies. The two weren't blaming their son; they feared he would be attacked if he was seen at the well.

At the same time, Liu Liben's third daughter, Qiaoling, was coming up from the gully carrying a book. She had just finished taking her college entrance exam and was staying at home while waiting for the results. She had gotten up early and gone deep into the gully to memorize her English vocabulary. As a result, she didn't know about the fight happening at home. She saw the gathering by the well and, curious, walked over to ask what was going on.

Someone immediately quipped, "Your eldest sister and her husband thought the water was unsanitary, so they put laundry detergent in it. Does your family usually drink laundry detergent? See how white it's made your face!"

A wash of red spread across Qiaoling's cheeks. Although she was still in her teens, she was already as tall as Qiaozhen and just as pretty as her sister, though Qiaozhen was a bit more elegant. Qiaoling had long ago noticed her sister's affection for Jialin—and now she knew that they were together for sure. She liked and respected Jialin and was happy that her sister had found such a partner. She had known about the plan to put bleach in the well, so she tried to explain the uses of bleach to the crowd, using what she'd learned in high school chemistry.

Before she even finished speaking, curses rained down on her: "Hmph! Yeah, right! Why don't you go take a sip! You and your sister's husband both put on that Beijing accent. You're practically sharing the same pair of pants, aren't you?"

Everyone burst into laughter.

Tears gathered in Qiaoling's eyes as she turned and fled home—ignorance had quickly defeated science.

By that time, Gao Minglou had heard the news and rushed over to Qiaozhen's home to check up on things there. He had originally wanted to ask Jialin, but he reconsidered and went to his relatives' home first.

The moment he entered their courtyard, he saw the four women of the house sobbing. There was no sign of Liu Liben, since Minglou's eldest son had gone and blabbed to his aunt and mother-in-law about what had happened.

Minglou told them not to cry. He would sort things out.

After he had gotten the details of what had happened from Qiaozhen and Qiaoling, he turned and strode out the front gate of Liu Liben's house toward the gully and the well.

The crowd grew silent when Gao Minglou arrived. They would see how the hardened village leader dealt with this problem.

Minglou buttoned his old uniform coat button by button, clasped his hands behind his sturdy back, and, his eyes glinting, walked around the well. The assembled crowd made way for him as he walked by.

He bent over and took a symbolic look down the well. Then he turned and looked at everyone. "Aiya! We really are a bunch of chumps! Jialin did a wonderful thing for us, but instead of praising him, all you do is swear at him. You've done wrong by him! The well has needed fixing for a long time—it's a wonder I didn't do something about it years ago! Why aren't you all collecting your water? The bleach has just been added so the water's at its cleanest! Fifth Uncle, here, give me your ladle!"

As he spoke, he took the copper and wooden instrument from the old man standing next to him, dipped half a ladle of cool water from the well, stuck out his neck, and drank it in one swallow.

He stroked his beard, now wet with the well water, laughed, and said, "I, Gao Minglou, am the first to drink! Practice is the test of truth! You're not going to reject this water now, are you?"

The crowd laughed nervously, but Gao Minglou's imposing presence had brought the crowd to heel. They immediately began jostling for a spot at the well and ran to take the water up into the mountains. The sun was already as high as a stalk of bamboo.

CHAPTER 11

Gao Jialin felt rather depressed after the disturbance caused by his "hygiene revolution."

Sometimes instead of his nightly meetings with Qiaozhen, he would go stand by himself under the old toon tree, staring entranced at the misty, unbroken line of great mountains lit up by the stars. The summer night's breeze tousled Jialin's hair while the rest of the village slumbered and dreamed.

And sometimes, in the midst of the solemn silence, he would think he heard a faint rumbling coming from the far horizon. He'd look up and see that the sky was clear, so it couldn't be thunder. What could be making that noise? Was it a car? A train? A plane? He never could say for sure, but he thought it sounded like it was coming toward their village. Beautiful fantasies and visions of the future would make him momentarily forget the unhappiness and weariness of his present: he'd smile faintly in the blackness and watch and listen with pleasant anticipation for the sound coming from far away. Though he'd strained to identify the sound's source, he never could hear anything more. It must have been a figment of his imagination. He would sigh softly, close his eyes, and lean back against the tree.

Then Qiaozhen would quietly come to him. He loved that she would visit him like this, not making a sound but simply appearing at his side. He'd place one arm lightly on her shoulder. Her love and kindness comforted him as always, but it couldn't entirely wash away his renewed sense of melancholy. His past yearnings were gradually bubbling up again, and he longed to leave Gaojia Village, to become a factory worker or cadre. Hopefully he could take Qiaozhen with him!

He wasn't sure why, but he didn't tell Qiaozhen what he was thinking.

Nevertheless, Qiaozhen was clever enough to see what was in his heart. She didn't want Jialin to leave Gaojia Village, or her; she was afraid of losing him. Jialin was educated, and he could fly away anywhere; she was illiterate and would be tied to this land for the rest of her life. If he went away to work, would he still love her as much as he did now?

But when she saw her beloved so depressed, she longed for him to get his wish to leave. At least then he would be happy. If he were happy, she would have some comfort. She thought that even if he found a job in a city, he wouldn't forget her; she could work hard at home and raise their child. And the child would have a father with a proper job and wouldn't be discriminated against by society. Also, she would share in Jialin's glory.

Considering all this, she rather hoped Jialin would go away to find work, since it would lessen his stress. But then again, she thought, that wouldn't be easy. Jialin would have to get going either way. He'd been a community teacher, but he'd been fired by that narrow-minded and stupid Gao Minglou. How was he ever going to find a real job?

That night Jialin was again under the toon tree, and when she saw him with brows furrowed and a bitter expression on his face, she blurted out, "Jialin, you simply must think of a way to leave! I know what's on your mind. I can see you're so worried. I wish you would go!"

Jialin grabbed her shoulders and stared at her for a long time. His beloved! When had she begun to study his mind, and at what point had she totally and completely understood him?

He kept staring at her, and then finally joked, "If you're telling me to go, that must mean you're not afraid I won't want you anymore?"

"I'm not afraid. As long as you're content, I . . ." She burst into tears, holding him close, as tightly as dodder seeds entangled in grass. "You never need to worry about losing me . . ."

Jialin rested his chin on top of her head and laughed. "Oh, look at you, it's like you think I've already found a position somewhere!"

Qiaozhen looked up and smiled. She wiped the tears from her face. "Jialin, truly, as long as there's a way, I'll support you finding a job! There's no way you'll reach your full potential hidden away here in Gaojia Village. And you haven't worked in the fields since you were little—you're not used to it, and it will be very hard for you. In the future, if you leave us, I'll just plant the allotment and raise our child myself; whenever you have time, you can come back and see us. When I have a break from farming, I'll bring our child to the city and we can stay with you."

Dismayed, Jialin shook his head. "We mustn't make any more foolish plans. I can't possibly leave to find work right now. We must think of something we can do here in the countryside . . . Look, your arms are freezing—they're like ice! Don't catch cold! It's late. Let's go back."

They kissed each other like always and returned to their respective homes.

Gao Jialin entered his house and discovered Gao Minglou seated on the edge of the family kang, talking to his father.

When he saw Jialin enter, his father said immediately, "Where have you been? Your Uncle Minglou has been waiting forever to see you!"

Gao Minglou grinned at him and said, "It's no problem! Oh Jialin! Our thinking is so backward here. You had such good intentions putting bleach in the well, but everyone thought you were trying to poison them! What utter idiots!"

His father laughed at Gao Minglou and said, "It's all thanks to you! If you hadn't taken control of the situation, something bad would have happened."

His mother quickly added, "Yes, it's true! Uncle Minglou takes care of everything!"

Jialin sat on a wooden stool and looked at Minglou. "Blame me; I didn't explain my actions to people before doing them."

Gao Minglou spat out some smoke from his cigarette and said, "It's all in the past now. Let's not bring it up again. In two days, both brigades will send workers to help repair the well and build up the sides. Aiya! This needed to be done. Why, a few months ago I saw an old sow bathing in the well!" He snuffed his cigarette out with his fingers and threw it on the ground. "I came tonight to discuss something with you. It's like this: We're getting ready to collect some night soil to sow the wheat. The second brigade is in the midst of tilling the soil and can't spare anyone, so we'd like to send two people from the first brigade. I've been thinking about it, and I'd like you and Old Deshun to go—what do you think?"

Jialin didn't say a word.

His father butted in from where he sat on the kang. "He'll go! Uncle Minglou has given you an easy job! Go in the evening— it'll only take two or three hours to collect the night soil, and you can stay home during the day. In years past, people would fall over themselves trying to get this job!"

Gao Minglou pulled out another cigarette, lit it on an oil lamp, and looked down at the silent Jialin. "You're probably afraid of running into someone you know in town, that you'll be embarrassed? Young people are so concerned with your reputations! But at night you won't run into anyone."

Gao Jialin looked up and simply said, "I'll go."

Having secured Jialin's agreement, Minglou got down from the kang and made to leave. Gao Yude hurriedly slipped down, too, barefoot, and his wife left the stove so they could both escort the secretary to the door.

Gao Minglou stopped them there and said to Jialin, "You probably don't know this, but it's customary for those who collect night soil to eat a meal while they're in the city, paid for by the team. This year Qiaozhen will prepare the meal, since her aunt has a place in town."

Gao Jialin nodded and grunted in assent.

When Gao Yude heard that Qiaozhen would prepare the meal, his mouth opened to several times its normal size. He stuttered, "Minglou! Cooking is no easy task; you had better send a man! Qiaozhen is young and very busy these days; the second unit hasn't finished the tilling . . ."

Gao Minglou had to stifle a laugh, not wanting to embarrass Gao Yude. "It's best that Qiaozhen goes. Since the dinner will be at her aunt's house, it wouldn't be appropriate for a stranger to go." With that, he turned and left.

Life

~

Later that day, Old Deshun, Jialin, and Qiaozhen readied their two donkey-drawn carts on the main road out of the village. It was already nearing twilight. Near and far had already begun to blend together. In the village, the sounds of workers coming home and children playing mixed with the bleating of the goats as they entered their pens, creating a raucous atmosphere.

Old Deshun swatted a fly away from the lead donkey's rump with the palm of his hand. He put a straw mattress over the shafts of the rear cart and said, "Don't worry—it doesn't smell, but it's not perfumed, either! Once you get used to it, you won't notice it." He walked around to the front of the cart, fished a flask of liquor out from inside his jacket, took a swig, and smiled conspiratorially at Jialin and Qiaozhen. "You two take the other cart, and I'll lead the way in this one. I'm an old hand with the animal—you all follow me, and everything'll be fine. It's not quite dark yet; you get seated, and we'll be off!" He winked, pleased with himself, and sat in the front cart.

Thoroughly embarrassed by Old Deshun's words, Jialin and Qiaozhen sat down together in the rear cart, each perched awkwardly on opposite shafts, as far away from the other as possible.

Old Deshun let out a shout, and the donkey began to walk forward steadily. The two carts moved into the twilight toward the city.

In front, Old Deshun took another nip from his flask, already getting a bit tipsy. With a mouth full of teeth so broken that liquid leaked from between them, he sang out a few *xintianyou.*

Aiyo! It's good for youngsters to see each other

White-bearded old men are good for nothing

In the back, Jialin and Qiaozhen couldn't help laughing.

But Old Deshun heard them and stroked his white beard and said, "Aiya, what are you laughing at? It's true! Young people really are better! Young men and women are so affectionate with each other; I'm old now, but seeing you two together, I can't help but be happy."

Jialin called out, "Grandfather Deshun, why didn't you ever marry? Did you court anyone when you were younger?"

"Court? Courting? When I was younger, I knew way more about courting than you two!" His wrinkled face flushed as he took another nip; his eyes narrowed as he gazed at the mountains off to the east, kissed with moonlight. He didn't say another word.

The donkeys snorted and stomped the ground rhythmically. The misty moonlight shone in patches on the crops. The earth was silent, but the sound of water in the river valley was much louder than usual. The Great Horse River disappeared among the fields and mountains just as the carts passed by the stone cliffs, giving them one last look at its glistening surface.

152

Gao Jialin asked from the rear, "Grandfather Deshun, tell us some love stories from when you were young! I don't believe you didn't do any flirting!" He made a face at Qiaozhen sitting next to him, to show her he was teasing the old man.

Old Deshun couldn't keep quiet any longer, and, after he had taken another nip, he said, "I can't flirt, eh? It's your father who can't flirt! I was with your dad and Gao Minglou's and Liu Liben's fathers, too—all of us were working for Liu Guozhang. Your father was the youngest and the shyest, snot always running into his mouth! It was really me that got your mother and father together . . . I was in my twenties by then. Liu Guozhang saw that I was a good worker, and, since there wasn't much to do on the farm, he sent me off with the livestock and a load of salt and furs. I stopped off at some stable along the way for a rest, ran into the owner's daughter, and we became friends. Her name was Lingzhuan, and she was even prettier than the boy in our opera troupe who played the lead girl. Whenever I drove the animals past their place, Lingzhuan would time my arrival perfectly. She'd wait until I appeared just at the edge of their village and welcome me singing *xintianyou* folk songs. She had an excellent voice, just like a silver bell!"

"What did she sing?" Qiaozhen asked.

"I'll give you all a taste!" The old man turned around contentedly and began to sing in a drunken voice:

The mule walks in the lead oh with three, three lamps

He wears that bell of copper oh with a wa-wa sound

If you are my brother oh then wave, wave your hand

If you are not my beloved oh then go, oh go on your way

When the old man finished singing, he let out a long sigh. "Whenever I stopped at their place, I never wanted to leave. Her father never realized that Lingzhuan gave me mutton and buckwheat noodles to eat . . . and when evening came, she would slip away from her house and find me in my room . . . one day, two days, then I couldn't delay any longer and had to take the herd back. When I got up to leave, Lingzhuan would cry as though she were made of tears. As she walked me back to the riverbank, she would send me off with another *xintianyou* . . ."

"Did she sing 'Walking through the Western Pass'?" Jialin laughed.

"She did!" he said, and couldn't help but sing it. His voice was rough, almost like he was choking back tears; as he sang, snot would drip down his face every so often, and he would snort it back up his nose.

154

Life

When you walk through the Western Pass, Elder Brother,

It's hard for Little Sister to remain;

Her hand in your hand,

With you until the main gate.

When you walk through the Western Pass, Elder Brother,

Little Sister will see you on your way;

Her heartfelt words of comfort,

Elder Brother you must weigh.

When you walk, you must take the highways,

You mustn't take the lanes;

Men and horses crowd the highways,

155

Lu Yao

Thieves and bandits own the lanes.

When go by ship, you must sit astern,

You mustn't sit at the prow;

There the waves crash and winds blow,

I'm afraid you'll fall into the river.

When the sun sets, settle down for a rest,

When day breaks, get on the road again;

On your own in the cold wind and rain,

Everything depends on your brain.

When you walk through the Western Pass, Elder Brother,

You mustn't make any friends;

For if you make too many friends,

You might forget me.

When you have money, they are your friends,

When you don't, all they do is glare;

How can they compete with me?

Who will be with you till the end.

Old Deshun gasped for breath as he sang. Toward the end he lost the melody and just spoke the lyrics. When he finished he began to sob, but after a while, he suddenly laughed. "Aiya, would you look at that! What am I doing?! I've gone off my rocker in my old age! Crying like a fool, I'm sure you kids are laughing at me . . ."

Qiaozhen didn't know how she ended up leaning against Jialin's chest with her face covered in tears. Jialin wasn't sure when he'd decided to put his arm around Qiaozhen's shoulders. The moon rose higher in the sky, and the mountains were black in the distance, concealing a layer of mysterious color beneath. On either side of the road, the corn and sorghum formed two green walls around them as they traveled. The carts crushed the broken stones on the road beneath them, giving off a light shushing sound; the densely growing wormwood by the roadside gave off a strong and fresh perfume that burrowed into their noses. It was a wonderful summer night!

"Grandfather Deshun, what happened to Lingzhuan after that?" Qiaozhen clung to Jialin's chest.

Dispirited, Old Deshun sighed. "I heard that she married a businessman from Tianjin. She didn't want to, but her father forced her . . . Tianjin, it seemed like the end of the earth! From then on I never saw my beloved again! And I never took a wife, ever. Marrying the wrong wife is like drinking cold water—tasteless and dull."

"Maybe she's still alive?" Qiaozhen said.

"If I'm not dead yet, then she's not, either! She's been alive in my heart all these years . . ."

The carts steered around a hill, and the road before them suddenly shone bright. All the buildings were lit with a mix of moonlight and lamplight, and the city appeared before them in a blur.

Old Deshun took another nip from his flask. Although he had dropped the reins, he still maneuvered the donkey successfully, shouting as his arms made circles in the air.

The carts sped quickly toward town. The donkeys' hooves knocked against the road as they turned onto Great Horse River Bridge and into the city.

CHAPTER 12

After Jialin and Old Deshun filled one cart with night soil from the latrines, the old man's strength failed, and between fatigue and the liquor he'd drunk, he began to shake and stumble as they walked. Jialin took him to Qiaozhen's aunt's house and helped him lie down on the warm kang. Then Jialin continued on by himself to collect more night soil to fill the other cart.

As he walked next to the donkey, he tried his best not to take the cart on main streets or walk underneath the streetlamps. Although it was night and almost no one was out and about, he was still nervous about avoiding people, afraid of running into someone he knew or an old classmate.

He led the donkey among the scattered brigade and work unit offices along the north side of the road. Many people came to collect night soil in the city this time of year—sometimes the bottoms of the latrines were even scraped clean. He had already been through a few unit offices, and the cart wasn't even half-full.

Ahead of him was the radio station. He stood still, hesitating in the shadows at the street corner. He thought of his old classmate Huang Yaping.

After standing there for a while, he decided not to collect night soil from the radio station.

He walked a large circle around the building, heading for the bus station instead; lots of people came through there, so maybe they'd have more night soil.

He walked down the street in and out of the lamplight and sighed: life changed just as the seasons did, from cold to hot, and such a great difference between them! Three years earlier, at this time on a night just like this, he might have been reading in his warm and comfortable study, or leaving the movies with a crowd of people, laughing with his classmates on their way back to campus. Or maybe wearing his bright-red sweat suit, running around the stadium's basketball court, hearing the cheers of the crowd.

But now he was carting around night soil, skulking out of sight like a ghost. He couldn't help searching the brightly lit radio station with his gaze. What was Huang Yaping up to now? Watching TV? Drinking tea?

He felt ridiculous. What was he going to do? He wanted to fill up the cart as soon as possible. Why was he worrying about what she was up to? The most important thing was to collect the night soil. Whenever he found a latrine that had been scraped clean, he got depressed, and whenever he found one that could be scraped out, he wanted to laugh! Old Deshun's temperament was contagious, and Jialin was aware that he was gradually learning more and more from the old man. Hard labor was difficult, but it had its own joys!

Gao Jialin parked the donkey and cart outside the main gate of the bus station and went in to see if there was any night soil inside.

When he went into the latrine, the sight delighted him as much as a bar of gold—there was enough night soil inside to fill several carts! Too much for him to move tonight, certainly.

But he got depressed again when he saw the back of the latrine: some work unit had created an access door in order to remove the night soil easily—but they had locked it!

Gao Jialin was enraged: *Must people claim ownership even of shit and piss? Must I fight hegemony even here?*

This sort of thing easily riled up Gao Jialin. He picked up a rock, but instead of bashing the lock, he used it to pry open the door.

He gathered his bucket and shovel from the cart and began to empty the bus station latrines.

He had just filled and emptied one bucket and was preparing to fill a second when two young men came in, also looking to collect night soil. They wore matching Dacron pants and red tank tops emblazoned with the word *Vanguard* across the chest in yellow.

Jialin knew that these were members of the city work unit. They were vegetable growers, and everyone in town knew how well off they were.

As soon as they saw Jialin collecting night soil, they put down their cart and marched over angrily.

"Why are you stealing our night soil?" One of them had already blocked Jialin's path.

"This is your night soil?" Jialin confronted them.

"Of course it's ours!" the other one yelled.

"How could it be yours? This is a public toilet, and it's not where your unit pisses anyway!"

"That's fucking bullshit!" the first one swore.

"Watch your mouth!" Jialin's whole body tensed up.

"Damn you! Don't you know that we give vegetables to the bus station cadre all year for this shit, and we don't ask for a penny in return! What gives you the right to steal it?" The second one furrowed his brow and squinted at Jialin.

"Give us two bucks—you broke our lock!" The first one crossed his arms.

"Give you money?" Jialin turned his head. "Get out of my way, you lords of shit!" He carried his load of night soil toward the cart as he spoke.

The two men raised their fists. The one in front was quick and punched Jialin in the chest.

Flames shot from Jialin's eyes. He set the bucket down on the ground, picked up his shovel, and flung night soil at the man.

The one in front jumped and ducked to the side, while the one in back quickly grabbed a shovel. The three night-soil collectors fought it out in the bus station parking lot: long-handled shovels flew through the air, and they were soon covered in muck from head to toe. Misty moonlight shone on the rowdy scene. One of the young men's feet went numb after a blow from Jialin, and he cried and knelt; Jialin received a blow on the back from the other man's shovel.

The fight only stopped when people inside the bus station came out to break it up. The bald station manager berated both sides and wouldn't let Jialin take any night soil. He said the station had already signed a contract with the Vanguards, and only they could use it.

Jialin swore silently. *How dare you talk about "contracts"? You eat for free all year off your toilets!*

He figured that if he wanted any more, he'd have to fight for it. They were two, and he was only one—he couldn't win. Besides, their work unit was nearby, and if they all came to help, it would be a wonder if he weren't beaten to death!

So he decided to pack up his buckets and lead the donkey and cart away from the station.

The only place left nearby he hadn't visited was the Luxury Food Company. He hadn't gone by yet because he knew his old classmate Zhang Ke'nan worked there.

But then he suddenly remembered: Hadn't Ke'nan transferred to the sales division? He quickly decided to take a look at the Luxury Food Company's latrines.

Splattered with shit from head to toe, he could sense the stink emanating from his body as he led the donkey and cart. His back smarted where the man had struck him with the shovel. But he didn't mind any of this. He was focused on filling the cart as quickly as possible—Grandfather Deshun and Qiaozhen were probably waiting anxiously for him so that they could all return to the village.

He parked the cart at the main gate and went in search of the latrines.

He had never been there before and had to look for a long while before he found the right place. When he got to the toilets, he saw there wasn't much night soil, and it was watery at that, but at least it would fill up his bucket. There was only one problem: the way from the latrine to the road was not easy, and there were several narrow areas, so he couldn't bring the cart directly to the latrine.

He decided to scoop the night soil out bucket by bucket, then dump it into the cart the same way.

Gao Jialin took his bucket from the cart and went to the rear of the latrine to retrieve his first bucketful.

As he carried the bucket across the company courtyard, he saw a few people sitting beneath a paulownia tree in the southeast corner. They were sucking their teeth and harrumphing;

it was obvious that his stench was interfering with their enjoyment of the cool evening.

Gao Jialin felt apologetic, but there was nothing he could do. He silently wished the cadres would forgive him.

The cadres acted the same on his second trip to and fro, but he forced himself to continue.

On the third trip, one of the women said within earshot of him, "Couldn't you have picked a better time to do your business, you evil-smelling man?"

Her words pierced his ears, and he stopped in his tracks. But he knew he still had one or two trips left to make before the cart was full, so he sucked it up and set off as fast as possible.

After he'd emptied yet another bucket into the cart and as he was carrying it back through the courtyard, the women suddenly stood up and shouted at him, "Hey, you, carrying that shit! You're killing us with the stench! Go somewhere else to do that—don't torment us here!"

Gao Jialin stood still in the courtyard, his hands trembling, biting his lip. It was she who was the tormenter, even as she insisted he was the problem.

Anger welled up in him, but he suppressed it again. He had already gotten in one fight that evening, and he didn't want to get tangled up in another; besides, he only needed one or two more buckets and the cart would be full. He just had to suck it up, and his responsibilities for the evening would be fulfilled.

So he went back for another bucketful.

When he came back through the courtyard, the woman stood up again, even angrier this time. Her words were cruder and her speech harder to take: "Is this guy deaf? Did you hear what I said to you? Why are you still here, you disgusting man?"

An older-looking cadre next to her said, "Don't waste your breath. Just let him finish up, and when he's gone, it won't smell anymore!"

"These country hicks . . . I can't stand them!" She swore again.

Gao Jialin couldn't take it any longer! His nose twitched, and he thought, *Country people are so mistreated! We work so hard all year long. We bear the sun on our backs from dawn till dusk, harvest the grain, dry and clean it, and pick the best of the harvest for the city people to eat. And after they eat it, they shit it back out for the country folk to come and clean up, to clean up their lives for them.* And they dare treat him like this!

His hatred for the woman grew.

He threw the bucket on the ground, steam nearly coming out of his ears as he strode toward the paulownia tree. He wanted to give this presumptuous woman a piece of his mind.

When he had almost reached the group, the woman froze, unsure what the rash young man was going to do. The old cadres around her also seemed nervous.

Gao Jialin stopped, suddenly frightened. Good lord, the woman was Zhang Ke'nan's mother!

He recognized her clearly from ten paces away. He cracked his knuckles, unsure if he should keep going or retreat. No matter what, he couldn't get into a fight with Ke'nan's mother; this was already too awkward! What should he do? Beg forgiveness? But he hadn't done anything wrong! Should he just say, "I'm sorry"?

In the midst of this impossible dilemma, Ke'nan's mother suddenly pointed at him and asked, "Where are you from? This isn't the time to collect night soil! Have you just come here to annoy us? What are you doing? Coming to eat us?"

She clearly didn't remember him. Of course, he was wearing tattered clothes and covered in sludge; his face was no longer the pale, clean face of a student. He was coarse and rough—a peasant, born and raised. He had only been to Ke'nan's house two or three times; how could he think she would remember him?

Given the present circumstances, he no longer had any desire to be polite. But out of respect for his old classmate, he did his best to keep a steady tone and explain the situation. "Don't be angry, I'm almost finished. I have no choice. We came into the city tonight to collect night soil since everyone is working during the day and we thought it would be unhygienic to do it then. I didn't think you all would be here in the courtyard this evening . . ."

The cadres said, "Forget it, forget it, just hurry up and finish . . ."

But Ke'nan's mother was enraged and said, "Get out of here! You're covered in shit! You reek!"

Jialin was furious. "I may not be very clean, but I can smell the stink coming off of you!"

Ke'nan's mother was so angry her face shook as she made to drag him away; luckily the cadres stopped her and told Jialin not to make a fuss, to just go and finish collecting his night soil.

Gao Jialin turned, collected his last bucketful, and held back tears as he exited through the main gate of the Luxury Food Company.

He dumped his load into the cart and, even though he needed another two buckets to fill it up, led the cart and donkey away.

He turned from the road onto the main street of town, his nose still twitching. The streetlamps were spaced farther and farther apart, and the buildings were for the most part wrapped in darkness. Only the lights on the hydroelectric dam were still on. Rays of orange light shone across the water and bobbed along with the waves like regiments of flames burning on the surface.

Gao Jialin's heart was also ablaze. He pulled the cart over to the side of the road, tears blooming in his lonely eyes as he gazed silently at the city. He said to himself, *I must come back here! I'm cultured, I'm educated. Are the young people here really any better than me? Why must I endure this kind of mistreatment?*

He shifted his gaze to the bobbing lights on the water beneath the dam and thought the scene was spectacular. Blood coursed through his veins as he threw the cart to the ground and ran toward the lights.

He passed through a plot of vegetables on his way to the dam. He knew it belonged to the Vanguard group, and the thought of his fight earlier that night made fury rise in his chest again. He ran through the garden with a vengeance, grabbing a tomato plant as he went.

He arrived at a brightly lit pool, threw the tomato plant in the water, then followed after it.

Holding his breath, he forced himself deeper, then let himself float slowly to the surface.

After swimming for a while, he fished the tomatoes out, washed them, and threw them onto shore. Then he climbed out, clothes sopping wet, and plopped down. He grabbed a tomato and began to gorge himself.

~

Gao Jialin went over the night's events again and again in his mind for half the night before he, Old Deshun, and Qiaozhen took the two carts full of night soil back to the village.

Qiaozhen went straight home. Jialin and Old Deshun took the carts to the pit near the village's entrance and covered the night soil with dirt.

Old Deshun took care of the animals by himself. Jialin returned home, unsettled.

His father was snoring at the edge of the kang; his mother got up and asked why he had returned at such a late hour.

He didn't answer, just looked in the chest for some clean clothes. His mother groped around for her sewing kit, fished a letter out from it, and gave it to Jialin. "Your uncle sent it. Read it and then go to bed. You can tell us what it says in the morning . . ." And with that she lay down and went back to sleep.

Jialin stopped his search for clothing, ripped open the envelope, and ran to the kerosene lamp to read the letter.

> *Elder Brother, Sister-in-Law,*
> *How are you?*
>
> *I want to give you some good news: my superiors have approved my transfer to the local office. According to their letter, as of now I will be the regional labor bureau chief.*
>
> *I'm thrilled, since I've been away for ten years and have often dreamed of returning. I'm almost fifty now, and as the villagers say, a falling leaf must return to its roots. It's been my*

greatest desire to spend my final years in my old home.

My children all work in Xinjiang, but I'll let them continue there so we needn't bother the party and they won't need to transfer. Their mother and I will come back, along with our youngest, Jiaping.

If I return home to wait for my position to be finalized, I'll be sure to plan a trip to see you in the village.

I'll wait to tell you everything else then.

Your younger brother,

Yuzhi

When Gao Jialin finished reading the letter, he shouted, "Father! Mother! Wake up!"

CHAPTER 13

Around breakfast time, a bright green jeep drove into Gaojia Village and parked in an empty space in the middle of town.

After serving in the army for ten years, Gao Yude's brother had finally returned! The news spread quickly throughout the village. Everyone, from old men to the youngest children, dropped what they were doing and streamed into Gao Yude's dilapidated courtyard.

Gaojia Village hadn't had something this exciting happen in many years. Old men and women leaned on their canes, young mothers held babies in their arms, farmers delayed going into the mountains, students shouldered their satchels, the whole town bustled, and everyone was shouting. They were all excited to see the great cadre. Even the dogs, clueless about what was happening, barked and ran around. The village was in disarray, more so than it had been for any family wedding.

The Gao home was full to bursting. More people stood in the courtyard and out on the hillside, taking turns at the door, curious to see this great personage who had left their village and now returned.

Jialin's mother was next door cooking, with many of the village's women and girls helping out. Some were pumping the bellows; some were cutting vegetables; others were rolling out dough for noodles. For such an important event, all the neighbors were happy to lend a hand.

Gao Jialin took some candy from his father's satchel and handed it to the children who had gathered at their home. He tried his best to maintain a neutral expression, but he couldn't conceal his excitement. A smile broke out on his face, and he was more scatterbrained than usual.

The two brothers, Yude and Yuzhi, were mobbed by a group of older men inside the Gao home. Yuzhi had changed into the uniform of a local cadre and didn't look more than ten years younger than his brother, although he was twenty years his junior. He wasn't tall and was rather fat, with a red face and very few wrinkles. His hair was still jet-black, with a smattering of gray at the temples. He smiled from ear to ear as he recognized his pals from his younger days. These middle-aged men enthusiastically, yet politely, accepted the cigarettes Yuzhi handed them. When Old Deshun and some other elders came in, Yuzhi led them over to sit on the edge of the kang and asked about their health. One after another the old men slipped off the kang to hug and pat him. They shouted over each other as they did.

"Ah, the old body's hangin' in there . . ."

"I heard you took some fire in the war?"

"There was a time when we didn't hear from you—heard you died a hero's death!"

"Aiya, you've become quite the big man!"

Gao Yuzhi laughed as he responded to their questions. Yude stood to the side, pipe in his mouth, laughing while he wiped away his tears with one bony hand.

Ma Zhansheng, assistant county labor bureau chief, had accompanied Gao Yuzhi to his home village. He briefly went outside to relieve himself, and when he returned, he couldn't even squeeze his way back into Gao Yude's courtyard.

Gao Jialin ran into Ma outside the courtyard and tried to help him force his way through the crowd. Ma Zhansheng responded, "Wait a second. This is your uncle's first time home in decades—of course the whole village wants to see him! If you're not busy, let's go sit in the jeep."

Jialin didn't have anything to do, so he was content to walk with Ma toward the jeep.

The jeep was crammed with children. Zhansheng started to shoo them off when Jialin held him back saying, "Hang on. These kids have never seen something like this—let them sit. We can talk under this tree for a while."

Zhansheng put his arm warmly around Jialin's shoulders. "I wanted to tell you that we promise to figure out the issue of your employment soon . . ."

Gao Jialin's heart started beating madly. It was too much for his nerves. Before he could respond, Gao Minglou appeared in front of them.

Minglou smiled. "Jialin, have you gone to greet your uncle yet? Your parents are old and slow on their feet, and there's no one else there to help." He turned and shook Ma Zhansheng's hand warmly.

Jialin said, "We couldn't squeeze through the crowd, so we're waiting here."

"You go home," Minglou said. "I'll take the bureau chief to my home to rest a while. Also, tell your mother that your uncle can have this meal at your house, but for tonight's, we'll have him over to our place—we've already started to prepare." He turned to Ma Zhansheng and said, "Yuzhi is a very prominent cadre from our village; he's the pride of Gaojia!"

"Comrade Gao Yuzhi is our regional labor bureau chief—my direct superior," Ma Zhansheng said to Gao Minglou.

"Yes, I know," Gao Minglou said as he gestured for Gao Jialin to head home. He then escorted Ma Zhansheng to his own home on the north side of the village.

After they had eaten, Jialin, his father, and his uncle went to visit the graves of his paternal grandfather and grandmother.

The ancestral tomb was on a sunny hillside behind the village. The two mounds were covered with dense brush and grass. Their elders had rested here for more than ten years now.

Old Yude removed a steamed bun and a fried cake from the wicker basket he had brought and put them on the stone offerings table; he also burned some yellow sacrificial paper. He pulled Yuzhi and Jialin to the ground to kneel with him. Yuzhi hesitated for a moment, but he saw his brother's face and knelt beside him. In this situation, the labor bureau chief had no choice but to follow local customs.

The three of them kowtowed three times. Jialin, his uncle, and his father stood up. Old Yude suddenly threw himself on the yellow earth and began crying with great heaving sobs, *"Ahhheiheiheihei."* The other two felt rather uncomfortable. Hearing his brother's tormented wails, Yuzhi took out his handkerchief and wiped away his own streaming tears. He had left home when he was little and hadn't seen his parents again until he put them in the ground. Thinking about how they had suffered and how he had never been at their side, he couldn't help but cry. Jialin furrowed his brow as he stood to one side, watching them both weep.

The two brothers sobbed for a while, then Yuzhi reached out and pulled his brother up. Old Yude managed to choke out, "We old people . . . our lives . . . are suffering."

Guiltily, Gao Yuzhi said, "I've always been away, and I didn't take care of our parents. It upsets me to think about it.

177

There's no way to make up for it, but now, since I've returned to work nearby, I'm going to do my best to take care of you all . . . Whatever problems you have, just let me know, brother! Whatever love I failed to give our parents, I want to give you and your wife."

Gao Yude stared at him blankly for a while. "My wife and I will soon be in the earth alongside our parents. There's nothing for you to worry yourself over. The new village laws are in place; we've got food and clothes and no great difficulties. Our biggest problem is your nephew!" He looked at Jialin. "A high school graduate doing hard labor in the village! Most people pull at the smallest string to get a job, but this one . . ."

Yuzhi turned and asked Jialin, "Aren't you a teacher in the village?"

Without waiting for Jialin to respond, Old Yude answered, "There aren't that many children in school these days—they don't need as many teachers, so he came back." He was afraid of Jialin mentioning Gao Minglou in front of his brother. He didn't want Yuzhi to know that Minglou had let Jialin go. Minglou was the leader of their village, there was no way around it, and they couldn't cause problems with him. After a slap on the wrist, or the ass, Yuzhi could pack up and leave, but they would have to live in the same village as Minglou for the rest of their lives!

Gao Yuzhi was quiet for a while, then he said, "Dear brother, normally I'd do whatever I could to meet your request.

But you mustn't trouble me with this. After I took this position, the prefectural party committee and the committee chairperson sat down with me and said that the previous labor bureau chief had done too much hiring behind closed doors. They had to replace him because people were furious with him. My boss said that giving me this position even though I just got out of the army and worked in government showed great faith in me! How can I let them down by violating the law right after I've been appointed? Anything else I can do, but I absolutely cannot do this. Brother, you have to understand my position . . ."

Old Gao Yude heard his brother's speech and mulled it over. "Well, if that's the case, then I won't trouble you. *Ai . . .*" The old man sighed and brushed the dirt from his knees, beckoning the other two to return with him to the village. He mentioned before they'd left for the cemetery that Minglou had repeatedly told him they wanted Yuzhi to come over and have dinner.

~

At that very moment, Gao Minglou and Ma Zhansheng were chatting in Minglou's parlor.

Minglou was panicking. He was afraid Gao Jialin would tell his uncle about him, that the young man would say Minglou had pulled strings to hire his own son as a teacher and sent Gao Jialin home to the labor brigade. At the time,

Zhansheng and he had agreed on this, and now the two coconspirators were discussing the issue.

"And if they tell Bureau Chief Gao? What then?" Minglou asked Ma Zhansheng, who was sipping his tea.

Zhansheng smirked. "If Jialin had a position even better than teacher, would he still complain?"

"A better position?" Minglou stared at Zhansheng. "No one's hiring workers or cadres from the countryside these days—how could there be a better job than community teacher?"

"It just so happens that the regional government has set some targets for our little county coal pit. Of course, these targets didn't originally include the rural areas, since everyone had left for the city by the time a commune got established there." Ma Zhansheng took the cigarette Minglou passed him, lit it, and took a drag.

"I don't think Jialin will want to mine coal!"

"Who's making him mine coal?" Ma Zhansheng replied. "The county committee's communications office needs a communications administrator. Jialin writes well, and we can easily promote a worker to cadre. If we get him this job, I guarantee he'll be satisfied!"

"I'm afraid this will be a lot of work."

"I've already arranged everything. When the time comes, you'll sign a form and approve it with the production brigade's stamp, and I'll worry about the commune and the county. In any case everything will have been done legally. Even mischief has to be worked out properly!"

Ma Zhansheng couldn't finish his little speech without laughing, clearly amusing Gao Minglou, too.

After the two had finished chuckling, Minglou asked, "Did Bureau Chief Gao ever bring up finding a job for Jialin?"

"Aiya! You really are one of the shrewdest men in Gaojia Village!" Ma Zhansheng joked as he stared at Gao Minglou. "Once we've tied all this up, what idiot leader is going to say a word? They just want their underlings to handle everything! If you take the initiative to do this for the leader—and do it well—even if he does criticize you in public, in his heart he'll wish he could promote you!"

Gao Minglou gaped. He thought, *No wonder Zhansheng has been promoted from a regular commune cadre to assistant bureau chief at only thirty years old! He truly is an amazing person with a great future ahead of him!*

While the two of them were talking, Sanxing was inviting Gao Yuzhi into the courtyard.

Minglou and Zhansheng hurried out to welcome him.

Gao Minglou received the district and county bureau chiefs in his parlor. His wife served tea, and his eldest daughter-in-law handed around cigarettes and lit them for everyone.

Gao Yuzhi initially had not wanted to come, but his brother wouldn't let him refuse; he had to have this meal! Minglou was the village leader, and Yuzhi couldn't offend him.

Also, sometime in the past, their ancestors were all Gaos! He had to go.

Gao Minglou insisted that Zhansheng drink and smoke with Bureau Chief Gao Yuzhi while he went to the kitchen to tell his wife and daughter-in-law not to rush the food.

He went out into the courtyard and beckoned to Sanxing, who had been smoking in the corner. Lowering his voice, he asked, "Why haven't you gone to fetch Gao Yude and Jialin?"

"You didn't tell me to go fetch them!" His son looked bewildered at his father's enraged face.

"You complete blockhead! You wouldn't know your ass from your elbow! Hurry up and go ask them over!"

Sanxing rushed off and came back right before the food was served, dragging Gao Yude by the elbow.

Minglou rushed out and warmly grasped the man's other arm. "Where's Jialin?"

Old Yude said, "That boy is stubborn as a rod. Don't worry about him."

Gao Yude was immediately escorted inside the cave house by Gao Minglou and his son and placed in the chair of honor, flanked on either side by Gao Yuzhi and Ma Zhansheng. Minglou sat in an inferior seat.

The food was about to be served. The enormous red-lacquered old-fashioned square table was laden with saucers and platters, big bowls and little bowls, "flavors from the mountains and the seas," as the saying goes: a spread far richer than anything served in the county seat. The guest had no idea where such delicacies had come from!

Minglou stood up to give a toast. Once someone had filled his cup, he lifted his glass respectfully and toasted Gao Yude.

Gao Yude's gaunt arms trembled as he toasted with his companions. The old man felt his stomach and intestines knot up after downing just one cup. He looked at Gao Minglou's face with its fawning smile, and at his brother at his side. He sighed sadly to himself—what need was there for this kind of fine display?

~

Two weeks later, all Gao Jialin, Gao Yude's only son, had to do to become a party cadre was to show up at the county coal mine. He would then be an official state worker and could be promoted to his new job. How had he found himself here? What behind-the-scenes maneuvers had there been? Even he didn't know. He just filled out an application; everything else was managed by Ma Zhansheng.

Life could change so drastically in an instant!

The villagers were numb to this sort of thing by now, so no one made much of a fuss. Gao Minglou's son had graduated from high school, so Teacher Gao Jialin was let go and became a peasant . . . and nobody was surprised. Gao Jialin's uncle became the regional labor bureau chief, so Jialin suddenly found work in the county seat . . . and nobody was surprised. Sometimes they grumbled at the unfairness of contemporary society, but their honest good natures prevented them from taking any further action. What could they do anyway?

When Gao Jialin left the village, his father had just fallen ill and his mother was taking care of him, so they didn't see Gao Jialin off.

Only the deeply devoted Liu Qiaozhen went with him as he left the village. She walked him all the way to the crossroads at the bend in the river. His bedding and suitcase had been sent ahead a few days earlier, and he carried only his satchel. Qiaozhen acted just like a city girl, walking nonchalantly alongside him holding one of the straps of his bag.

When they came to the crossroads, they looked behind them, then at each other. He had kissed her here before. But now, in broad daylight, he couldn't do it.

"Jialin, please think of me often . . ." Qiaozhen bit her lip as tears streamed down her face.

Jialin nodded.

"We belong together, right?" Qiaozhen looked up at him, weeping.

Jialin nodded at her again, a dazed look in his eyes, and slowly turned away.

As he walked along the main road, he turned and saw Qiaozhen still standing at the bend in the river, watching him. Tears suddenly blurred his vision.

He stood there for a long time, looking at Qiaozhen's lovely, slender figure; he looked at the irregular outline of the cottages of Gaojia Village and at the Great Horse River wreathed in green, and he felt a sudden sense of regret at his departure. Although he had longed to leave this place and broaden his horizons, he still felt a deep passion for the village that had raised him.

He wiped the tears from his eyes and turned resolutely toward the county seat.

Where would the road of life take him next?

PART TWO

CHAPTER 14

It had already been a number of days since Gao Jialin arrived at the county seat, and he still didn't feel settled. It was all like a dream. He was deliriously happy, but also anxious. He had once again come from the farmland to the city. But this time wasn't quite like the last. When he'd moved to the county seat last time, he was basically still a country boy, cowering, terrified of the big city. A few years of active student life made his outlook, sensibilities, and lifestyle more and more like those of a city-dweller. He became an urbanite to the core. He grew indifferent toward the countryside; it was like a backdrop on the stage of his life—something he only got a taste of during winter or summer vacation.

Then, at the very moment he finally felt one with the city, he found out he hadn't tested into college, so after he graduated high school, he had no choice but to return to a land that felt strange to him. The distress of a young person with such high hopes is easy to imagine, even to understand. But the country was going through a difficult period just then, and not every citizen's demands or desires could be satisfied.

If all parts of a society are healthy, doubtless it will correctly guide its young people, helping them see how the interests of the nation and their own future are related. Thus, looking back at how my country solved society's problems in the fifties and early sixties, one might remember real people like Ma Zhansheng and Gao Minglou. For their own benefit, they would harm those who loitered at the crossroads of life, leaving them hopeless. Yet sometimes, also for their own purposes, these same men turned around and set individuals like this afloat on the ship of life with a good wind at their backs. In a flash, things can change for the better. Yet while people may feel happy with their accomplishments, they may also feel a sense of loss at the suddenness of their success.

Gao Jialin was deliriously happy because he realized that this time he wasn't just passing through; he was truly a citizen of the city. Of course, given his current circumstances, he wouldn't be able to live there his whole life, but for the moment his place was there and he had achieved his heart's desire. And he was so visible in his current position! He was a communications cadre, which is to say the county journalist, and he went around doing interviews, writing reports, and taking photos. His every word might appear in the newspaper. If the county government held a big meeting, he would shoulder his camera and dare to come and go freely on that hallowed ground, the chairman's platform.

He knew he owed his current situation entirely to Ma Zhansheng. Gao Yuzhi swore to Jialin that he hadn't done anything. But if it wasn't him, it could have been someone acting on his behalf. Jialin felt he had gone to heaven, and he finally knew what it meant to go through the back door—it truly was mightier than the front! He couldn't help but feel a bit anxious knowing that was how he'd gotten his current position; everyone seemed opposed to that kind of thing these days.

But he quickly comforted himself with the thought that they didn't manage to catch that many people. Zhansheng said all cats smell fishy and told Jialin to relax. If anything happened, he, Zhansheng, would take the blame. So Jialin did his best not to think about it anymore. Since he was a national cadre now, he just had to work hard and make his deadlines. That's what he really felt. He sometimes credited the party with the change in his circumstances and resolved to work hard for them. He even thought, *Next year, I must write and apply to join!*

His superior was Jing Ruohong. Old Jing was more than ten years older than he was, skinny, tall, with a pair of white-framed glasses perched on his nose. The year the Cultural Revolution began, he'd graduated from the provincial normal university with a degree in Chinese. Before Gao Jialin came, Old Jing was the only communications cadre in the county.

When he first met Old Jing, Jialin thought he seemed very kind. He didn't say much, but when he did speak he revealed his education and the depth of his character. Gao Jialin quickly grew to like him, and called him Teacher Jing. Old Jing had never become an official, but he was clearly a leader.

For the first few days after Gao Jialin arrived at his new job, Old Jing wouldn't let him work; he made him organize his things and his office first, and if there was nothing else to do, then he let him go out and amuse himself.

His working and living quarters with Old Jing were in the four-walled compound of the county committee's hotel. They both had their own offices in a five-room mud building built into the earth. The rooms were built to high specifications— each had four walls and a door to which they alone had the keys. The other rooms functioned as the county's best hotel, accommodating provincial party leaders on the random occasions when they came to the city for a few days. They had set up an office for the communications cadres here, to demonstrate the importance the provincial leaders placed on propaganda work. Conditions were comfortable, and it was quiet and suitable for writing.

Gao Jialin aired his bedding and put away his suitcase. Old Jing then took him to the county committee office to get some office supplies. A table and chairs as well as a filing cabinet had been delivered the previous day.

After all this had been accomplished, Gao Jialin walked back and forth in his cave, looking here, poking there, humming his favorite Soviet tune, "The Dnieper River Rages," and glancing at his own jaunty expression in the mirror.

He felt supremely comfortable. The west-leaning sun shone in through the great glass window and spilled its glittering beams onto his writing desk, the sunlight a perfect, harmonious reflection of his mood.

Everything was taken care of. After eating lunch in the canteen, he went for a leisurely stroll and found himself at his alma mater.

They had let out for vacation so there was no one on campus. As he wandered around the place he knew by heart, events of his past appeared before his eyes. The winsome tones of an accordion and the clamor of a school sporting event rang in his ears. The faces of his classmates passed before him. Finally, the ship of his memory came to rest on the figure of Huang Yaping. Where the two of them had discussed some issue, what they had talked about—he could imagine it all so clearly.

Everywhere he went, he did just what he used to do in his school days, sitting down, or lying down, his eyes brimming with tears all the while. The mind lovingly preserves each tree and blade of grass of one's youth, and it's easy to get choked up when these memories come flooding back.

He left the school and walked to the county sports stadium; he was fond of exercise and had been a member of many teams in his school days. He and Ke'nan were the stars of the basketball team, and he had spent many exciting evenings here in the stadium.

He then turned out of the stadium and walked along the road, taking in all the main sites of the city like a tourist. When he was done, he climbed up the hill at the east end of town.

The hill was covered with saplings, some of which had been planted during the Grave-Sweeping Festival earlier that year. At the top of the hill was the Heroes' Memorial Garden, where more than a hundred revolutionary soldiers were buried. There was a mottled plinth that explained to visitors that more than thirty years had passed since they had lost their lives fighting in this very county.

This was the most beautiful place in town. The average resident spent most of their time at the theater or the stadium—it was mostly the schoolteachers, doctors, and other intellectuals that came up here. But since the hill was high and not many people visited, it made for a peaceful retreat.

Gao Jialin sat beneath a great locust tree. He could see the entire village through the gaps in the foliage. Not much had changed since he had left three years ago—there were a few foreign-looking multistory buildings along the road, and there was a new bridge across the river that connected a few communes on the opposite side of the water with the sports stadium on the other bank.

The sun was just setting in the west, and its red light smeared across the blue-tiled roofs of the buildings. It was an extraordinarily dazzling scene. The yellow plains outside the city extended to the mountains, which rose endlessly like so many waves toward the distant horizon.

When the city lights lit up like stars, Gao Jialin stood up and made his way down the hill. Once he was on the road, he couldn't help but spread his arms in an embrace of the shining city, saying, "I'll never leave you again."

∽

Gao Jialin's first professional opportunity came when a thunderstorm erupted over the southern part of the city.

The rain started that morning, and while quite a bit fell over the city, the most affected area was the South Horse River Commune, according to the reports coming in via telephone. Several villages in the area had been flooded, and initial estimates suggested that more than thirty people had been carried away, yet to be found. Homes had been destroyed, and many residents had nowhere to go. The entire commune was doing what it could in terms of disaster relief.

Jing Ruohong had decided to go himself to the South Horse River Commune to report on the relief situation, despite his suffering from a cold. Gao Jialin was determined not to let him go and begged Old Jing to let him take his place. He said this would be his first job—it was a test—and if the report was unsatisfactory, he would bring back his notes so that Old Jing could rewrite it. Jing Ruohong was forced to agree.

Gao Jialin didn't take his bike because he heard that the roads by South Horse River were mostly washed out. He borrowed a raincoat from the office, rolled his pants up to his knees, and set out in the rain toward the South Horse River Commune.

He could hear the blood rushing in his ears the whole way there. He was the kind of person who liked to take risks, who liked to play the hero. In everyday situations, this quality could reveal itself in regrettable ways, but now it came into its own.

In this kind of situation, he could be vigorous and energized, and completely focused, with quick reactions and a clear mind. He was prepared to make any sacrifice at any moment.

He left before twilight, but within a few miles, night had fallen.

The rain soon soaked his head, and it was so dark he couldn't see his hand in front of his face. He practically jogged there, although he didn't really know the way. At one point he was so thirsty he thought his throat might catch on fire, so he drank some water from a puddle on the side of the road. He also banged his foot on something, feeling the pain in his bones. Despite all of that, and perhaps because of it, he felt absolutely elated! At that moment Gao Jialin felt like a real journalist. Although he had never done a single day's work as a journalist, he understood the honor of the profession, which aligned perfectly with his spirit of fearless self-sacrifice. According to what he had read, some journalists would even charge alongside soldiers on the battlefield and send missives from prisoner of war camps. Amazing!

Gao Jialin was the first cadre from town to reach South Horse River Commune. The disaster relief team headed by the deputy secretary of the county committee got there five hours later, around dawn.

When Jialin arrived, none of the commune cadres recognized him. He introduced himself as a newly appointed county-level communications administrator who had come as quickly as possible to conduct interviews and report on emergency relief efforts. When they saw the barely twenty-something young man covered in mud, with bleeding feet, they were deeply moved and hurried to get him something to eat. The commune cadres had just returned from working with a production brigade in a place where the flooding was the worst, and after they ate they would get ready to go out with yet another brigade. They were soaked to the skin, their faces so covered with mud that only their eyes were still visible. The commune secretary, Liu Yuhai, had sustained seven injuries, which were all wrapped in gauze. He looked like he had just returned from the front lines of battle.

They forced Jialin into a change of clothes and bandaged his feet. Then the commune clerk told Jialin he'd give him a full report at his home, while everyone else left to work in another disaster area.

But Jialin was determined to go with them. He took out a plastic bag in which he had wrapped his fountain pen and notebook, which he'd taken from his satchel, and forced his way in with the departing group. The commune clerk, Little Ma, joked that he should give a report to the communications administrator praising Jialin's work ethic.

Once on the road, the muddy party divided into groups to go to different production brigades to investigate and organize relief efforts.

Gao Jialin, Little Ma the clerk, and Secretary Liu Yuhai went to meet with the Buddhist temple brigade. Making their way blindly, unable to see each other through the downpour, they groped slowly forward. The roar of the torrent in the riverbed was deafening, and rain was still dumping on them. As the clerk kept falling and scrambling back up, he was simultaneously discussing everything he knew about the disaster and the commune's relief measures. Gao Jialin memorized it all. Secretary Liu Yuhai didn't say a word; he just kept moving forward.

Just as they joined the Buddhist temple brigade, a crowd of sobbing villagers ran toward them, shouting at Liu Yuhai that several caves had collapsed, livestock had been swept away, and crops had been ruined.

Liu Yuhai's face was ashen as he asked the brigade cadres, "And the people?"

"Everyone's fine!" they all said.

Liu Yuhai whirled his uninjured arm around and shouted, "If the people are all right, there's no need for fear!"

His words garnered an immediate roar of approval from the crowd. Liu Yuhai then gathered everyone around the stove of the communal cave, and they sat on the ground in a circle, debating the best rescue methods.

Gao Jialin was also moved by Liu Yuhai's words. He turned his head and saw the secretary among the group of farmers on the floor: he was just as down-to-earth and spirited as Zhu Laozhong from *Keep the Red Flag Flying*. His body was covered in wounds, yet he was still so attentive toward the commoners. Jialin was very inspired. Life was full of treacherous cadres like Ma Zhansheng and Gao Minglou, but there were also good cadres like Liu Yuhai. Even though Ma Zhansheng had pulled strings for Gao Jialin, he still didn't like him. And even though this was his first time meeting Liu Yuhai, Jialin felt drawn to him.

He thought of Liu's earlier call to arms and had a sudden burst of inspiration. Pulling out his fountain pen and notebook from the plastic bag, he wrote down the headline of his first report: *There's No Need to Fear Disaster If the People Are All Right.*

By the weak light of the communal cave, he concentrated on writing his report. Outside, the rain gurgled and the flooding riverbed roared, but he heard none of it. His pen trembled as it flew excitedly across the pages of his notebook. He understood the conventions and requirements of a news report well—he often read the paper and had long been familiar with different genres of writing.

After he finished the draft, he went with Liu Yuhai to one of the disaster zones to work with everyone else in the mud and the rain.

The next morning, he gave his report to the commune's mailman to take to Old Jing in town.

In the evening, he went with Liu Yuhai and the clerk to the commune headquarters to attend an emergency meeting. At the meeting, a cadre from each brigade gave a report on the situation. This was Gao Jialin's first time at a meeting like this, and he was uninhibited as he questioned everyone and collected specific details along with examples of heroism.

Later, Liu Yuhai ordered everyone to rest for three hours, except for those currently on duty; at midnight, they'd go out again.

Gao Jialin didn't sleep at all. He wrote three more short dispatches and a summary report by the light of a kerosene lamp.

After he finished, he stood in the doorway of the commune headquarters and stretched his arms and legs.

Then he heard a sound over the PA. It was a program from the city, broadcasting Huang Yaping's smooth Mandarin: "Comrade Du Yuan, now let's listen to Jialin's interview and report, *There's No Need to Fear Disaster If the People Are All Right*." Yaping sounded excited. When she read the part about Liu Yuhai, she was especially dynamic, and the pace of the broadcast seemed livelier than normal.

Gao Jialin stood under the eaves of the house, his heart racing, listening to his first-ever broadcast from beginning to end. Old Jing hadn't even changed one word!

Happiness welled up in him, and he sighed softly amid the pounding rain.

The next day, Jialin received a note from Old Jing with just a few words written on it: *Remarkable job. Waiting for your next report. Return whenever you see fit.*

Gao Jialin did as he was instructed and sent a series of reports back from South Horse River. Evening and morning, Huang Yaping's smooth, beautiful Mandarin came over the cable radio: "Now we give you Jialin's first string of reports on the disaster at South Horse River . . ."

It was like this for five days, until finally Gao Jialin returned to the city with a group of cadres who had gone to the country to convey the condolences of the county committee.

CHAPTER 15

Gao Jialin arrived back in town and fell into bed without a thought.

He slept soundly the whole night, even sleeping through breakfast the next day.

Eventually, half-awake, he heard what sounded like someone knocking on a door. At first he thought it was someone standing outside Old Jing's room, but, listening closely, he realized it was his door they were knocking at. He thought it must be Old Jing looking for him, so he jumped out of bed and shouted while he was getting dressed, "Teacher Jing, come in!"

A chuckle came from outside the door. It sounded female.

He called again quickly, "Please wait a moment!"

He finished dressing and went to open the door.

When he opened it, he was so surprised he took a step back: it was Huang Yaping!

Yaping was leaning her arm against the doorframe, smiling at him. He again noticed that she no longer resembled the fragile, delicate girl of their school days—she had filled out. Her face seemingly hadn't changed, but her eyebrows, like two curving strokes of a brush, had become more pronounced—a common mark of a southern lady. She wore a fine red short-sleeved blouse that looked new and milk-white straight-legged trousers with ochre kitten heels. Gao Jialin took this all in with a glance.

Huang Yaping walked into Gao Jialin's room and said, "Why didn't you tell me you had come to the city to work? You're such a great journalist now—did you already forget your friends?"

Gao Jialin hurried to explain that he had only recently moved to town and that'd he been busy; he had just gotten back from South Horse River and was planning to visit her and Ke'nan in the next few days.

"Why didn't Ke'nan come?" Jialin asked as he poured some water for his old classmate.

"He's an industrialist now—he doesn't drop by on old friends anymore," Huang Yaping said.

Jialin put a teacup in front of Huang Yaping, walked over to his bed, and sat down. "Yes, Ke'nan is quite the industrialist. I've known since we were young that he had a promising future. Our country needs talented people like him right now."

"Forget about Ke'nan. Let him go industrialize," Yaping joked. "Let's talk about you! You must be exhausted. Those disaster reports from South Horse River were excellent—I sometimes teared up reading them . . ."

"They weren't that good. It's my first time writing that kind of thing; they're really very amateurish. I owe everything to Teacher Jing's editing," Jialin said modestly, but he was secretly giddy with delight.

"You've gotten skinnier since school. But you seem sturdier, taller somehow." Yaping appraised him while she drank her tea.

Jialin felt a bit embarrassed by her gaze and tried to make light of it. "Doing hard labor for a day or two might have made me a bit sturdier . . ."

Yaping quickly took notice of Jialin's discomfort and felt embarrassed herself. She looked down at her tea.

They were silent for a while.

Huang Yaping took a sip before saying, "I'm happy you've come to the city so I have someone else to talk to here. You probably don't know this, but these past few years I've felt so isolated. Everyone's so busy, and no one has time to ask how anyone else is doing. I tried my hardest to find someone to chat with, but couldn't."

"You're exaggerating. There must be someone—you just haven't met them yet. You can come off as rather intimidating, you know—it's hard for us regular folk to get close to you," Jialin said, smiling.

Huang Yaping smiled, too. "Maybe you're right, but I really have been depressed lately. I'd like to have some romance in my life."

"Luckily you have Ke'nan . . ." Jialin didn't know why this sprang so suddenly to his lips.

"Well, aren't you the Ke'nan expert! He means well, but I've always felt that he was a little emotionally shallow. Still, he has done a lot for me over the years . . . You probably know about our . . . situation." Huang Yaping blushed.

"I've heard a bit," Jialin said.

"You should come have lunch at my family's house today!" Huang Yaping said, warmth in her voice.

"I'm sorry, I can't," Jialin quickly replied. "I'm not used to going to strangers' homes to eat."

"Now I'm a stranger?" Huang Yaping asked, hurt.

"I mean to say that I don't know your parents."

"If you come over, then you'll meet them!"

"Thank you, but . . ."

"Are you afraid of them?"

"Uh . . ."

"Such a country boy!" Huang Yaping laughed.

Gao Jialin wasn't upset by her teasing tone; instead, he was happy that Yaping felt close enough to joke around with him.

When they were in school together, she would always joke that he was a hillbilly.

"Yes, I'm a country boy. What else could I be?" He gazed happily at Huang Yaping.

Yaping stared back at him. "You really don't look it. But sometimes there's a naivete about you; it's funny . . . If you don't want to come eat with us, then forget it, but you'll probably have to come by the radio station for work, and then we'll get to chat, just like in school, all right?"

Gao Jialin didn't know how to respond. Scenes of their school days flashed before his eyes. But they were children then, and innocent. Now that they were both in their twenties, could they have the same carefree relationship as before? Honestly, he would love to talk with Yaping. They had a lot in common and agreed on most things. But he knew it would be hard to reestablish their old relationship. They were both cadres now, and they might attract attention. And she and Ke'nan were already dating—he would have to take all this into account.

He hesitated a moment and saw Yaping looking at him, waiting for him to speak. He hedged. "If I have time, I'll definitely call on you at the radio station."

"So diplomatic! What do you mean, call on me? You might as well just come pay me an official visit! I know you research international affairs and you're practicing your diplomatic rhetoric."

Gao Jialin couldn't help but smile. "You're just as sharp-tongued as always! OK, I'll definitely come find you at the radio station."

"It's OK if you don't come. I'll just find you here!"

"Yaping, I beg you not to come here too often. I just started this job, and I'm afraid that it might cause a stir . . . I'm really sorry . . ."

Huang Yaping stood up quickly, having realized that she had overstepped the bounds of propriety. She couldn't think of anything polite to say, so she simply said, "I was joking! Please go back to bed. I'll leave . . . but really, if you have time, please come see me at the radio station. It's already been three years since we graduated . . ."

Gao Jialin nodded earnestly.

When Huang Yaping left the courtyard of Jialin's building, she felt a warmth spread across her chest and forehead as if she was coming down with something. Gao Jialin's sudden appearance had turned her peaceful world upside down.

After she'd graduated from high school, she had found work in the county seat, Jialin had returned to the countryside, and the two had naturally gone their separate ways. That first year, she would think of him and their close relationship not infrequently; he would often pop up in her thoughts. She missed him terribly. Moving around with her father so much, she had gone to many schools, but out of all her male schoolmates, no one had made the impression on her that Jialin had.

Before, she had looked down on her classmates from the countryside, knowing they wouldn't amount to much. But getting to know Jialin changed her mind. She appreciated his character, outlook, intelligence, and spirit.

After leaving school, they lived only ten *li* apart, but it was as if they lived in two different worlds, and neither was brave enough to make plans to meet up. In this way, three years passed in an instant. That is, until the day she was seeing Ke'nan off at the bus station and they'd run into Jialin. She was distracted for days after their meeting.

She and Ke'nan became closer after graduation. He would constantly visit the radio station to bring her snacks and drinks. And whenever some fashionable new product arrived in his store, he would buy it for her. At first, she despised him for this. At school, Ke'nan would always find some excuse to compliment her, and she avoided him assiduously—she was primarily interested in spending time with Gao Jialin. But now that she had a job and everything about her work unit was unfamiliar, her intimidating personality made it difficult for others to get close to her. And anyway, Ke'nan had been her classmate for so many years, and they understood each other to a certain extent, so eventually she began to enjoy his company. She discovered that he was capable and enthusiastic in his work, kindhearted, and considerate, especially when it came to daily tasks. He was aware of what displeased her about him, and he did his best to overcome those things when they were together. He was also very relaxed. When she was sick, she usually wouldn't bother her parents and would just take a rest at her work unit. But she couldn't keep it from Ke'nan. He would become like an attentive nurse or housekeeper, protecting and caring for her. He was a good cook and would make her several meals a day.

He made more and more of an impression on her, and she grew to accept his love. Their parents were all very satisfied, and over the past two years they had developed a stable relationship. She had begun to fall in love with him, too. He might not be elegant or refined, but he wasn't unattractive, with his broad shoulders and masculine physique. After a few years at the Luxury Food Company, he had plumped up, but he wasn't what you would call obese; on the contrary, the weight made him manlier somehow. When they went to the movies together, they attracted their fair share of attention.

Not long ago, the military subdistrict had approved Yaping's father's request to transfer to his hometown in Jiangsu. Her father had been in contact with his workplace in Nanjing. Yaping was an only child, so according to the law, she could get a job in the same town as her mother and father. An old army buddy of her father's was high up in the Jiangsu provincial government, and last year when she went home to Nanjing, this uncle heard her broadcasts and offered her a job at the Jiangsu People's Radio Station. So if she went back to Nanjing now, she would have a great job; the only hitch in this plan was Ke'nan. But her father had written many letters to his old army buddy to find a job for Ke'nan as well and to make it easier for their two families to come together.

So, her life was calm and predictable, progressing normally and to her satisfaction. But then, out of the blue, Gao Jialin had reappeared!

Yaping didn't know that Jialin had become a communications administrator with the county until she heard from Old Jing and broadcast Gao Jialin's first report on the disaster at South Horse River. As she read the piece, she could see how talented he was, and suddenly her heart was ablaze as all her memories of them together flashed before her eyes. As she recorded the broadcast, staring at the spinning reel, she cried, but not entirely because of the report. Rather, she cried as she thought of her student days with Jialin. After all this time, it became clear; she finally understood she had been in love with him all along! He was her true love, and the only reason she had gotten together with Ke'nan was because Jialin had returned to the countryside, leaving her without hope of a future together. There was no need to hide that or be ashamed; she couldn't marry a peasant—even for love. She knew she couldn't cope with that much suffering for the rest of her life.

Now that Jialin had gotten a job in the city, she didn't need to worry about that anymore. All things being equal, if she weighed Jialin and Ke'nan against each other on the scales of her love, Ke'nan was far from measuring up to Jialin . . . And since she had heard that Jialin had returned, she couldn't help but go first thing that morning to see him.

As she walked along the path to the radio station, she felt both excited and disappointed. She could see that Jialin had grown even more attractive: he was tall and handsome, with a chiseled jaw and bright eyes. He looked a little like the illustrations of Pavel Korchagin from the novel *How the Steel Was Tempered*, or Julien Sorel from the film *The Red and the Black*.

How wonderful it would be if we could spend our lives together. Yaping daydreamed as she walked. But she immediately felt sad again, because just then Ke'nan came to mind.

"Aiya, keep your head down as you walk—be careful you don't fall!"

Surprised, Yaping looked up: just as she had been thinking about Ke'nan, his mother appeared before her eyes. She didn't like Ke'nan's mother; the assistant manager of the pharmaceutical company put on the airs of a city woman and an official simultaneously.

Ke'nan's mother pulled a few plump fish from her satchel and said, "It's noon! How we southerners suffer here in the north, not eating fish all year. The Luxury Food Company got these from the reservoir of the commune on the other side of the mountain."

"Auntie, I'm afraid I can't come to lunch. I've already eaten at your home far too much." Yaping tried her best to smile as she responded.

"Why, child, what are you saying! When did our home become 'your home'?"

Yaping found the awkward phrase funny and shot back with, "When did your home become 'our home'?"

Ke'nan's mother cracked up at this.

Yaping said, "I'm not feeling so well today. I don't think I should eat anything. I should go lie down."

"Do you need some medicine? My company just got some new pills in for stomachaches. The results—"

"I have some—I don't want to bother you."

Yaping quickly took her leave of Ke'nan's mother and continued on toward the radio station.

She fell onto her bed as soon as she got in the door. She pulled the pillow out from under her and covered her face with it.

Not long after, she heard a knock at the door. Frustrated, she answered, "Who's there?"

"It's me," Ke'nan responded.

Annoyed, she got out of bed and opened the door.

Ke'nan entered and said cheerfully, "Come over and join us for some fish! It's fresh, and I bought several. My mother's taking them home now—"

"That's all your mother ever talks about—food! You're such a pig! The collar on the sweater I knit for you last year is already so stretched out after only one winter that it looks like the rim of a bucket!" Huang Yaping fell angrily on the bed again, and covered her face with the pillow.

The hailstorm of her words pelted Zhang Ke'nan and broke him like a stalk of millet. He didn't know what to do. What had happened to his dear Yaping?

After wringing his hands in distress for a while, he walked over and softly lifted the pillow from Yaping's face.

Yaping snatched back the pillow and shouted, "Go away!"

Zhang Ke'nan cowered, anxious and confused. "What the hell happened to you?" It sounded like he was crying.

After a while, Yaping sat up and wiped her face with the pillowcase, having calmed down a bit. "Don't be angry," she said to the mute Ke'nan in front of her. "I'm just feeling a little sick today . . ."

"Can you still go to the movie tonight?" Ke'nan said as he pulled the tickets out from his pocket. "I've heard it's good. It's parts one and two of this Pakistani film, *Eternal Love*."

Huang Yaping sighed and said, "Yes, I'll go . . ."

CHAPTER 16

Gao Jialin quickly became something of a celebrity in the county seat. All his talents came to the fore in that particular environment. Several of his news reports were published in the local and provincial papers, and he even published a story on the local people and customs in the provincial paper's supplement. He quickly mastered the techniques of taking, developing, and printing photographs, which he learned from Old Jing. Whenever there was an important social event, Jialin would march through the assembled crowds with a camera (complete with flashbulb) hanging from his neck, looking particularly conspicuous. Not to mention the fact that he was quite a handsome young man, which made him even more of a phenomenon. People had recently started to ask, "Who is that young man? What's his background? How old is he? Where is he from?" Girls would bat their eyes at him whenever they had the chance, thinking of any excuse to run into him.

Late nights he would cause quite a stir at the athletics stadium. The various county-level work units would take turns organizing basketball tournaments. Gao Jialin had been the star of his high school team, and now he was the star of the county committee's team as well. With the sole exception of the movie theater, the sports stadium was the most popular destination in that mountain city. The basketball courts were brightly lit, and the mud-brick seating platforms were often crowded with spectators. Gao Jialin wore a sky-blue jersey with two stripes down the arms and legs: he looked like a warrior. He was as good as anyone in the city, and spectators were very quickly drawn to him.

In a mountain city of about ten thousand people, it was rare to find a young man of his talents and charm, and it wasn't surprising that he became an object of infatuation.

Soon, whenever he went to the government canteen to buy food, the female workers would give him more food than everyone else, even though he gave them the same amount of money or food coupons. When he went to the department store, the salespeople would all come up to him and ask what he wanted to buy; when he walked down the street, he could hear people say as he passed, "Look, it's the county journalist! He's always got a camera with him. And his essays are always in the paper!" Or maybe, "It's number 11, the forward. He's fast and accurate."

Gao Jialin had become a superstar.

Needless to say, he was feeling livelier and more animated than usual as a result. His job never felt too tiring or difficult, and no matter where he had to go to conduct an interview, he would either bike or run there. When he got back to the city, he would hunch over his desk all night, writing. He was living a bit more comfortably now. He not only got a salary, but also fees for his essays. Of course, the newspaper didn't pay him nearly as much as the radio station—he got two yuan per piece at the latter, and he wrote a piece just about every day, since his program, *Our County*, ran daily, and there weren't that many people writing for it.

He felt pride and self-confidence every moment of every day; his self-esteem was the highest it had ever been. He sometimes felt light as a feather. He was incisive when he talked to his colleagues, his literary skills were self-evident, and he generally looked pleased with himself. Sometimes he would break out in a sweat and worry he shouldn't be so conspicuous; he warned himself not to boast or brag. He had bigger ambitions and ideas that couldn't be satisfied by his current position, and if he wasn't careful, his future might be thwarted—he already felt others' envy at his rise in popularity.

In this way, he was able to moderate himself. He began to avoid places in which he might attract undue attention. When he wasn't busy, he'd run to the little forest in the eastern hills and sit in quiet meditation, or else he'd go to the fields to run sprints and do calisthenics to express his irrepressible inner happiness.

He had only gone to the radio station once to look for Huang Yaping. But Yaping would often come to him without waiting for an invitation. At first, her forwardness worried him, since he didn't want to be too familiar with her. But Yaping kept finding opportunities to come discuss anything and everything with him. It appeared she had been reading a lot these past few years; her knowledge was broad and her thinking always clear and logical. She even brought some of her poetry for him to read. Gradually, Jialin became more engaged in their discussions. He got along better with her than anyone else in the city. Old Jing was extremely erudite, but he was older, and Jialin didn't dare position himself on the same level as his elder in a casual discussion. He mostly just asked for advice.

Yaping and Jialin quickly regained the relationship they'd had in their school days. However, Jialin was prudent and steered the conversation only toward current affairs and academic topics. Of course, sometimes other thoughts would flash across his mind: *If we were a couple, our lives would be incredibly happy; we understand each other so well, it's like we share a secret language.*

This thought was quickly suppressed by a different one—Qiaozhen's dear, adorable face appearing before his eyes. And every time this happened, he yearned more and more for her. Ever since he had come to the town, he had been so busy he hadn't been able to visit her. He heard she had come to town a few times to look for him, but he had always been away in the countryside. He had been trying to find the time to return home.

One day after lunch, Jialin went to the cultural center to read magazines and happened to run into Yaping—she had come to borrow a book.

They sat down on a bench and quickly began talking about all sorts of international issues. This was a strength of Jialin's: from Solidarity in Poland to the Iranian leader, Khomeini, and Banisadr, the former president of Iran who had claimed asylum in France. They also discussed Reagan and his decision to stockpile nuclear weapons, and the resulting outcry from Europe and the USSR. Finally, he led her in a detailed discussion of an issue that had been overlooked by the general public: the strike of American air traffic controllers and the American government's hard line against negotiation as well as the support of European and non-European air traffic controllers for the strikers.

Yaping listened keenly, her beautiful face watching his, warmth and admiration in her gaze.

When Jialin finished talking, Yaping—not to be outdone—spoke to him about international energy issues. She first told him about the shift from coal to oil as the world's main energy source, and how ever since the seventies, the cost of energy had increased drastically and the reserves of a few important oil-producing regions had been almost entirely used up. There would most certainly be a global energy crisis. Moreover, according to a report published by the United Nations news service, in 1950 one-quarter of the earth's land was covered by forests, but now half of that forest had been destroyed by ax, bulldozer, chainsaw, or fire. In Africa, fifty million acres of forests were burned every year for fuel. According to the UN Food and Agricultural Organization, one hundred million people were suffering from a serious lack of fuel.

The words flowed confidently from Huang Yaping's mouth. She went on, telling Jialin that besides oil there were now fourteen forms of renewable energy, including solar energy, geothermal energy, wind energy, hydroelectricity, bioenergy, wood energy, charcoal, oil shale, oil sand, ocean energy, wave energy, tidal energy, and energy from peat and livestock . . .

Gao Jialin listened to her fluent narration, amazed at how much she could talk. He'd had no idea of the breadth and specificity of her knowledge!

Later they returned to the topic of literature. Yaping hesitated a moment, then pulled a sheet of paper from her pocket and gave it to Jialin, saying, "It's a poem I wrote yesterday—take a look."

Gao Jialin took the paper and read it:

"For Jialin"

I wish you were a winged wild goose

Free to love all corners of the sky

Wherever you can best survive

Is where you should make your roost

His face grew hot as he finished reading. He held the paper out to Yaping and said, "It's well written. But I'm not sure I understand why I'm a wild goose . . ."

Yaping wouldn't take the paper back. "Keep it. I wrote it for you. You'll understand eventually."

They both found it hard to change the topic after that, and there wasn't much else they could say about the poem, so they stood up and made to leave, excited by their conversation.

Yaping left first. Jialin put the poem she'd given him in his pocket and left through the back door of the reading room.

He stood a while in a melancholic daze, thinking about maybe doing an interview at the county cement factory, when a tractor hauling a trailer rumbled to a stop next to him.

He looked up, surprised, as he saw that the driver was none other than Gao Minglou's son Sanxing, the new community teacher.

Sanxing had already jumped down from the driver's seat and was now standing in front of Jialin, laughing.

"Why are you driving a tractor?" Jialin asked.

"Not long after you left, Uncle Zhansheng sent me to work on the mechanization and production team of the county's agricultural machinery bureau. Now I'm doing agricultural infrastructure in the Great Horse River Valley."

"If you left, then who's teaching?"

"Qiaoling," Sanxing said.

"She didn't test into college?"

"No . . ." Sanxing hesitated a moment, then said, "Qiaozhen came to see you. She rode here on my tractor. I was passing through the village and saw her working on the side of the road. She asked me to bring her along . . . She's waiting just ahead at the post and telecom office. She said she had to go to the county committee offices to find you . . ."

Jialin's chest felt hot. He said goodbye to Sanxing and hurried toward the committee offices.

Gao Jialin walked through the main gate and saw Qiaozhen hovering near the doorway, staring across the courtyard. She hadn't yet seen Jialin coming toward her.

Jialin stared at her from behind and saw that she was still wearing that beige short-sleeved shirt. Everything was the same as before; her graceful figure was still just as lovely, and her raven hair was still bound up with a flowered kerchief—only today it looked a bit messy, probably because she had been working right before she got on the tractor and hadn't had time to comb it. Seeing her like this really turned him on.

When Qiaozhen finally saw him standing in front of her, her eyes lit up immediately and she beamed. "I wanted to go inside to look for you, but the guard at the door said you weren't here and wouldn't let me in . . ."

Jialin said, "Let's go to my office." He walked ahead, and Qiaozhen followed.

Once they reached Jialin's office, Qiaozhen threw herself on his chest. Jialin quickly pushed her away, saying, "We're not in the field! My boss has a room right next door . . . Please sit down, I'll pour you some water." He brought out a cup.

Qiaozhen didn't sit and simply stared affectionately at her beloved. "You left and never came back . . . I came to the city looking for you a few times, but people said you'd gone to the countryside . . ."

"I've been busy!" Jialin said as he put the cup on his desk for Qiaozhen to drink.

Qiaozhen didn't take it. She went over to the bed and stroked it with her hand, testing out the comforter and pinching the mattress. "Your comforter's too thin—I'll help you pad it with some new cotton. And this felt cover is no good—I'll bring you the dog-skin mattress from home . . . ," she prattled.

"Aiya," Jialin said. "I can't have a hairy dog-skin mattress here at the office—everyone would laugh at me!"

"But dog skin is warm . . ."

"I'm not cold! You are absolutely not to bring it!" Jialin said, rather severely.

Qiaozhen saw the unhappy expression on Jialin's face and dropped the subject. But now she didn't know what to talk about. "Sanxing has been driving the tractor, and now Qiaoling is teaching. She didn't get into college."

"I know all that; Sanxing already told me."

"The village well has been fixed! And the weir was raised!"

"Oh . . ."

"Our old sow gave birth to twelve babies. One was crushed to death by the mother, but there are still—"

"Aiya, do you really need to spell it out? Of course there are eleven left. Please, drink!"

"Yes, there were eleven left, but the next day one more died . . ."

"Aiya, be quiet already!" Jialin grabbed a newspaper from his desk and stared at it without reading. He thought of the wide-ranging discussion he had just had with Yaping and how engaging it was. But his conversation with Qiaozhen was so tedious. A feeling welled up inside him that he could not put into words.

Qiaozhen saw how agitated he was, but didn't know what she had said wrong, nor did she know what Jialin was thinking, though she could tell that he didn't feel the same affection he used to have for her.

What else should she say? She didn't know. What *could* she say anyway? After all, she couldn't name fourteen kinds of new or renewable compound energy!

Jialin noticed Qiaozhen's discomfort as she sat at the edge of the bed, silently watching him. She looked pitiful—wanting him to want her but not knowing how to make it so.

At this moment he loved her deeply again. "It's almost lunchtime," he said. "You wait here in the office while I go get us something to eat from the canteen. We can eat together."

"I'm not hungry! And I have to hurry back. In my rush to catch Sanxing's tractor, I left my hoe in the field and didn't tell anyone."

She stood up from the edge of the bed and pulled a roll of cash from under her shirt. Walking over to him, she said, "Jialin, you have a lot of expenses here in the city, and you don't make a lot of money. Here's fifty yuan; if there's not enough in the pantry, you can take this to the canteen or the street corner to get something to eat. I also bought a pair of sneakers for you, since Sanxing said that you play basketball and often wear out your shoes . . . They gave out midyear bonuses, and I got ninety-two yuan . . ."

Gao Jialin choked up as tears welled in his eyes. He grasped Qiaozhen's hands, still holding the money, and said, "Qiaozhen! I have money now and plenty to eat. I don't need your funds . . . Take this and buy some new, fashionable clothes . . ."

"You have to take it!" Qiaozhen pressed the cash into his hands.

"I'll get angry if you keep acting this way!" was all he could say.

Qiaozhen saw that he really was displeased and had no choice but to take back the money, disappointed. "I'll leave it for you, for whenever you might need a little something extra . . . I should go."

Jialin walked her to the door. "Go to the Great Horse Bridge and wait for me there; I have something to do in town, but I'll meet you in a little while."

Qiaozhen nodded and left.

Gao Jialin ran out quickly to the supermarket and used the earnings he'd received that day from the radio station to buy a red kerchief. He folded it into his bag and hurried off to the Great Horse River Bridge.

Gao Jialin had been wanting to buy Qiaozhen a red scarf. The first time he was with her, she reminded him of a beautiful woman from a foreign oil painting, except the girl from the painting had her hair wrapped in a red scarf. So out of some sense of romance and nostalgia, and even though it was a very hot summer, he wanted to wrap Qiaozhen's head in a red scarf.

At the bridge, he saw Qiaozhen standing right where she had waited for him when he'd been heading home from the market with his unsold basket of steamed buns. This memory instantly stirred up a warm current of loving feelings in him.

The two walked side by side over the bridge and turned toward the Great Horse River Valley.

They followed a bend in the road behind a hill, and seeing that there was no one around, Jialin stopped, pulled the red scarf out of his bag, and gave it to Qiaozhen.

Qiaozhen didn't understand why her dearest was acting this way. She thought this must be Jialin's way of telling her that he loved and adored her.

She hugged him close without saying anything, happy tears pouring down her face. After seeing Qiaozhen off, Jialin walked along the street, thinking how the passion between him and Qiaozhen was nowhere near as strong now as it had been when they were in the fields.

At this unhappy realization, he looked up and sighed a long sigh into the gray and drizzling sky.

CHAPTER 17

Huang Yaping was in turmoil. She had fallen passionately in love with Gao Jialin and was determined to find a way to be with him. She had already decided that she would break off her relationship with Zhang Ke'nan.

The problem was how her parents would react. She was their only child, and they'd both spoiled her her whole life. They would never let her suffer, but they also loved Ke'nan. For the past few years, Ke'nan had treated them like his own parents, and they had treated him like a son. If she broke up with him, it would also be a blow to her parents. What's more, her parents and Ke'nan's had already become like family. Her father was a soldier, and loyalty was very important to him; he would think of the breakup as incredibly immoral.

She mulled the issue over and decided that, no matter what, she had to break up with Ke'nan. It didn't matter what her parents or society thought; she had her own ideas.

Huang Yaping was one of the city's few modern youths. In her opinion, people should be free to pursue happiness on their own terms. She was her own person, and no one had the right to interfere in her pursuits, not even her very loving parents. They were looking at the situation from the point of view of potential in-laws, while she was seeing it from the perspective of a lover. Breaking up with him now would be easier than waiting—even if they were married, she would divorce Ke'nan if she fell in love with someone else!

She had made up her mind. The vexing thing was, did Gao Jialin love her or not?

From what she could tell, Gao Jialin liked her a great deal, and back in their school days, they were closer than most classmates. Really, it only made sense that Gao Jialin must love her! Even though she didn't look like a movie star or anything, she was one of the most attractive girls in the city—at least, from her point of view. And her family was better off economically and socially than Gao Jialin's. Even more important was the fact that her family was about to move to Nanjing, where she would be a broadcaster at the Jiangsu People's Radio Station. She knew Jialin had great hopes for his future, and a move to Nanjing would certainly be attractive to him. Unlike Zhang Ke'nan, who didn't dare speak of it in front of his parents and in private begged her not to go, saying they already knew the people and the land here and could live very happily. She saw no real future for that kind of person!

Although she was relatively confident in Jialin's love for her, she wasn't completely sure—sometimes he acted strangely or did bizarre things.

No matter, she would figure it all out with him soon, since she couldn't stand this state of uncertainty much longer. Recently she had stopped eating and could barely sleep, and she wasn't doing well at work, either. Three days earlier, it had been her turn to work the morning shift, but she hadn't slept the night before, and finally fell asleep just before dawn. She hadn't heard her alarm so the broadcast was delayed fifteen minutes. Her boss had had to send several people by to knock on her door to wake her up, and she had been reprimanded.

That day, she ate only a few bites. After mulling it over for a while, she decided she couldn't put it off anymore—she would go to the committee offices and find Jialin.

She was just getting ready to leave when Ke'nan stopped by. She was so angry she could have cried.

"What's the matter?" Ke'nan's face was a mask of worry. "Have you been sick? I'll take you to the hospital for a checkup," he said with his brows furrowed.

"I don't want a checkup! I know what's wrong—heart disease!" Yaping said bitterly as she lay down on the bed, refusing to look at him.

"Heart disease?" Ke'nan said, confused. "When did this happen?"

"Aiya, who has heart disease? What an idiot! You don't even get a joke!" Yaping said, irritably.

"From my viewpoint, it didn't seem like a joke; it seemed real." Ke'nan sighed and smiled.

He poured himself some water and sat on the chair by the desk. "Yaping, it hasn't been that long since Jialin came to the city for work. Today, it occurred to me that we should invite him to dinner. At school, we were pretty good friends, and you and Jialin got along well. There aren't many of our classmates working in the city now . . . We'll invite him to the state-run canteen. I know everyone there, and it's a convenient place to eat . . ."

Huang Yaping lay on the bed, not saying a word.

"Well, shall we or not?" Ke'nan asked again.

Still lying on the bed, Huang Yaping looked at him and implored, "My dear Ke'nan, you mustn't meddle in these things. I'm so upset, please don't torture me anymore! Go to work. Let me sleep . . ."

With Yaping in this kind of mood, Ke'nan had no choice but to get up and leave. He walked over to the door, then turned, moving back to kiss her. Yaping buried her head in the blankets instead and shouted, "No, don't! Go away!"

Ke'nan sighed, depressed and irritated, then left.

Huang Yaping lay on the bed for a long time. She was depressed that Ke'nan was such a simpleton—he was oblivious

Life

to the fact that she loved Jialin, so she obviously didn't want to invite him out to eat!

She wondered if she had been a bit too cruel to Ke'nan. But for now, at least, she decided to go talk to Jialin at noon.

After lunch, she went to her parents' home, still anxious and distracted.

Her father, wearing reading glasses, was poring over an editorial in the newspaper, a red pencil underlining each line as he read. Her mother saw her come in and rushed to get a piece of clothing out from a trunk. "Ke'nan's father went to Shanghai on a business trip and bought this for you. Ke'nan's mother just brought it over; try it on . . ."

Yaping pushed it back into her mother's hands and said, "Put it away for now, I don't feel well . . ."

Her father turned to look at her, his eyes peering over his glasses. "Yaping, you don't seem like yourself lately. What's going on?"

Yaping didn't look at her father. Instead, she picked up her brush and started diligently brushing her hair in the mirror. She said, "I might make a big decision before long. But I'll tell you all now."

"Is it that you want to marry Ke'nan?" her mother asked.

"No, I want to divorce him!" She couldn't help smiling at what she had said.

Her mother smiled as well. "You always were a naughty child! You're not yet married, and you already want a divorce!"

Her father looked back down at the paper, grinning from ear to ear and mumbling, "You really are a naughty child . . ."

The two older people didn't take their daughter's words seriously—but before long they would know what she meant.

Huang Yaping was more determined than ever to tell Jialin what was in her heart. She couldn't keep putting it off! The sooner she resolved this mess, the sooner everyone involved would be free of it. She couldn't keep deceiving Ke'nan, either. She didn't want to torment him any further.

When she had finished brushing her hair, she changed into her dark-blue school uniform and, without eating dinner, set off for the committee offices.

When she arrived at the communications bureau, Gao Jialin wasn't in his office, and his door was locked.

Had he gone to the countryside? She felt defeated. She hurried to Jing Ruohong's room next door. Old Jing told her that Jialin hadn't left for the countryside. He had been writing in his office all day and had just gone for a walk after eating dinner.

Where could he have gone? She felt bad pestering Old Jing.

She hesitated a moment, then asked, "Old Jing, do you know where Jialin went?"

Jing Ruohong eyed her closely and said, "I couldn't say. Is there some emergency?"

"No . . ." Huang Yaping's face felt hot all of a sudden.

She was about to leave when Jing Ruohong suddenly slapped his forehead. "He might have gone to the eastern hills. He likes to take walks around there."

"Thank you." Yaping nodded toward him and left the courtyard.

~

Gao Jialin had gone to the eastern hills.

He was leaning against a locust tree, a cigarette between his fingers. He had been smoking a lot lately.

He had been writing all day, and he couldn't think straight. Now he could feel the wind, and that paired with his cigarette quickly helped him clear his head.

His thoughts turned to Huang Yaping and Qiaozhen. He didn't know why, but whenever he had a free moment, he would always think of the two of them. True, Yaping had implied that she loved him, but he still felt strange: Hadn't she been with Ke'nan this whole time?

His heart told him that Yaping was his ideal wife. He hadn't dared believe it before, and though he did now, the situation was still complicated. She was with Ke'nan, and he was with Qiaozhen. It all seemed irreconcilable, and he told himself to forget about it. But Yaping kept coming to find him, and her words, her expression, and her gaze told him she loved him!

He had already been in love, and so he saw all this clearly; plus, Yaping had practically confessed to him already.

His heart surged with emotions; he felt a storm coming—he was excited, but also nervous.

Gao Jialin leaned on the tree trunk, smoking. He felt as though he had been thinking of so many things, but that somehow, at the same time, he hadn't really thought of anything at all.

A sudden downpour passed overhead, and the earth cooled. The hottest days of the year hadn't yet passed, although it was already well into summer, almost the twentieth day of Liqiu, by the lunar calendar. Although it was still blisteringly hot at midday in the mountains, it was cooling down a little in the mornings and evenings now.

Gao Jialin hadn't worn a long-sleeved shirt, and his arms were too cold to stand being outside much longer, so he walked back down the hill.

A faint layer of fog slowly rolled in from the gully, bringing with it a cold, eerie energy. He looked out over the city as he slowly descended. It was bright with streetlights. There weren't many people out and about; the streets and alleys were quiet, like a river after a flood. Tangerine-colored lamps, lined all in a row, lit the empty streets. Only the intersections still contained people, with a few peddlers listlessly selling street food.

Gao Jialin kept to a dirt path and had just reached the bottom of a small slope when he saw someone coming toward him.

He stopped automatically. He waited until the person got closer, and he was surprised to see it was Huang Yaping.

"Why are you up here?" he asked, both excited and astonished.

Yaping smiled, her hands stuck awkwardly in her pockets. "Why shouldn't other people come up here? This isn't the tomb of your ancestors . . ."

"No need to get testy!" Jialin said. "It's dark, and you're up here alone . . ."

"Who says I'm alone?"

Jialin glanced at the road and said, "Ke'nan? Where is he?"

"He's not my tail. Why would he be following me?"

"Well, then, who's with you?"

"Aren't you someone?"

"Me?"

"Uh-huh!"

Jialin felt like his heart was going to leap out of his chest.

Yaping turned suddenly tender and said, "Jialin, don't be afraid. Let's sit down together."

Gao Jialin hesitated, but then walked with her over toward a small cluster of apricot trees.

They sat down. They picked a few apricot leaves. They pinched them, stroked them, and tore them, not saying a word.

"I have to go . . . ," Yaping said suddenly.

"Are you going on a work trip?" Jialin turned to ask.

"No, not on a work trip. I'm leaving forever!" Yaping said, looking off into the distance toward the twinkling lights of the city.

"Huh?" Jialin couldn't help but shout.

"My father is being transferred to Nanjing soon, and I'm going with him." Yaping turned to look back at Jialin.

"Do you want to go?" Jialin stared directly into her eyes.

Huang Yaping turned away slightly and gazed at the bright starlight as though she was trying to see the future. She murmured, "Of course I want to go! The south is my home. I've lived there since I was little, and even though I came to the north with my parents, I've always dreamed of the beauty of my homeland." Tears glinted in her eyes as she quietly recited the poem by the great Bai Juyi:

> *The Southland is best, long ago I knew the scenery:*
>
> *at sunrise, the river's flowers red like fire,*
>
> *in spring, the river so green it is almost blue.*
>
> *Who wouldn't miss the Southland?*

Jialin couldn't help but continue:

> *Remembering the Southland, it is Hangzhou I most recall,*

among mountain temples, I search for the Osmanthus petals,

from which the moon did fall. When will I return there?

Yaping looked warmly at Jialin. "Nanjing is close to Hangzhou. In the north is heaven; in the south are Suzhou and Hangzhou. Suzhou is Jiangsu Province's . . ."

"Uh-huh . . ." Jialin sighed. "I'll go my whole life without seeing those places."

"Don't you want to see them?" A small, enigmatic smile appeared on her face.

"I want to see the UN!" Jialin threw away the leaf he had been holding and wrenched his head to one side.

"I'm asking if you want to visit Nanjing, Suzhou, Hangzhou, and even Shanghai."

"I won't get to go to those places for work."

"It's no fun to go to those places alone," Yaping said.

"If you go, you won't be alone. You'll have Ke'nan . . ."

"I don't want him. I want you!"

Gao Jialin turned back around and stared at Yaping, his eyes blazing.

Huang Yaping's eyes shone with tears, and she said excitedly, "Jialin, ever since you came to the city, I haven't had a moment's peace. I adored you when we were at school, but we were so young and didn't really understand these things. Then you went back to the countryside . . . and now, seeing you here again, I know you're the one I love. It's not that I don't like Ke'nan, but I can't make myself love him—my parents love him more than I do! You and I can be together! Come with us to Nanjing. You have a great future ahead of you, and it'll be even greater in a big city. I'll probably work at the provincial radio station, and I'll find a way to get you a job through my father. You can work at the *Xinhua Daily* or as a journalist at the provincial TV station . . ."

Gao Jialin looked down, yanked on a stalk of ram's horn grass, and flung it casually down the hill; he pulled out another blade as he stood up.

Yaping stood up, too, and stared at him, her eyes still shining with tears.

Jialin rubbed his arms with his hands and said, "It's so cold up here I can't take it anymore. Let's go . . . Yaping, don't worry, let me think about it . . ."

Huang Yaping nodded at him. The two of them turned onto a small dirt path and walked down the path single file.

CHAPTER 18

The storm Gao Jialin had sensed had finally arrived. He couldn't ignore the fierce battle that raged within him. He was only twenty-four years old, but he took things seriously, and his thoughts and feelings were more complex than those of most people his age.

He was about to make a very important decision.

The differences between Huang Yaping and Liu Qiaozhen were clear. And he knew he was being pulled one way.

Of course he wanted to be with Huang Yaping. He felt that he and Huang Yaping were compatible in every respect. She was cultured and insightful, came from a good family, and was a beautiful southern girl. Her body held some mysterious attraction for him. He knew girls from around here, like Qiaozhen, girls from the countryside. He knew them through and through. He thought they were innocent, but boring.

Sometimes he understood Huang Yaping, and sometimes he didn't. Although they had spent a lot of time together, there was still much about her that he didn't know. The differences in their family backgrounds and economic circumstances, the different lives they had led and their experiences—all this should have naturally separated them, but in reality it increased her aura of mystery. He thought of her as something he couldn't get close to, like a wisp of cloud. In school, their relationship was like a beautiful rainbow in a blue sky after a storm: it disappeared quickly and left nothing but an impression in his memory. Sometimes this impression would rise to the surface of his mind and he'd feel melancholy, as though he had lost something, but it would quickly disappear without a trace.

But now, the gossamer threads of his past fantasies had suddenly become real. Huang Yaping had demonstrated her love for him, and as long as she was willing, he wanted to be with her. Ah, life, which sometimes made reality into fantasy, also made fantasy into reality.

But his relationship with Qiaozhen also deserved his full consideration. They had loved each other ardently for some time now. Qiaozhen's love for him was no less than Ke'nan's love for Yaping. The difference was that Yaping said she didn't have feelings for Ke'nan, while Jialin loved Qiaozhen quite deeply. Qiaozhen's beauty and goodness, her affection and warmth, her selflessness, the way she loved him with all her heart, how she had awakened youthful passions and kindled the flame of love in him—he was so grateful to her for all of this. Because of her, even though he had endured suffering, his life was still rich with affection.

Now, since Yaping had confessed her love for him and was even preparing to bring him with her to Nanjing, he was finally considering how love might impact his future. He thought that Qiaozhen was an exemplary woman from a rural family, but she would most likely never amount to anything more. He and Qiaozhen could be very happy together if he were a peasant his whole life, but he was a public figure now, and if they got married, they wouldn't have any shared interests, or even a shared language. He thought about writing essays, whereas she thought about things that mattered to mothers and wives. The last time she'd come to see him, he had already started to worry that they didn't have enough in common. And if they got married, he would be forever tied to this county, his hopes and aspirations spinning ever further out of reach. Ever since he had arrived in the county seat, he knew he couldn't spend the rest of his life here. He wanted to travel far and wide and to expand his horizons beyond this city . . . Now, all he had to do was say yes!

He mulled it over for a while and decided that he couldn't miss an important opportunity simply for Qiaozhen's sake—an opportunity that might determine the course of the rest of his life! And besides, as a lover, Yaping was an ideal choice. Even though he had never loved Yaping like he had loved Qiaozhen, he felt their love would be better, richer, more dazzling!

After he had weighed everything, he decided to end things with Qiaozhen and move away with Yaping.

Of course, his conscience was uneasy—he knew he was an unpardonable bastard. He had hardly even thought about what this would do to Ke'nan, focusing as he had on Qiaozhen. He paced back and forth in his room like a madman, beating his fists on the desk and banging his head on the wall.

Thinking about what he had done to Ke'nan by sneaking around with Yaping, he mocked himself, *You bastard! You lost your conscience, and now you're trying to be kind?*

He did his best to harden his heart. He ground his teeth and warned himself, *Don't look back. Don't be weak. You have to make sacrifices in order to have a great future. And sometimes you have to be cruel to yourself.*

The hard-hearted Jialin now had to decide how to break up with Qiaozhen. He expected that it would be a heartrending experience, and he wanted to say goodbye as efficiently as possible. The problem was that Qiaozhen couldn't read, or else he would write her a note to avoid seeing the pain on her face.

He spent the whole day in bed racking his brain about how to end things.

Huang Yaping took this opportunity to visit and ask if he had made a decision yet.

He paused for a moment and then explained his relationship with Qiaozhen.

Huang Yaping didn't say anything at first. Then, with a surprised expression on her face, she asked, "So you wanted to marry an illiterate girl from the countryside?"

"Uh-huh." Jialin nodded.

"Well, that's self-destructive! An educated high school student, full of potential . . . How could you marry an ignorant peasant? What were you were thinking?!"

"Shut up!" Jialin jumped angrily off the bed. "I was just a regular person—living in a modest house with a face covered in yellow earth. How could I have thought a city girl like you would love me?"

Huang Yaping was startled by his anger and paused for a long while before saying, "How vicious! Ke'nan was never so horrible to me!"

"Then go find Ke'nan!" Jialin lay back down on the bedding and closed his eyes. He thought to himself, *Ugh, Qiaozhen never talked to me like this . . .*

Before long, Yaping came over and placed her hand softly on his shoulder.

Gao Jialin opened his eyes and saw her eyes glinting with tears.

He ignored her, still angry.

"Jialin! Don't be angry! When you act like that, not only am I not upset, but it actually makes me happy! Zhang Ke'nan couldn't get angry if you stabbed him in the neck with a knife! Sometimes, I wanted to make him angry, for him to spit beautiful fire at me, swear at me, but no matter how much I swore at him or cut him down, he would just laugh until I got so angry I would cry. I much prefer your temperament. You're a pillar of manhood and integrity, with real vigor coursing through your veins," Yaping said eagerly.

Gao Jialin couldn't tell if she was speaking the truth or just trying to make him feel better. But when he saw Yaping's eyes brimming with tears under her two slender, curved eyebrows, his heart softened. "I have a bad temper . . . and when we live together, I'm afraid you won't be able to take it."

"Jialin!" Yaping grabbed his shoulders and asked, "So you want to live with me?"

He nodded at her distractedly.

Yaping sat down on the bed, close to him. Jialin quickly wriggled away from her. He didn't know why, but just then he was thinking of Qiaozhen, and it didn't feel right to accept Yaping's affection at that moment.

Gao Jialin was quiet for a while, then said, "I need to explain all this to Qiaozhen . . . I'm not lying to you, I feel terrible about this . . . Please forgive me, I'm not trying to deceive you."

"Yes, you should end your unhappiness quickly!"

"But it could also be an unhappy ending!" he said dramatically.

"It'll be easy with Ke'nan. I can write him a letter, and that will be that. I don't feel that torn up about it—just sorry for him, is all. Since you really and truly love me . . ."

"Ke'nan will suffer terribly . . ." Jialin sighed.

"I'm not worried about Ke'nan. I'm mostly worried about my parents. They adore Ke'nan, but they're old cadres, and they have an old-fashioned sense of ethics . . ."

"There is no way your father will accept me! They want someone who's a match for their daughter socially and economically. I'm a country boy—I'd be a disgrace to them!" Jialin shouted.

Very gently, Yaping said, "Look at how angry you are. My parents aren't necessarily those kinds of people. The problem is just that they think I've been with Ke'nan for so long now that the whole town knows, and with our families having gotten so close, I'm afraid—"

"Then forget it!" Jialin cut her off.

Huang Yaping burst into tears, stood up, and said, "Jialin! Don't be so angry, OK? I'll deal with this. My parents will eventually respect my decision . . . All I want to know now is if you want to be with me." As she spoke, she scooted closer to him.

~

When Huang Yaping returned home, her ever-punctual parents were already asleep in their bedroom.

She went into her room, turned on the light, and sat down at her desk, but didn't do anything, just sat there quietly. Her heart was beating out of her chest.

Getting up quickly, she stood in front of the mirror. She looked at herself and smiled.

She lay down on her bed, then got right back up again.

She didn't know what to do with herself. Waves of thought crashed against the shores of her mind: first a montage of past events, then the recent scene with Jialin, recounted in minute detail, and finally scenes of the future she dreamed of for herself.

She finally calmed down a bit as she washed her face.

She knew she wouldn't be able to fall asleep easily. Well, so be it! She wasn't on duty in the morning—someone else was doing the broadcast, so she could sleep in. As for whether or not she'd be able to sleep at all, she wasn't sure.

So now what should she do? Write a letter to Ke'nan? Or "issue a statement" to her parents?

Her parents were already asleep, so she would write the letter.

As soon as she had gotten out the paper, envelope, and pen, she changed her mind: No! She should talk to her parents first. This was too important. It was better to let them know as soon as possible.

She opened her door and went out into the courtyard.

The insomniac was determined not to let her parents sleep.

She knocked on their door and called, "Father, Mother, wake up and come out here. I have something important to tell you!"

Their light turned on, and she heard nervous whispering. The willful girl gave a wry smile and returned to her room.

Her mother came in first, followed by her father, who was putting on his coat as he stumbled into her room. They both took a seat, her mother sitting in front of her father, and asked simultaneously, "What happened?"

Huang Yaping saw how nervous her parents were and couldn't help smiling. She sobered up eventually, though, and said, "Don't worry, nothing bad has happened, I just have some news that might shock you."

Her father stared at her, not yet reacting to the fact that his headstrong child had gotten them out of bed in the dead of night.

Her mother rubbed her eyes and said anxiously, "Aiya, little Pingping! If you have something to say, then say it. You're going to worry us to death!"

Yaping thought for a moment and said, "It's confusing, but I'll sketch it out for you tonight. I'll give you all the details later, since you'll probably want to know . . . So it's like this: I've met another man; I want to break up with Ke'nan . . ."

"What? What? What?"

Her parents stood up abruptly and stared at their daughter, panic-stricken.

"You won't change my mind. I know you love Ke'nan, but I don't like him . . ."

A long silence.

Her father finally pulled himself together and gulped with great difficulty. Sadly, he said, "Weren't you the one that first brought Ke'nan over here? That was over two years ago, and the whole city knows about you two now. Me and Old Zhang, your mother and Ke'nan's mother—these relationships . . . God, you stubborn thing! Your mother and I spoiled you, and you repay us like this . . ." He beat his chest, and his lips, swollen as though stung by bees, trembled with rage.

Her mother was bent over the bed sobbing.

Even though her father loved her more than he loved himself, he shouted at her, "This is typical bourgeois thinking! You young people are killing me! You're a decaying generation. Undisciplined and out of control. We should hold a funeral for the revolution!" Crazy things were flying out of the old man's mouth, he was so worked up.

Huang Yaping was now sobbing, too, hunched over the desk. Her father had never yelled at her like this, and she couldn't handle it.

Yaping's mother saw her daughter crying and cried along with her. She addressed her husband: "Even if Pingping is wrong, you can't yell at our baby like that . . ."

"It's because you've spoiled her!" the military man shouted again.

Yaping's father walked out, but instead of going back to his room, he stood in the courtyard, pulled out a cigarette, and tapped it on the box. Yet he made no move to light it.

Yaping stood up and pushed her mother out of her room, then closed the door.

She grabbed a towel to wipe the tears from her face and then sat down and began to write to Ke'nan.

> *Ke'nan,*
>
> *For both of our sakes, I have to tell you that I've fallen in love with Jialin, and so we must break off our relationship. We'll go back to what we were before—friendly classmates and comrades.*
>
> *I know this will hurt you. But it's not worth pining over a woman who doesn't love you. You should look for your true love—and I believe you will find this person. I wish you happiness.*
>
> *Jialin and I got along well in school. I now realize that he is the man I truly love, not you. The only reason you and I fell in love is because you paid attention to me at the right time, which was very touching, but it wasn't love.*
>
> *You're a good person, a remarkable person. I don't want to get in your way. And I don't want you to hate Jialin. If you feel you've been*

wronged, then it's me who caused it. I pursued Jialin. You should hate me!

In my heart, I'll always be thankful for you. And I need to tell you that besides my lovers, of all my friends you are the best. If you can forgive me, then I'll ask for your blessing.

Written in haste,
Yaping

CHAPTER 19

Gao Jialin parked his bicycle on the side of the bridge and leaned over the railing. He looked down at the eddies in the river and the current as it flowed under the bridge and into the Great Horse River.

He was waiting for Qiaozhen. Yesterday he had asked Sanxing, whom he'd met on his way back to the village, to tell Qiaozhen to come to the city today. He had decided to end their relationship. He didn't want to go back to Gaojia Village to do it, nor did he want to do it in his office. He thought Qiaozhen might try to hurt herself or make a scene.

Old Jing had ordered him to take a trip to the Liujiawan Commune. He was supposed to interview experts on the autumn harvest there, so he decided to deal with this other bit of business on the way, since the road to Liujiawan Commune passed over the Great Horse River Bridge before making its way into another valley. After this conversation, they could each go their own way, and neither would have to see the other again.

Gao Jialin leaned against the railing and thought about how he would break the news to Qiaozhen. He had considered many different ways to start, but none seemed right. He might as well be as blunt as possible. Even if he beat around the bush, in the end he'd still have to break up with her, right?

While he was thinking this over, he heard a voice from behind him. "Jialin . . ."

The sound was like a dagger plunging into his heart.

He turned and saw Qiaozhen standing in front of him holding her bicycle. She'd come so quickly! She always did her best to satisfy his desires.

"Jialin, is everything all right? Yesterday Sanxing told me you wanted me here, and I couldn't sleep a wink. I asked Sanxing if you were sick, but he said you weren't . . ." She leaned her bicycle against Jialin's and walked toward him as she was talking. She leaned over the railing beside him.

Gao Jialin saw she was wearing a new outfit. She looked beautiful. He suddenly felt sad.

He was afraid he would lose heart, so he quickly brought up the issue at hand.

"Qiaozhen . . ."

"Hmm?" She noticed his gloomy expression. "How are you?"

Jialin turned to her and said, "I want to tell you some-thing, but I'm finding it difficult . . ."

Qiaozhen looked at him sweetly. "Jialin, spit it out! If you have something on your mind, just tell me. Don't bottle it up!"

"I'm afraid you'll cry if I tell you."

Qiaozhen stared at him. "Say it. I . . . I won't cry!"

"Qiaozhen . . ."

"Hmm?"

"I might be transferred thousands of miles away for work. We . . ."

Qiaozhen stuffed her fingers in her mouth and bit down on them. After a while, she said, "Then you . . . you should go."

"What will you do?"

She said nothing.

"I've been thinking a lot about this . . ."

A long silence. Two streams of silent tears slid down Qiaozhen's face. Her hands clenched and unclenched around the railing. Choking with sobs, she said, "Jialin, don't say any more. I get it. You . . . go! I certainly won't keep you here. Jialin, after you left, I thought of you . . . I don't know how many times. And though I love you with all my heart, I know I can't go with you. I can't even read a single word. I can't help you. I'd be a burden to you and your work . . . You should go your own way, find a more suitable partner who's not from around here . . . but be careful. You'll be a stranger in a strange land, far from our fields . . . Jialin, you don't know how much I love you . . ."

Qiaozhen couldn't go on. She pulled out a handkerchief and stuffed it in her mouth.

Gao Jialin's eyes were filled with tears. "You're . . . crying . . ." He didn't look at her.

Qiaozhen shook her head, tears painting watery swaths across her face and falling into the current below her. The Great Horse River, clean and bright on this summer's day, flowed by the bridge and into the muddy County River.

Silence . . . silence . . . it seemed like the whole world had fallen silent.

Suddenly, Qiaozhen turned around and said, "Jialin . . . I'm leaving!"

He tried to hold her back, but couldn't stop her. Rather than face Qiaozhen, rather than face the whole world, his head dropped low.

She swayed back and forth as she walked away, and after mounting her bicycle with some difficulty, she fled toward the village without looking back. By the time Jialin glanced up again, all that remained were green fields and a long, empty road of yellow earth.

Gao Jialin quickly got on his bicycle and turned toward the road heading for Liujiawan Commune. He pedaled madly, with the wind blowing in his ears and the road ahead of him hazy, like a yellow ribbon flapping in the breeze.

He rode until there was no sign of anyone nearby, then steered his bicycle over to a ditch at the side of the road. He threw it to the ground and doubled over in the grass, his hands covering his face, wailing like a child. He hated himself in that moment.

After an hour, he washed his face with water from the ditch, then pushed his bicycle back onto the road.

He felt a bit more relaxed now. In front of him were green mountains and water, fresh and bright; the cloudless sky looked as if it had been washed clean. An eagle circled above him for a while and then set off like an arrow toward the far-away horizon.

~

A few days later, Gao Jialin returned to the county seat from Liujiawan Commune and began his new life as Huang Yaping's lover.

Their method of courtship was entirely modern.

When it got to be noon, they would put on their bathing suits and go swimming in the pond outside the city. After they swam, they would lie by the river wearing sunglasses and tan themselves on the sand. At night, to pass the time, they would go to the eastern hills, where they would talk about everything under the sun—they would even sing together, one song after another.

Huang Yaping quickly reoutfitted Gao Jialin according to her own aesthetic: a brown jacket with a large foldover collar, sky-blue straight-legged pants, and a beige windbreaker. She permed her hair and tied it up with a red ribbon, looking very romantic. She was a vision in the latest fashions from Shanghai.

Sometimes, when they came back into town, they would ride together on one bicycle, as if asking people to look. Huang Yaping pedaled happily through the streets, while Jialin sat in back.

They really attracted a lot of attention. The whole city was talking about them. Some people called them part-time foreigners.

But they didn't take notice of public opinion. They were obsessed with their new *liaison romantique*.

At first, Jialin didn't want it to be like this, but Huang Yaping said that they wouldn't be around the city for much longer, so why not let people see? She wanted Jialin to be more laid back so that when they moved it would be easier for him to adapt. So Jialin became like Yaping's apprentice and followed her lead.

He was excited, of course, since Huang Yaping was introducing him to a new way of life. Everything felt fresh and exciting, just like when he was fourteen and rode in a car for the first time.

But he also felt frustrated. As he and Yaping deepened their connection, he began to notice how stubborn she was. Being with her was different than it had been with Qiaozhen, who took her cues from him and deferred to him in everything. Huang Yaping wasn't like that. She would do as she pleased, then tell him what to do, even wanting him to defer to her.

Sometimes, when they were at their happiest, he would happen to think of Qiaozhen, and the thought would be like a knife stabbing at his heart. His temperament would instantly change from boiling to freezing. His shifts in emotion rubbed off on Huang Yaping. Since she couldn't guess the reason for his sudden change of mood, Yaping felt increasingly annoyed, though she would try to distract him with silly behavior. This only ended up intensifying his mood swings, which would make hers worse as well. Sometimes, they both felt their love was unrequited.

One morning, it was raining hard, and there was a general meeting of the propaganda division of the county committee. Someone from the telephone office next door called Jialin over to take a call.

Jialin picked up the receiver and heard Yaping's voice. She told him that she had left her special imported apple-peeling knife where they had been hanging out the day before. She wanted him to go look for it as soon as possible.

Jialin told her that he was in a meeting, and plus, it was raining hard. He would go during the afternoon break.

Yaping threw a fit and said his indifference was making her unhappy. She began to sob.

Gao Jialin was exasperated, but felt he had no choice but to go to the meeting and lie, saying that a friend of his was outside with an emergency he had to handle.

The chairperson let him go, and he went back to his dorm to get his windbreaker and bike.

He was soaked through before he even got to the street, but he braved the rain and made his way to the little pool they had visited south of the city. He got off his bicycle and began searching for the knife.

After looking for a while and turning over what seemed like every blade of grass, he still hadn't found it.

He finally gave up, feeling like he had done his duty, then headed back through the rain to the radio station to tell Yaping he hadn't found the knife.

He pushed open Yaping's door and saw her there, smiling happily. "Did you go?" she asked.

"I went. I didn't find it," he said.

Yaping began to giggle. She pulled the knife out from her pocket.

"You found it?" Jialin asked.

"I never lost it! It was a test to see if you would do what I asked. Don't be angry—I just wanted to be romantic . . ."

"Son of a bitch! What a complete cliché!" Gao Jialin shouted furiously at her, his lips quivering. He whirled around and left.

Huang Yaping sobbed alone in her room. She knew that she had gone too far and was petrified that she wouldn't be able to fix the situation.

Gao Jialin returned to his office, changed out of his wet clothes, and lay down on his bed. Qiaozhen appeared before his eyes: her beautiful, honest face and her gentle, sweet smile. He cried into his pillow, murmuring her name over and over . . .

The next day, Huang Yaping bought some cans of food and other snacks and brought them to Jialin's. She cried and begged for his forgiveness, promising to never make him angry again.

So Jialin made up with her. Huang Yaping intoxicated him like high-proof liquor—but she also gave him a headache. He knew all her irrational behavior stemmed from her love for him; he had experienced this firsthand. And from a financial perspective, she was very generous with him. She seemed to spend her entire salary on him: she bought him trendy new clothes for every season, and she had someone in Beijing buy and mail him a pair of fancy military-style leather shoes (which he hadn't yet dared wear). There was also an endless stream of canned food, cakes, expensive milk candy, coffee, cocoa powder, malted milk powder—things that not even the secretary of the county committee could reliably get. She bought him an imported digital watch with a calendar, even though she herself wore a Shanghai brand. She would sacrifice anything for him.

They quickly reentered that most romantic stage of their relationship.

Right around that time, Jialin's father and Old Deshun came to visit.

As the two old people entered Gao Jialin's office, their faces looked grim.

Gao Jialin set out a display of milk candy, fruit, and cakes on the desk and put two cups of very sugary water in front of them.

No one ate or drank.

Gao Jialin knew they wanted to say something, but he simply sat respectfully across from them, looking down and rubbing his face with his hands to try and lessen his stress.

"Oh, Jialin, you sold out!" Old Deshun said. "Qiaozhen is such a good girl, and you've thrown her away like garbage on the side of the road! You messed up. Oh, Jialin, I've known you since you were little and watched you grow up. Now I need to give you a piece of my mind. After all, ever since you were a little sprout of grass, your roots shared our land. But now you're like a bean sprout, without any roots, floating in the breeze, no idea where you're headed. You . . . what can I say? You hurt Qiaozhen, and in the process you hurt yourself . . ." The old man couldn't continue. He closed his eyes and took long, deep breaths.

His father picked up where Deshun left off: "Remember, I told you not to get involved with Liben's daughter—they've got a reputation to maintain. But now you've raised yourself up; you can't be so heartless. Qiaozhen is a good girl: ever since you left, she brings us water, helps your mother cook, pushes the grindstone, feeds the pigs . . . *Ay*, what a good girl! And no matter how successful you become, if you treat this girl badly, the whole valley will detest you. Your mother and I already can't show our faces in public since everyone's saying what a stuck-up boy you are. I heard you found a foreign woman—what will she think when she finds out how poor we are? You should put a stop to that relationship immediately!"

"It's said that the higher you climb, the harder you fall!" Old Deshun advised him. "No matter how much time passes, you mustn't lose touch with your roots . . ."

"I haven't been to the city in a long time, but I dragged Grandfather Deshun here today to make you come to your senses! You're still young, and you don't understand the ways of the world. People are living longer and longer these days—I was nearly forty when I had you. Now I'm afraid you're making a mistake that might affect the rest of your life . . ." Tears filled his father's eyes as he spoke.

The two old men went back and forth like this, both highly emotional the whole time.

Gao Jialin kept his head down as they spoke, like a convict at his trial.

He finally looked up, sighed, and said, "Maybe everything you've both said is true, but I've already jumped off the cliff and there's no going back. You have your ways of living, and I have mine. I don't want to be the same as you, making a living by digging up the earth in Gaojia Village . . . I'll go get you some food . . ." He stood up to go tend to his guests, but the two old men got up as well, complaining of sore legs, and said they should get on the road soon to make it home before dark. They refused to eat anything, though they would have liked to share a few more of their thoughts with him, but they could tell it wouldn't be any use. Jialin would do what he wanted to do—their philosophizing wouldn't persuade him. So they said goodbye.

When Gao Jialin saw that they were determined to leave, he decided to accompany them at least as far as the Great Horse Bridge. The old men walked with heavy hearts.

Gao Jialin was also upset. He knew that what Grandfather Deshun and his father had said made sense. Their words weighed heavily on him.

Not long after, news came that greatly improved his mood: the provincial newspaper was holding a monthlong training class in reporting and had asked each county to send a representative. The propaganda bureau of the county committee had decided to send Jialin.

As soon as he heard this news, the air of unpleasantness that had been left in the wake of his father's and Old Deshun's visit instantly dissipated. He was so happy he didn't sleep at all that night—this would be the first time he would travel far from home, visit the provincial capital, and see what life was like in a big metropolis, *ya*!

Yaping saw him to the bus station when he left. Everything he was wearing and everything in his bag had been picked out for him with the utmost care by Yaping. She had even insisted he wear the military-style leather shoes. He felt awkward but excited to walk in leather shoes for the first time.

As the bus went through the gate and Yaping's smiling face and waving hands disappeared behind him, Jialin was carried along by the speed of the bus through endless open country and toward the bright city lights.

CHAPTER 20

The people of Gaojia Village hadn't seen Qiaozhen go to work in the mountains for a few days. That was strange because Qiaozhen was a hardworking girl, and she rarely went so long without leaving home. She often made a lot more money in one year of hard labor than her father did with his business.

But eventually people found out that their lovely Qiaozhen had encountered misfortune.

They discussed the situation endlessly, just as they had when they'd first found out about Qiaozhen and Jialin. Most people pitied her, but some took pleasure in her misfortune. But everyone agreed that Liu Liben's second daughter was completely ruined. If she didn't commit suicide, she'd definitely go insane. Everyone knew what something like this meant for a girl; it didn't matter how much she was in love with Gao Yude's son.

But after a few days, the villagers saw her come out of her house, like a sick, overworked mare. First, she tended to her family's allotment and repaired the broken fence around the vegetable garden. Then she went to work with the rest of them, though she didn't say much. But besides that, she was the same as before, doing what she was supposed to do.

What a strong girl! Not only did she not kill herself, but she stayed sane. Life had been cruel to her, but she had picked herself up. Even those who had taken pleasure in her misfortune couldn't help but respect her now.

Everyone kept a close eye on her. The general impression seemed to be that she had gotten quite skinny.

How could she not? Those past two weeks, she had hardly been able to eat or sleep. Every night she would stay up late crying into her bedding. She would weep from unhappiness, because of her misfortune, and for the dream of love that had been buried alive.

She had thought about dying. But when she looked at the mountain valley she had lived and labored in for more than twenty years, when she looked at the earth and plants that she had kept green with her own sweat, those thoughts dissipated instantly. She was reluctant to leave this world; she loved the sun, loved the earth, loved work, loved the clear and bright Great Horse River, loved the grasses and wildflowers that grew on the riverbank . . . She couldn't die! She should live! She wanted to work the land. There was something in the earth that could be found nowhere else.

Having experienced this kind of once-in-a-lifetime emotional pain, she realized how naive her romance had been. Her tragic circumstances weren't due to fate, but simply because she and her beloved Jialin were different people. All she could do now was accept reality.

But no matter what she did, she couldn't forget about Jialin. She would never be able to hate him; she would love him no matter how much it hurt!

She went to work in the mountains every day; no one at home could persuade her otherwise. To her, the bosom of mother earth was so broad that it could accommodate all the world's suffering.

In the evenings after she returned home, she would go quietly to her room, and without washing her face, brushing her hair, or eating, she would lie on her bed and let the tears softly fall. Her mother and big sister and Qiaoling took turns spending time with her, encouraging her to eat, crying along with her. They cried because they thought she might be depressed, that she might take her own life.

Liu Liben would sigh and moan as he slept in another room. He had been ill ever since this whole thing started; there were black marks on his forehead from several rounds of fire-cupping. Ever since they'd started courting, he had been furious at Qiaozhen and Jialin, but now, seeing what had become of his daughter, he couldn't bring himself to admonish her anymore. His family's enemies were already sniggering at Qiaozhen; they said it served her right, since she had only managed to make it halfway to the top of the social ladder. Well, let them talk! How could a father further twist the knife in his child? But he silently cursed Gao Yude's rotten son, who had hurt his Qiaozhen so badly.

It's hard to predict how things will turn out in life. Right around then, an official matchmaker showed up with a request from Ma Shuan to marry Qiaozhen. Several matchmakers had already been by, but as soon as they sat down and caught wind of the family's circumstances, they got up awkwardly and left.

One evening, a few days after this visit, Ma Shuan himself dropped by.

Liu Liben's family noted Ma Shuan's sincerity and welcomed him into their home. They were very moved that the young man would ask for Qiaozhen's hand under her present circumstances. As for whether or not anything would come of it, Liu Liben hadn't given it much thought. As matters stood, Liben had decided not to force his daughter to marry anyone. She had already gone through so much; he didn't want to cause her any more pain.

While his wife prepared a meal for Ma Shuan, he dragged his sick and withered frame to see Qiaozhen.

He sat on the edge of the kang and groped for a cigarette, took two puffs, then pinched it out. His daughter cried into her bedroll. "Cheer up, Qiaozhen . . . God will have his revenge on Gao Yude's rotten son!" As soon as he mentioned Jialin, he grew angry. He scooted off the kang and stood up to let out a stream of abuse: "That son of a bitch! Asshole! Motherfucker . . . You'll rue the day you were born! May you be struck down where you stand! I'll torch you until you're a pile of tinder."

Qiaozhen sat up suddenly and gasped into her pillow. "Daddy, don't curse him! Don't curse him! Don't . . ."

Liu Liben stopped and sighed heavily. "Qiaozhen, let's not bring up the painful experiences of the past. You don't have to be sad anymore. Forget Gao Jialin! Above all else, you mustn't be depressed; you'll just make things worse for yourself. It's like you're not quite alive anymore . . . I have always tried to do what was best for you, but from now on, I won't force you into anything. You're not a little girl anymore, and you should find your match yourself. You don't need to set your sights too high—I was wrong not to let you learn to read, but you can still marry a good farmer who knows his place. Aiya, Ma Shuan has sent a matchmaker . . . but I won't force you into anything. If you don't agree, I'll tell him to drop it . . . though he himself came today."

"Is he still here?" Qiaozhen asked her father.

"Yes . . ."

"Have him come in . . ."

Her father stared at her without understanding, but then got up and left.

Not long after, Ma Shuan came in.

He stared at Qiaozhen sitting on the kang and quickly sat beside her, rubbing his hands.

"Ma Shuan, do you really want to marry me?" Qiaozhen asked.

Ma Shuan looked away. "I set my sights on you long ago, tormented ever since! But then I heard you and Teacher Gao were together, and my passion cooled. Teacher Gao is educated, and I'm just an ordinary guy. I wouldn't dare compare myself to him, and so I thought there was no hope left for me. Then a few days ago, I heard that Teacher Gao had fallen in love with a girl from the city and didn't want you anymore, and I got excited, so . . ."

"My reputation is ruined, don't you hate—"

"I don't hate you!" Ma Shuan shouted. "What does any of that have to do with us? Who doesn't make a few mistakes when they're young? You shouldn't hate Teacher Gao; he's a national-level cadre now, and you can't even read—you two could never end up together. We have a saying in our village, 'Gold flowers go with silver flowers, and zucchinis go with pumpkins.' You and I go together so well because we aren't educated! Qiaozhen, I promise that you will never again suffer! I'm strong but not inflexible; I'll work tirelessly and never betray you. Whatever joys there are to be found in our village,

I'll help you enjoy them . . ." The rough farmer had said his piece and became very emotional. He got out his matches and struck one with a *pah* before realizing he hadn't yet taken out his cigarettes. He pulled the box out of his pocket.

Tears suddenly streamed from Qiaozhen's swollen, red eyes. "Ma Shuan," she said, "don't say anything else. I . . . I'll marry you. Let's do it soon—in a few days!"

Ma Shuan stuffed his cigarettes back in his pocket and jumped up on the kang, his face red with excitement and his lips trembling.

"Go tell my father to come in. But don't come back."

Ma Shuan hurried to leave and almost fell on his way out the door.

Soon a smile broke out on Liu Liben's face, which was drawn with illness. He went to Qiaozhen.

Qiaozhen said quickly, "Daddy, I've agreed to marry Ma Shuan. I want to do it right away—within four or five days."

Liu Liben didn't know how to react. "That's . . . quite soon. Do you want us to plan it with his family?"

"Daddy, just tell Ma Shuan that everything should be done according to our family's customs. Tell our family to prepare as well. Do exactly what you and my mother did when you got married."

"We were married according to the old customs—"

"Then we will be, too!" she shouted bitterly.

Liu Liben hurried out. First, he relayed his conversation with Qiaozhen to Ma Shuan. Ma Shuan said it was no problem and quickly went home to hire a flute player and prepare the sedan chairs. As for the rest of the wedding, he'd had it all planned out for the past two years.

After Liu Liben saw Ma Shuan off, he went to find Gao Minglou.

At first, Minglou was surprised to hear that Qiaozhen had agreed to marry Ma Shuan. Then he said, "But it's good! Gao Jialin has an important position now, and our child has no hope of climbing so high. But Ma Shuan is a farmer . . . They go well together."

"The biggest issue now is that Qiaozhen is acting a bit rashly. She wants the wedding to follow the old customs. This—"

"Don't worry!" Minglou cut him off. "The party's restrictions have relaxed; they won't consider this a superstitious event. Just do as she says! If you're too busy to take care of everything, my sons and Qiaoying can come over to help."

~

On the day of the wedding, the villages of Gaojia and Madian were brimming with an air of festivity. Most of the farmers in the two villages stayed home from the mountains that day. In Gaojia Village, in addition to the marriage go-betweens, some non-family members were asked to help. The adults and children were all dressed up. Even those who weren't attending the ceremony changed into clean clothes to see the display and show their faces in the crowd.

Gao Jialin's mother and father were, of course, the exceptions. Old Gao Yude worked in the mountains to hide from the event. Jialin's mother went to a relative's house in a neighboring village—also hiding from a potentially ugly scene.

There was only one person in the entire village who stayed home and didn't go out, and that was Old Deshun. The old man, overcome with emotion, lay on his kang unable to staunch the flow of tears from his eyes. He mourned for Qiaozhen's misfortune and for Jialin's betrayal of her.

The first part of the ceremony took place in Madian Village. Ma Shuan's maternal and paternal aunts were the hosts. Ma Shuan's uncle played the most important role—the maternal uncle's families on both sides were always the revered guests. A party of five flutists and drummers walked before them, and behind them came a big, strong horse saddled and bridled and bedecked in red, to welcome the new daughter-in-law. Ma Shuan rode atop the horse, looking as imposing as a black iron tower. This was called *yama*, or "pushing the horse," according to which custom the new son-in-law had to "push" the horse to the edge of the village, and then return to his own home to await the coming of his bride.

Behind Ma Shuan came his maternal and paternal aunts on donkeys; their husbands pulled the donkeys along by the reins. After his maternal uncle had done his part as the "commander," he walked back with the matchmaker; the matchmaker was the guest of honor, and she both received the guests and saw them off.

The flutes sounded a long note, and the drums accompanied them smartly to announce the troops' entrance into Gaojia Village. The two *suona* players' cheeks swelled to the size of fists as they played "The Great Line" on their wind instruments. At the same time, on the hill by Liu Liben's house, fireworks popped in welcome. Soon after the groom's guests had been welcomed, the first meal began—buckwheat noodles, in accordance with tradition. The musicians formed a circle in the corner of the courtyard and began to play a slow melody.

Everywhere inside Liu Liben's house and in the courtyard, spilling outside and onto the roof, were people coming to enjoy the festivities. The children shouted, and the old women and girls chatted and laughed.

Because they were pressed for time, as soon as the first meal was finished, the next one began. At the bridal party's table, there were the traditional eight bowls: four nonvegetarian and four vegetarian dishes, four cold and four hot, and a bottle of *shao* liquor in the middle. Eight porcelain liquor cups were displayed around the lazy Susan on the traditional red-lacquered eight-person square table. The two maternal uncles' families sat in the seats of honor; next came other close relatives, and last the marriage intermediaries (those who'd helped with the event) and Liu Liben's close friends. The musicians played continuously throughout; they had to wait until everyone else was done before they could eat.

Amid all this raucous celebrating, Qiaozhen stayed alone in her room.

She sat at the head of the kang, staring blankly at a space on the opposite wall, not moving. Outside, the sound of the instruments, the clamor of the guests, and the rattle of the dishes all sounded very far away.

She didn't know how her twenty-two years could have led her to this point. She would be with this man for the rest of her life. She certainly hadn't expected that her fate and Ma Shuan's would be intertwined; Gao Jialin was her true love! She had cried for him and laughed with him and dreamed of him so many times. Now, the dream was over . . .

She sat and stared wearily for a while, propped up on her bedding, then shut her eyes.

Drowsiness crept over her, and she finally fell asleep.

The creaking of the door woke her.

She turned her head and saw her mother come in, holding a stack of clothing.

"Let's change your outfit, wash your face, and brush your hair. Hurry, get up," her mother said softly.

She wiped the cold tears from the corners of her eyes with her fingertips and slowly rose from the kang.

Just then, the music picked up, the musicians playing enthusiastically, which meant that the feast was just about finished—and the musicians could eat soon.

Her mother quickly sat her in a chair and helped Qiaozhen change clothes. After that, she poured some hot water into a basin and washed the tearstains from her daughter's face, then began to brush her hair.

At that moment, her younger sister, Qiaoling, came in. She had just finished teaching school for the day, and though she hadn't had anything to eat, she came directly to see her older sister.

Lovely Qiaoling looked like Qiaozhen used to: She had a tall, slender frame like a white poplar tree, and a vivid face that portrayed her inner gentleness and warmth. Long eyelashes framed two large eyes, which spoke volumes even when she stayed silent.

When Qiaozhen saw her sister, she grasped Qiaoling's hand and said fervently, "Qiaoling, my dear sister, don't forget your second sister . . . You must come see me often. I may not have been to school, but I love educated people. I'll be happy as long as I can see you . . ."

It was Qiaoling's turn to cry. "Second Sister, I know you're suffering . . ."

"Don't worry—I'll survive, no matter what. Ma Shuan and I will raise our children together and experience the rest of what life has in store . . ."

Qiaoling squatted down in front of Qiaozhen and held her hands. "Yes, of course I'll come see you. I've loved you ever since I was little, and even though you didn't go to school, you know a lot; and even though I've been to school, I've been greatly influenced by you. If not for you, I would be stubborn and not as mature as I am today . . . Sister! You mustn't dwell too much on the past. We often say society must look to the future, but that's also true for each of us. People should never rest easy; we must keep striving to succeed. There's so much for you to love in life. You mustn't get discouraged just because you've hit one roadblock. Take me, for example—it was my dream to go to college, but even though I didn't get in, does that mean I won't survive? I'm the best teacher I can be, with the hope that some of the village children will later get into college themselves. Even if I couldn't teach and had to return to work in the village, I would still do what I had to do to survive . . ."

Qiaoling was very mature in many ways, and her speech made Qiaozhen's eyes brighten. She clasped Qiaoling's hands tightly and said, "You absolutely must come visit me and remind me of these words when you do . . ."

Qiaoling kept nodding at her sister and exclaimed, "Gao Jialin has no conscience!"

Qiaozhen shook her head and shut her eyes.

Qiaoying came in to escort them outside. She told her mother to hurry up; everything was ready for their departure.

Their mother told Qiaoling to go get something to eat. After Qiaoling left, their mother looked around the room and removed a red silk cloth from a chest in the back. She pinned it to Qiaozhen's hair and let it hang down in front of her face as a veil.

When the sun began to slant toward the west, the bridal party, along with their horses, made their way from Liu Liben's house down the mud slope. The sounds of the *suona*, gongs, drums, people's cries, and the pops of the firecrackers all melded together. Villagers gathered along the edge of the road to watch the display as it passed by. Children and dogs ran wildly around the procession as it left the village.

The musicians led the way cheerfully; right behind them came the male attendants and their horses. The bride rode in the middle on the great horse bedecked in celebratory red, a red silk veil covering her face. Last came the bride's family; according to custom they numbered twice as many as the groom's party, which in this case amounted to Liu Liben, his wife, and nearly all his other relatives attending the wedding. In accordance with tradition, Liben escorted the group to the bottom of the slope and then returned home. Once he walked through the gate, he gave a long, relaxed sigh.

The groom's party advanced very slowly through the village—as though they wanted the lively event to linger importantly in the villagers' memories.

As Qiaozhen rode along, she kept hoping her frail body wouldn't fall; her face, covered with the red silk veil, twitched painfully.

When she guessed that they were about to leave the village, she couldn't help lifting a corner of the veil to peek at Jialin's house. How many times had she gazed at it! She also caught sight of a pear tree on the opposite shore of the river—it was beneath that tree, in that green valley, that they had lain together, embraced, kissed . . . Everything else was in the past.

She let her veil fall to cover her face, the tears once more surging from eyes that she thought had wept themselves dry.

CHAPTER 21

Zhang Ke'nan was taking out his stress on an elm tree. The tree now lay in his family's courtyard next to piles of coal and wood.

His family had more than enough kindling for their cooking needs. He really didn't have to chop more wood. And if they did need some, they wouldn't have had to chop it themselves. They could buy it; they really didn't need Zhang Ke'nan to put in so much effort.

No one knew when the thick trunk had first appeared in their courtyard, or who had brought it to them. Regardless, it seemed like it had always been there, propping up the woodpile and preventing the stack from falling over.

The day after Zhang Ke'nan received Huang Yaping's breakup letter, he left out the back door of the Luxury Food Company carrying a long-handled ax without saying a word, ready to destroy the tree.

Elm trees had the toughest, most fibrous bark of all the local trees. Most people wouldn't choose elm for firewood since it was too hard to cut.

Zhang Ke'nan attacked the tree as soon as he got home. He hadn't tried to chop firewood in many days, but he didn't really care if he was able to cut much—the idea was just to chop. He was covered in sweat, and he breathed heavily like a bellows, but he didn't put down his long-handled ax.

When he was so tired he really couldn't continue, he went inside and lay down on his bed silently, his head resting on his clasped hands and his eyes closed.

His mother occasionally checked on him, gazing at him with sad eyes, but didn't say a word. She had her own inner turmoil, and had started smoking again after a year of abstaining. Ke'nan's father was studying at the county party school and didn't come home much. Their house was utterly quiet.

One day after he had hacked at the tree for a while, he lay down on his bed and shut his eyes as usual. He lay so still, it was as if his tall, sturdy frame had no more breath in it.

His mother came and this time called out, "Nan-nan, get up!"

Zhang Ke'nan seemed not to have heard. He continued to lie still.

"Get up! I have something to tell you. You're just like your worthless father, twenty-something and still good for nothing!"

Ke'nan opened his eyes and stared at his mother's gloomy expression, but he remained silent and motionless.

"Let me tell you, two days ago, I found out that young Gao Jialin pulled some strings to get his job! He's cozy with Ma Zhansheng. I've got all the proof we need!" A strange smile crept across her face.

Zhang Ke'nan still paid no attention to his mother. He didn't know what any of this had to do with his heartbreak. He said, indifferently, "It doesn't matter who he's cozy with, it doesn't change anything . . ."

"Coward! I spent the past few days at the Central Commission for Discipline Inspection of the prefectural party committee filing an official complaint. Today, your Uncle Jiang, head of the county discipline committee, said that the central committee takes these matters very seriously and that they've sent someone to investigate. The investigator arrived today. Gao Jialin is finished!"

Zhang Ke'nan bolted upright, his eyes boring into his mother. "Mother! How could you do this? Let the authorities handle this—why would we get involved? Now we look like the petty ones!"

"You're such a loser! How can you talk such nonsense when your girlfriend was stolen by someone else? Why shouldn't I file a complaint against that son of a bitch; that hillbilly took advantage of us, so why not repay him in kind? He cheated the system, violated the law, and I'm a national cadre—it's my responsibility to safeguard the rules of the party!"

"Mother, you're technically correct. But morally speaking, if we do this, we'll be beyond help. People have eyes, Mother! They won't think you're being patriotic—they'll think you're trying to get revenge! Two wrongs don't make a right—"

His mother rushed at him and slapped him. Then she dropped onto the bed and began to sob. "What a horrible life I lead! To have given birth to such a hopeless boy!"

Zhang Ke'nan rubbed his face with his hands and, tears streaming from his eyes, said, "Mama! You know that I adore Yaping . . . I feel like someone tore my heart apart . . . I want to die! And yes, I did hate Gao Jialin. But I thought hard about everything, and I decided there's nothing to be done! There's a saying, 'An unripe melon is hard to dig up.' Yaping wants Gao Jialin, not me, and no matter how upset this makes me, I have to accept it. You know I have a soft heart—as a child I couldn't even watch chickens being slaughtered. There's nothing I fear or hate more than the slaughterhouse. My hair stands on end when I hear the squeals of pigs, and I get so upset. For the same reason, I don't want to see people around me destroy each other . . . You think you know me, Mama, but you don't really know me. Maybe I am stupid sometimes, but I also have my principles. I know I'm just twenty-five years old, but I've still lived a fair amount. People like to be around me because I'm honest and generous . . . Yes, I have my faults—I can be weak and cowardly and I don't have lofty ambitions. Yaping may not have liked these things about me, but she didn't know she was choosing someone worse! Yaping! You didn't really know me!"

Zhang Ke'nan clasped his chest with his hands as he addressed his mother and an invisible Yaping. His face was frighteningly contorted. He finished speaking and collapsed on his bed like a sack of grain.

After a long time, he got up and left. His mother didn't know when or where he had gone. Their yard was as quiet as a neglected old temple.

Ke'nan went out the gate and paced back and forth outside for what seemed like forever.

After throwing dozens of cigarette butts onto the ground, he left and went straight to the radio station.

There, he found Huang Yaping and immediately told her everything: how his mother had written to the prefectural commission for discipline, and how the commission had sent someone down to the county to investigate. He also laid his heart bare. He wanted Yaping to see if there was any way to remedy the situation.

At first, Yaping couldn't see the forest for the trees: "What a vile woman your mother is!"

But then tears shone in her eyes and she said, "Ke'nan, what a good person you are . . ."

~

The commission for discipline quickly came to a decision on the issue of Gao Jialin getting his job dishonestly. At the same time, Gao Jialin's uncle found out about the situation and twice called the prefectural party secretary to tell them they must send Gao Jialin back to the village.

People were riveted by the drama. The news about Jialin's situation spread to all corners of the county, and the topic was on everyone's lips.

It was an agenda item at the meeting of the standing committee of the county party. The investigators were in attendance, and they gave a detailed report of their findings.

The standing committee's decision was immediate: they revoked Gao Jialin's offer of employment as well as his city residence permit in order to send him back to his production brigade. Ma Zhansheng, the vice chairman of the county labor bureau, was determined to have acted against the laws of the party and used back channels and other improper methods many times. His leadership responsibilities would be revoked, and he would be transferred out of the labor bureau until the personnel bureau could find him a new permanent position.

The official documents were quickly distributed to all relevant work units. Ma Zhansheng danced like an ant on a hot pot, paying visits to local leaders, calling in favors, asking to be allowed to conduct a self-criticism, anything to keep the committee from punishing him.

But eventually he figured out that it was no use, and he had no choice but to be the fall guy: "Aiya, someone's been kissing someone else's fucking ass to make this happen . . ."

Besides Ma Zhansheng, another interested party was also making the rounds, inquiring discreetly of her father's friends, seeing if they could remedy the situation and not force Gao Jialin to return to the countryside: Huang Yaping.

But when she saw the documents that had been distributed by the committee, she knew there was no saving him.

"It's over! It's over! It's all over . . . ," she wailed to herself, feeling utterly helpless.

She hadn't thought that life could change so quickly, like a flash of lightning—she had only just begun to feel happy; now she was suddenly in the midst of despair.

She pulled at her hair and thrashed in her bed. She couldn't bear the pain of her dilemma.

What was the cause of it?

Obviously, she loved Gao Jialin, but she did not want him to become a peasant! She felt horribly conflicted.

If only she knew her mind one way or another: for example, if she stopped loving Jialin, then he could go to hell and it wouldn't bother her at all; on the other hand, if she was willing to give up everything for love, well, then if he went to hell, she'd go right along with him!

But there was no reconciling the two positions. She felt strongly, both that she loved Gao Jialin and that she feared becoming a peasant.

Life was merciless to people like her, people who—if they didn't hold firmly to their principles—would be endlessly confronted with these sorts of dilemmas. She had to make a choice! Life's inherent tensions are omnipresent, like God: no one could escape them.

Huang Yaping didn't know what was best. Jialin wasn't around, and she didn't have any close friends to talk it over with. In the past, she could have talked to Ke'nan, but given their current situation, she absolutely could not go see him now.

Then she thought of her dear father. She could talk to him.

How should she approach him? He had originally opposed her leaving Ke'nan for Jialin. How would he treat her now, after she had broken his heart?

No matter what, she still had to talk to him.

She returned to her parents' home, but he wasn't there. Her mother said he was at his office.

So she ran there.

Her father was wearing his glasses and reading the *People's Liberation Army Daily*. When he saw her come in, he took off his glasses and put the paper down.

"Daddy, do you know what's happened to Gao Jialin?"

"How could I not? All the standing committee members were there . . ."

"What should we do?"

"What do you mean, what should we do?"

"What do I do?"

"You?"

"Uh-huh . . ."

Her father stared out the window silently for a while.

He lit a cigarette, still staring out the window, still not looking at her.

"I don't understand you young people these days. You love to be spontaneous. You never got the strict training we got with revolutionary life. You bear the marks of petit bourgeois thinking. It's these things that have led you to your present condition . . ."

"Daddy, please don't lecture me on politics right now! You know how much pain I'm in . . ."

"You brought it on yourself."

"No! Life is just too harsh and always playing with people's fates!"

"Don't complain about life. Life is always fair. You should complain about yourself!" the old military man shouted, standing up from his chair. His eyes were gleaming under his long eyebrows as he glared at his daughter.

Huang Yaping stamped her foot and cried out, "Daddy, I never imagined you would become so cruel so quickly! I hate you!"

At that, her father seemed to soften. He walked over to her and caressed her hair with his rough palms. He made her sit down on the chair and wiped away her tears with his handkerchief. He prepared a cup of powdered malted milk, added a spoonful of sugar, and set it before her. "Drink. Your throat must be sore."

He sat back down in the armchair by his desk and rapped the surface with his fingertips as he watched his daughter take small sips of her drink.

After a while, he leaned back in his chair, sighed, and said, "I don't doubt your feelings toward that young man. Although I haven't met him, I know my daughter wouldn't love a mediocre person. At a minimum, he must be very talented. That's why we didn't force you to break it off with him after you so abruptly cast aside Ke'nan, which made both your mother and I unhappy and rather embarrassed around the Zhang family. I fought through a forest of artillery fire in distant lands, using up most of my nine lives, and only now, after nearly half my life has passed, I finally have you, my treasure. As far as I'm concerned, you're the most important thing, and I never want to see you suffer. That's why I've only thought of your happiness and haven't taught you much about how to live life properly . . ." He suddenly stopped, waved his hand in the air, and chastised himself. "Why am I prattling on about this? It's too late now!"

He took a drag off his cigarette, turned, and looked at his daughter sitting there quietly.

"I'm your father, and I've given plenty of thought to the situation, so you must listen to me. We need to leave for Nanjing right away. That young man is a peasant—how could we take him with us? Even if we got him a place in a commune on the outskirts of the city, how could you live together for the rest of your life? Feelings are feelings, yes, but reality is also reality, you must—"

"You're making me break up with Jialin?" Huang Yaping looked up, her lips trembling.

"Yes. I hear that he's currently in the provincial capital at a meeting. As soon as he's back, you must go see him."

"No, Daddy! Don't say that! How can I break up with him now? I love him! We've just begun our relationship! I've suffered enough—how can I hurt him like this? I—"

"Pingping, you mustn't disobey me on this. I will not tolerate your stubbornness! If you two can't be together forever, then it's best to break it off as soon as possible! That's the only way to spare you both some pain."

"Hardly! I'll feel this pain forever . . ."

Her father stood up and walked toward the door, head lowered. As he left, he sighed repeatedly. "I've suffered a good deal, but never as much as what you're going through." He shook his head. "You and Ke'nan used to get along so well . . .

Oh, by the way, the day before yesterday I received a letter from an old army friend, saying that they've been in touch with a Nanjing work unit on behalf of Ke'nan . . ."

Huang Yaping jolted upright. She shouted, "Don't you dare mention Ke'nan right now! Don't say his name . . ." She walked over, sat in her father's armchair, and pulled out a piece of clean paper.

"What are you doing?" her father asked.

"I'm writing a letter to Jialin, telling him everything!"

Her father rushed to her side. "You mustn't write him a letter! This is serious! What if something happened to the letter? Besides, won't he be back soon?"

Huang Yaping thought for a second and pushed the paper to the side. She would listen to her father. "According to his original orders from the provincial capital, he'll be back next week."

She walked over to the calendar on the wall and ripped off seven days.

CHAPTER 22

After being immersed in big-city life on the plain, Gao Jialin felt refreshed and excited to return home to the county seat nestled in the mountains.

He got off the bus and left the station, surprised that the city felt somehow different, stranger. The walls were so small! The streets so narrow! It felt like something bad had happened. Few people were about, and all was quiet, with hardly a sound to be heard.

The town hadn't really changed at all; it was his feelings that had. Whenever someone returned from a big, bustling city to a lonely mountain town, they always had this kind of reaction.

Gao Jialin walked along the main road, his stride steady and carefree. He felt even more confident in his future. Although he hadn't been gone long, he felt like now he basically understood the outside world. As he compared the little town in front of his eyes with the big universe beyond it, he felt he no longer had to live a shrunken life. He could stretch his arms and legs . . . It was like he had returned to his small pond after a trip across the ocean.

He hadn't gone far before he ran into Sanxing. Dressed head to toe in greasy work clothes, Sanxing came over and shook his hand enviously. "You're back?"

Gao Jialin nodded and asked, "What are you doing?"

"My tractor broke. I came in this morning to get it repaired. I'll go back in the evening."

"And nothing big has happened in the village, or with our families, has it?" he asked casually.

"No . . . just . . . Qiaozhen got married not too long ago . . ."

"To whom?" Gao Jialin heard a buzzing inside his head.

"To Ma Shuan . . . Well, you're back! I should go!" As soon as Sanxing saw the pained expression on Jialin's face, he hurried away.

An unspeakable sadness filled Jialin's chest when he heard the news. He stood still in the middle of the road for a long time, as though he had lost his way. He never thought Qiaozhen would get married so quickly. It was always troubling to hear that a woman who once loved you was now married to someone else.

He quickly realized that he couldn't keep standing in the middle of the road like that, so he picked up his bag and headed toward the committee offices. He walked slowly, his feet heavy. He thought that everyone was looking at him strangely, like they knew he was unhappy.

Of course, everyone *was* looking at him like that, but for an entirely different reason. He would have to return to the committee offices before he realized why.

When he got back to his office, he put his things down, and soon after, Old Jing stopped by. He first asked about Jialin's trip and then became suddenly quiet; his expression seemed off. Gao Jialin felt very strange. He thought that Old Jing wanted to tell him something, but that whatever his news, it was difficult for him to say.

Old Jing sat down on a chair and kept silent for a while. Finally, he opened up and told Jialin everything: about how the scandal of his pulling strings to get a job had been exposed and about how the county committee had already ruled definitively that he should return to the countryside. He even told him that it was Ke'nan's mother who wrote the letter to the discipline committee and that he had also heard Ke'nan and his mother had gotten in a fight, since Ke'nan disagreed with what she had done.

Gao Jialin's mind went blank.

He stood there, numb, unaware of his surroundings. He caught bits of what Old Jing was saying, that he had gone to the county secretary and told him that Jialin had done outstanding work and begged him to let the young man stay on.

But the secretary couldn't agree; he said the scandal had a long reach and that they had to get rid of him quickly and send him back to his old labor brigade. Old Jing even heard that his uncle had made a call, ordering the office to send Jialin back to the countryside.

Jialin's mind drifted. When had Old Jing left? Jialin didn't know. Around the same time he began to grasp what exactly he was facing, he also came to the realization of what he should do.

First, he took out a cigarette, but instead of smoking it, he tossed it behind him. For some reason, after he had thrown away the cigarette, he pulled out his box of matches and threw them all on the ground. Then he bent down to pick them up and rearranged them carefully inside the matchbox. After they were rearranged, he spilled them back onto the ground, then picked them up again . . .

After an hour of this, he pulled himself together.

Things seemed much simpler now: He would just go back to the countryside, return to the land, and rejoin the commune, right?

Then he remembered Qiaozhen. He pounded his desk with his fists and shouted in despair, "It's too late! What a bastard I am . . ."

Only after that did his thoughts turn to Huang Yaping. Thinking of her didn't cause him so much pain. "Ah, life, what a joke," he murmured.

Was life playing a trick on him, or was he playing a joke on life? There was no way to tell. Just as Qiaozhen thought that her relationship with Jialin was like a dream, he felt that his relationship with Huang Yaping was also a dream. It was undoubtedly true that he was now a peasant and that an uncrossable gulf had appeared between him and Yaping. To marry Yaping, to go with her to Nanjing . . . This was all impossible now. Even if Yaping still held on to her love for him, he decided that he wouldn't pursue her anymore. They should both go back to where they had come from. Although he was an idealist, he was practical when it came to concrete problems.

Actually, he didn't have much time to ponder this sudden, complicated shift in the course of his personal life. In fact, he felt like the ending before him was rather inevitable: if it hadn't happened today, then it could have happened tomorrow. He'd had a premonition, but he always avoided thinking about it. He knew that he had followed a rainbow, but he had preferred to see it as a bridge!

He wished that bridge had never existed; the rainbow was resplendently colored, but it had disappeared quickly. Now he was facing his own reality.

True, one couldn't change reality at will. Trying to deny reality is like trying to leave the earth itself. People ought to have ideals, even fantasies, but one can't deny real life in the blind pursuit of something unachievable. This was an especially important realization for a young person who had just begun his journey on the road of life.

But society must take care of its own. We must eradicate the countless irrationalities of life and let light shine in its every corner; we must encourage those young people who loiter at the crossroads of life to walk the straight and narrow because only then can they mature and fully achieve their goals. The future of our homeland rests on the younger generation!

Of course, as far as young people are concerned, the most important thing is to balance ideals with reality. Even if one's pursuits are reasonable, they mustn't be achieved by way of a crooked path! Because even one failure can bring suffering and even ruin to the rest of a person's life!

Gao Jialin's tragedy was complex, and the public should discuss the many contributing factors impartially. We will now continue to narrate our story of life.

Jialin couldn't bring himself to think of anything else. He had to figure out how to handle his relationship with Yaping.

Yet he had already decided what to do: he would go find Huang Yaping and break things off himself!

After washing his face, he took off his leather shoes, tossed them under his bed, and picked up the cloth shoes Qiaozhen had made for him. Oh, they were made stitch by stitch, thread by thread—what warm feelings were sewn up in those shoes! He clutched them to his chest even though they were tattered and covered in dust, and tears poured down his face.

Then he prepared to go look for Huang Yaping. It was the afternoon, and since she should have been off work by then, she would certainly be at home. He realized that this was the first time he would ever visit Yaping's home . . . and also the last.

Just as he was about to leave, Ke'nan suddenly entered his office.

They stood silently facing each other.

After a while, Gao Jialin finally said, "Please sit . . ."

Ke'nan sat on the chair by the desk. Jialin sat on the edge of the bed.

"Jialin, you must hate me right now . . . ," Ke'nan said without looking at him.

Gao Jialin similarly avoided Ke'nan's gaze. "No . . . you should hate me!"

"You look down on me! You think Zhang Ke'nan is a villain!"

"No." Gao Jialin turned and said sincerely, "I understand you . . . and this thing, it has nothing to do with you. I know this now. Truthfully, even if you *had* written the letter exposing me, I would still understand. Because I hurt you first . . . Even if you retaliated, it was still fair . . ."

Zhang Ke'nan glanced up suddenly at Jialin. "You're a hot-blooded person. But even though we have different personalities, I've always respected you. And I still respect you now. What's past is past . . . but I don't know how to help you. I know you're suffering. Yaping is suffering, too . . . I don't want you two to suffer . . ."

"You are suffering even more!" Jialin stood up. "Let's end this terrible time! You and Yaping can still get back what you had before. The only thing I ask is that you forgive what I've done to you . . ."

"No!" Ke'nan stood up next to him. "Even if I loved Yaping, Yaping is still in love with you! My suffering has passed, and I've thought through everything . . . Yaping shouldn't leave you . . ."

"I want to leave her! I want to break things off with her. I've already made up my mind."

"She loves you . . ."

"But I love someone else!" Gao Jialin shouted.

Zhang Ke'nan stared at him in surprise. He didn't say anything for a long time.

Gao Jialin sat back on the bed, dispirited. A lock of disheveled hair fell across his pale forehead.

Ke'nan eventually sat next to Gao Jialin and said, "Jialin, let's not talk of this. Right now, I know you have to return to the countryside, where a difficult life awaits you. I know that your family isn't well off . . . My family is doing OK, if you ever need anything . . ."

Ke'nan hadn't finished speaking before Gao Jialin stood up angrily. "Don't insult me! Get out! Get out!"

Ke'nan fell silent.

Tears shone in his eyes as he looked at Jialin. He slowly turned away.

Gao Jialin suddenly ran forward and put his arm around Ke'nan's shoulders. In low tones he said, "Ke'nan, I'm sorry. But how can you say that? If I didn't know what an honorable man you were, I'd punch you . . . Forgive me, but please leave! I need to find Yaping and put an end to this. Forgive me."

They shook hands outside the door and parted silently.

～

Huang Yaping heard that Gao Jialin had returned and was just then getting ready to go see him, unaware that he was already at her gate.

After she discovered him there, she took him back to her room. Her father and mother brought cakes, cigarettes, a teapot, and cups and placed them on the table. Then they left.

Yaping put a cup of tea in front of him and immediately asked, "Did you hear?"

Gao Jialin sipped his tea and said quietly, "I heard."

Huang Yaping doubled over on the table beside him and began to whimper.

Gao Jialin gazed at her bent, trembling shoulders and her soft, fluffy hair, and he felt a pain in his chest. He remembered the young men and women walking arm in arm on the streets and in the parks of the provincial capital. Back then he had thought it wouldn't be long before Yaping and he walked hand in hand down Nanjing's great promenades, watching the red mist mingle with the clouds in the morning light as they strolled along the banks of the Yangtze, going to Yuhuatai to collect colorful *yuhua* stones . . .

He choked down tears at the thought. Right when the life he had always dreamed of seemed close enough to touch, it had disappeared in a flash. An acute pain pierced his chest again, and he thumped it with his fist to suppress it.

Yaping looked up, her face covered with tears.

"You must go to the countryside tomorrow and find your uncle and make him get you another job!"

Jialin lit a cigarette and took a resolute puff.

"He didn't want me to come here in the first place. He even made a phone call telling the authorities to send me back to the countryside. He thinks it's the right thing to do, and that I have no grounds to complain. I can't go to him now. In the end, I have to go my own way. It's simple: my only choice is to go back to the village . . ."

"You can't go back!" she wailed.

Jialin forced a smile. "It's not a question of whether I can or can't; I must!"

"What will you do if you go back?" Yaping looked up at the ceiling, a distressed expression on her face as she muttered, almost to herself, her hands anxiously stroking her hair.

"What will I do? What *can* I do? Become a peasant again!"

"What will *we* do?" Yaping faced him. She seemed to be asking both Jialin and herself.

"I've already thought it through. I came here to talk to you about it." Standing up, Jialin walked over to the wall and leaned against it. "We should end our relationship. You should go back to Ke'nan! He loves you so much . . ."

"No, I want to be with you!" Huang Yaping also stood up, then leaned against the table.

"That's not possible. I'm a peasant; I can't have a life with you anymore. And you'll have to leave for Nanjing soon for work."

"I won't work! And I won't go to Nanjing! I'll quit! I'll go be a peasant with you! I can't be without you . . ." Yaping suddenly covered her face with her hands and sobbed into them. Poor girl! Not everything she said was impulsive exaggeration. She was incredibly individualistic, and, things being as they were, she was able and willing to make such a noble sacrifice. She loved Gao Jialin just then more than ever!

Gao Jialin dragged on his cigarette with each breath.

"Yaping, how would that work? I don't deserve your sacrifice. If you really came with me to be a peasant, do you think you'd ever truly be satisfied? You've been spoiled since childhood—life in the countryside would be too difficult for you. I know your feelings are genuine, Yaping, and I thank you for that. I've always adored you. But deep in my heart, I know that I love Qiaozhen more, even though she can't read. I realize now that I shouldn't have kept this from you . . ."

Huang Yaping was floored. She stared silently, desperately at him. Wiping her tears away with the cuff of her sleeve, she took a couple of steps toward him. Slowly, she said, "If it's like that, then . . . I wish you both . . . happiness." Tears silently ran down her face as she stretched her hands out toward him.

Jialin grasped them. "Qiaozhen married someone else . . . so I should simply wish you and Ke'nan happiness!"

He pulled his hands from hers and turned to leave.

Yaping reached out to stop him. "Just one more kiss . . ."

Gao Jialin turned and kissed her tearstained face. Then he hurried out over the threshold, the bitter taste of her tears on his lips. After leaving her house, he didn't go directly back to his office. Instead, Jialin went to the county agricultural machinery repair yard to ask Sanxing to take his bedding back to the village that night. He and Old Jing completed the necessary procedures for him to leave his position, then he shut himself up in his room and lay down on the bed, alone.

~

Most people in Gaojia Village knew what had happened by the time Gao Sanxing returned with Jialin's things. Everyone was devastated. No one had thought the young man would be brought so low so suddenly!

Yude and his wife calmly accepted the bedclothes Sanxing brought them, just as they serenely accepted their son's return. They'd never believed in anything other than fate, and there was no arguing with destiny.

Liu Liben was quite satisfied with the whole situation. He thought God had finally come to his senses and given Gao Jialin what he deserved. That night he trotted over to Minglou's house to get all the details from Sanxing.

But their family didn't seem that excited about the situation. In fact, Minglou seemed rather depressed after hearing the news. That didn't mean he sympathized with Gao Jialin, but he'd become acutely aware of how society now posed an ever-greater danger to people like himself. Even a capable member of the elite like Zhansheng had fallen from grace, so what could he, an illiterate peasant, really do? Who knew when the other shoe would drop and he might have to stand up for himself? Plus, he would be an old man before long. And no matter what he did, Gao Jialin would still hate him. He knew that their meetings in the future would give him headaches. So Minglou didn't want Gao Jialin to come back—he would rather the young man achieve great success, somewhere far, far away!

That same evening, while everyone in town was discussing Gao Jialin's return, Liu Liben's wife and his eldest daughter, Qiaoying, were in a corner of their house hatching their own scheme.

The next morning, Qiaoying left the village, basket in hand, and went to the crossroads at the Great Horse River to collect grass for the pigs. In reality, there wasn't much for the pigs to eat around there—by the time Qiaoying had spent half the day looking, she still hadn't filled her basket.

But Qiaoying wasn't really looking for pig grass. She was carrying out the plan she and her mother had hatched the night before. They were so infuriated by Gao Jialin's behavior that they'd decided Qiaoying should confront him and mock him mercilessly. The whole village was working in nearby fields that morning, so it was the perfect place to execute their scheme. When the time came, everyone would come out from the fields to see what was going on, and the news would spread like wildfire up- and downriver. They would drag Jialin's reputation through the mud!

Qiaoling had overheard them scheming the night before, and, educated girl that she was, she implored her mother and sister not to do it. She told them that people wouldn't laugh at Jialin; they would laugh at the two of them instead! But the two illiterate, old-fashioned women gave her such a chewing-out that Qiaoling ran back to the school where she taught to stay with another female teacher that night.

Qiaoying was a mother and no longer as pretty as she had been when she was younger. Still, she was prettier than most, and whenever she went to the market, there were always young men from out of town who took her for a young single girl and chatted her up; she would immediately unleash a torrent of abuse on them in the coarsest language possible. Unlike her two younger sisters, she had inherited all her mother's and father's traits: she could be narrow-minded and too acerbic; but she was ultimately good, if a bit of a shrew. Her current behavior was entirely due to the anger stirred up deep in her belly.

Now she was watching the road ahead of her as she absent-mindedly picked grass. She was calculating exactly how to make Jialin look as bad as possible. She worked herself into the appropriate role, just like an actress, adopting a gloomy expression, lips pouted.

Suddenly, from behind came the sound of hurried footsteps. When she turned to look, she was surprised to see her sister Qiaozhen, wearing a plain printed jacket, blue pants, and cloth shoes she had made herself. She wore her hair in the typical country bowl cut. She was a country wife in every way, but somehow she was even more magnetic, even more beautiful, than most. After all, simple clothing highlights natural beauty. And although Qiaozhen's face didn't have the glow of a new bride, it also didn't carry the shadows of her recent misfortune.

"What are you doing here?" Qiaoying asked.

"Sister, come back! Don't do this! People will laugh!" Qiaozhen tugged on her sister's sleeve.

"Why would they laugh at me?" Qiaoying stupidly feigned surprise.

"Good sister! Last night Qiaoling came and told me your whole plan. I was so anxious that I couldn't sleep a wink. This morning when I went to our house, I had it out with Mother, and she agreed we shouldn't do this, so I came here . . ."

"You really are a nuisance!" Qiaoying cut her off, suddenly so angry that she couldn't speak anymore, only gnash her teeth and gnaw her lips. Finally she got the words out: "Gao Jialin humiliated you! He threw pig urine on our family, and now we all smell like piss! If you can bear that, do so on your own! We can't. I'm going to make this as difficult as possible for him."

"Good sister! He is pathetic enough now; if you shame him in front of everyone, how will he be able to go on . . ." Tears welled up in her eyes as she spoke.

Qiaoying wrenched her head away stubbornly. "Don't worry about it! This is my affair." She threw her basket onto the ground as she spoke and sat down on a stone next to it, angrily hugging her knees like an insolent little boy.

Bending down in front of her sister, Qiaozhen bowed her head. "I kneel before you, Sister! I beg you—don't treat Jialin like this! No matter what, I will always love him dearly. You will be stabbing me in the heart if you do this!"

Qiaoying's resolve was softened by her sister's goodness and empathy in the face of such misfortune. With one hand she wiped away her own tears, and with the other she affectionately stroked Qiaozhen's head. "Don't cry, Zhenzhen! I understand. I can't . . ." She stopped, unable to speak for a while, then sighed and continued: "I know in my heart how much you love him. *Ai!* If only that rascal had been expelled from society long ago . . . but now what can we do? I see that he is your true love. I'm not sure if he'll still want you, but now . . ."

"No!" Qiaozhen looked up, her face tearstained. "It's impossible, I'm already married. I must stay with Ma Shuan forever. Ma Shuan is a decent person and is kind to me. I've already had my own heart broken; I cannot break Ma Shuan's heart now, too . . ."

Qiaoying took another deep breath. "Why don't you go back home? I'll come with you . . ." She stood and picked up her basket.

Qiaozhen also stood and asked, "Is your husband at home?"

"Yes, why?"

"Last night I heard Qiaoying say that the commune might hire a new teacher for the village school. When Jialin comes back, he won't be accustomed to hard labor, and I'd like to see if he could be the new teacher. Ma Shuan is on the Madian school's regulatory committee, and he said that if they were hiring there, he could speak on Jialin's behalf. Since your husband has a lot of power in the village, I wanted you both to come with me to talk to Uncle Minglou and get him to hire Jialin again. You must help me talk to him. You're his daughter-in-law, and he has more respect for you."

Qiaoying's jaw dropped in astonishment as she gaped at her sister. She adjusted her basket with one arm, then put her other arm around Qiaozhen's shoulders. "Well then, let's go! Sister, you really do have the heart of a bodhisattva . . ."

~

It was not yet light when Gao Jialin left the large courtyard of the committee offices empty-handed.

He stumbled numbly through streets empty of people. His tall, thin frame didn't look as elegant as usual, and he was slightly stooped. His lifeless eyes were sunken in their sockets and gave off no hint of light. His hair was as messy as a bunch of thatch. His entire face seemed to be covered in a layer of dust, and several fine wrinkles lay across his forehead.

Such a handsome, carefree young man had aged so quickly!

Gao Jialin thought of himself now as a beggar with nothing to his name. He felt he was completely alone, in search of something he would never find. He didn't know by which road he had come, or by which road he should continue.

By the time he reached the Great Horse River, he was so exhausted that he collapsed against the railing. The clear river water reflected the murky predawn light as it passed under the bridge and merged with the County River, swollen and wide in the early autumn. The muddy yellow water of the creek circled around the town and flowed toward some invisible, distant place.

As he held on to the bridge railing, he thought back to that time he'd come to sell buns and how Qiaozhen had been standing here waiting for him; then he thought of how he had left her there so callously not long ago . . . and now he was back at this same place again, but with what? His dreams of a job and life in the big city were destroyed, Huang Yaping had returned to the fringes of his world, and he had cruelly tossed aside his dear Liu Qiaozhen, who was now married to someone else. He wanted to throw himself over the bridge and into the river!

Who was there to blame? After careful thought, he decided there was no one. His tragedy was of his own creation. He had thrown away his principles for the sake of vanity and so had fallen to where he was now. He'd learned the hard way that he couldn't avoid life's punishments forever—and that next time, he might be completely destroyed . . .

The grim reality of life can teach us the most, and although life had dampened some of Jialin's fervor, it had also made him do some true soul-searching. Even if he had gone with Huang Yaping to Nanjing, he wondered if he really would have been happy. Would he have been able to rise to the level of his dreams? Would Yaping have loved him forever? Who knows how many more remarkable people than him were in Nanjing? There was no guarantee she wouldn't eventually run off with one of those other men, tossing him to the side just like she had

Zhang Ke'nan. It would be difficult to live in the countryside for the rest of his life, though there would be happy times, too. But he had thrown away the most important thing! He had violated his conscience! His father and Uncle Deshun's predictions had come true—he had hurt others and himself. He had thrown others' lives into turmoil and had made a complete mess of his own.

Without him noticing, dawn had silently arrived. The lights in town were extinguished one after another, and the earth threw off its black nightclothes to reveal its face in the gentle, natural light of day. It was already autumn, and from the mountaintops to the river valley farms, the green leaves of the trees were beginning to turn yellow.

The town was bustling with activity. The rhythm of daily life continued as it always had.

Gao Jialin stared at the town covered in blue fog. He turned around, walked over the bridge, then continued toward the Great Horse River Valley.

He walked along the road between the fields, and a sadness he had never experienced before welled up inside him. He had taken this route countless times. He had walked to town on this road, and he had returned to the village on this road. This short, ten-*li* dirt road seemed endless to him. It symbolized the path of life that he had walked to this point—short, but winding!

He broke off the branch of a willow tree and whipped the wild grasses growing alongside the road as he went, wondering how people would treat him after he returned to the village. How would he begin his life there anew? His dear Qiaozhen was gone! If he had her, he wouldn't be suffering like this. Her love was as hot as fire and as gentle as water, and it would wash away all of his distress. But now . . . he hurt so much he wanted to die . . . He couldn't help it, he stopped in the middle of the road and opened his mouth to scream . . . but no sound came out. He clutched wildly at his chest, and the buttons on his overcoat flew off like bullets.

The early morning sun shone on the autumn fields, and the land was revealed in a swath of gorgeous color. The crystalline dew glittered on the green grass, and the dirt road beneath his feet was damp and threw off no yellow dust. Gao Jialin stumbled along the route, walking a few paces, then stopping, standing still awhile before going on . . .

When he had about one more *li* to go before he reached the village, he heard a group of children chattering on the hillside on the other side of the river. He heard one of the boys shout, "Teacher Gao's back . . ." He knew these children—they were all his former students, probably sent from his village to chop wood.

Suddenly, one of the children on the hillside began to sing a *xintianyou*—

Older Brother, what a hack

Sold his conscience, then came back

The children all laughed and then, still twittering among themselves, made their way down into the gully.

Although that ancient rhyme had come out of a child's mouth, it carried the force of a scathing critique and shook Gao Jialin to the core. He knew that the child had sung it so he would hear.

So! The children all hated him. He had no doubt that the adults in the village hated him even more.

Before long he was there. A dense date plantation concealed one part of the village, while the other side stretched toward the gully and out of sight.

Again, he couldn't help but stop and mourn for the place he knew so well. Everything was as it had always been—but to him it had changed completely.

At this moment, the villagers were walking down the mountain and weaving their way out of the fields, all running en masse toward him.

He didn't know what was going on. Everyone came up to him, surrounding him, asking him all sorts of questions. Their speech, their faces, their glances betrayed no mockery or derision, just sincerity. They were fighting among each other for the chance to comfort him.

"If you are coming back, then really come back—there's no need to feel discouraged!"

"There are as many peasants in the world as there are grains of sand. Those who go out into the world and become cadres are few and far between!"

"Sure, life is difficult here, but it has its advantages! Our food is always fresh! Don't worry about everything else."

"Take a good, long look. You'll go away again someday."

~

Dear old villagers—when you were doing well, they were nowhere to be seen, but when you were down on your luck, they'd extend a rough hand to help you up. They had huge hearts and would always help those less fortunate.

Hot tears streamed down Jialin's face. He didn't say a word, but reached for his cigarettes and handed them out one by one.

When the farmers had finished greeting and comforting him, they returned to the fields.

By the time Gao Jialin began his walk toward the village again, he felt relaxed, like a breeze had blown through him. He looked up at the lush fields and tiny hamlets surrounded by dense greenery and was moved by the sight of the simple, rich farmland. He had been away a long time, and now he was back . . .

But when he reached the crossroads at the bend in the river, his legs suddenly weakened and he couldn't move a muscle. He realized that the first time he and Qiaozhen had walked back together from the city, this was where they had said goodbye—and now they had said goodbye forever. He also remembered that when he had gone to the city for work, this was where Qiaozhen saw him off. Now he was returning, but she would never again be here waiting for him.

He felt like his whole body was on fire. Sitting down on a rock, he covered his eyes with his hands. His head dropped to his chest. He had no idea how he would go on living. "My love!" he murmured to himself. "If only I hadn't lost you . . ." Tears gushed from between his fingers like a spring.

After a long while, he finally looked up. He was surprised to see Grandfather Deshun squatting in front of him. He didn't know when the old man had come, but he must have squatted down very quietly, smoking his pipe.

When he saw Jialin look up, he beamed and said, "Any tears left?" The wrinkles on his face crept back toward the corners of his eyes, and he shook his snow-white head back and forth. "Oh child, don't be afraid of coming back here—hard labor's not so bad. But you've lost your gold! Qiaozhen, she really is a piece of gold!"

"Grandfather, I'm so depressed. Please, let's not talk about this. I know that I had a piece of gold and that I threw it away like a clump of dirt. Now it feels like life has no meaning and I might as well die."

"Nonsense!" Grandfather Deshun stood up suddenly. "You're only twenty-four years old, how can you have such shameful thoughts? If I thought like you do, I'd have died a long time ago! I'm almost seventy, with no son or daughter, a bachelor all my days. But my heart still beats, and I plan to keep it going a few more years! You're still young and tender. Even though I have no wife or children, I still think life has meaning. I've loved and I've suffered, I've used these two hands to do hard labor, I've planted the five crops, I've planted trees, I've repaired roads . . . Don't these things also create a meaningful life? To use a word you young people like, it's called *happiness*. Happiness! You young people don't realize, but when I pick the fruit from my trees and give it to the children, my heart is so . . . happy! How much of my fruit did you eat when you were little? You're too young to understand, but when I plant a tree, I think about how when I die, later generations will pick fruit from that tree, and they'll say, 'This is one of the trees that old bachelor Deshun planted.'"

Old Deshun spoke with great emotion, as though trying to teach Jialin something, but also summing up his life; he seemed as full of passion as one of the old poets or philosophers. His aging hand trembled violently as it held his pipe.

All of a sudden, Gao Jialin stood up. He was a proud high school graduate who had researched a number of international issues, lectured on many books, knew who the Ayatollah Khomeini and Banisadr were, and understood Reagan's neutron bomb regulations. He never imagined that this old bachelor peasant whose clothes were covered in patches would teach him about life's most profound issues. He stared at dear, wrinkled Old Deshun whose lightless eyes had once again sparked.

Grandfather Deshun used a patched sleeve to wipe the tears from his eyes. "I heard you were coming back today so I came here to wait for you to tell you a few things. You mustn't lose hope! You also mustn't look down at our little town." He used a shriveled finger to point at the mountains and rivers and land around them. "This place—it has taken care of us for generations. Without land, we'd have nothing! Nothing! And as long as we love labor, things will be OK. Besides, the party's laws are correct, and life continues to get better for us. The future looks good for our village—you'll see! My boy, don't lose heart! A strapping young lad such as yourself shouldn't fear falling. Just don't stop climbing, or else you really will be as dead as mutton."

"Grandfather, your words have helped me understand. I will remember them, and they'll help me start a new life. By the river earlier, I ran into some other people from the fields, and they spoke to me kindly as well. But I'm worried that Gao Minglou's and Liu Liben's families will make trouble for me."

"Aiya, don't worry! I just went to Minglou's house to see him about this exact issue. Years ago, his father and I were sworn brothers, so I'm not afraid to give him advice. I got him to agree not to pester you anymore. Oh! And I forgot to tell you. At Minglou's, I saw Qiaozhen imploring him to go work his magic at the commune and let you keep teaching. Tears were streaming down her face. In the face of her pleading, Minglou relented. His daughter-in-law, Qiaoying, also helped Qiaozhen convince him, though I don't know why. So don't worry. You'll teach or you won't—either way, focus on your new beginning . . . Ah, Qiaozhen, what a wonderful girl! A heart of gold . . . like gold . . ." Tears leaked out of Old Deshun's eyes, and he was suddenly too choked up to go on.

Gao Jialin fell down at Old Deshun's feet and clutched the yellow earth in his fists as he howled, "My love . . ."

First draft written in Ganquan County, northern Shaanxi Province, summer 1981.

Revised in the autumn in Xi'an and Xianyang, and in the winter in Beijing.

ABOUT THE AUTHOR

Photo © Beijing October Publishing House

The Chinese novelist Lu Yao (路遥) was born Wang Weiguo (王卫国) in 1949 in Shaanxi Province. He grew up in a very poor family, together with six siblings, and began writing novels when he was a college student at Yan'an University. In 1982, Lu Yao published his novella *Life*, which won the National Excellent Novella Award and was then adapted into a film of the same name, which won the Hundred Flowers Award (the Chinese equivalent of the Academy Awards) for Best Feature

Film in 1984. Lu Yao became a national celebrity. In 1991, he published his magnum opus, *Ordinary World*, which won the Mao Dun Literature Prize. His writing was closely related to his own experiences, and it focused mostly on young people striving to change their lives. He died in 1992 at the age of forty-two, having published only two works, both considered masterpieces. Despite how well known Lu Yao is within China, he has remained untranslated until now. *Life* is the first translation of Lu Yao's work to appear in English.

ABOUT THE TRANSLATOR

Photo © Elliot de Carvalho

Chloe Estep was born in West Virginia, grew up in Florida, worked in Shanghai, and now lives in New York, where she is pursuing her PhD in modern Chinese literature at Columbia University.